ACCLAIM

"*The Faces of War*" is a daring, heart wrenching, pulse pounding story of hope emerging from misery, triumph springing from despair and sustained love. Jane McCarthy's sterling story set at the height of World War ll is the best novel in recent memory, with echoes of Tim O'Brien, Phil Caputo and even classics on the level of *All's Quiet on the Western Front* and *The Red Badge of Courage.* McCarthy has fashioned a story etched from the power of the human spirit and the darkness of the human soul. An emotionally wrought story that gives no quarter and never opts for easy choices. Not to be missed.

Jon Land, *USA Today* bestselling author of the *Caitlin Strong* novels.

"Jane does a wonderful job showing the awfulness of war and its effect on both the soldiers and the loved ones they leave behind. Reminiscent of the classic William Wyler movie, *The Best Years of Our Lives,* this is a great addition to the universe of World War II literature

Jeff Ayers, bestselling author of *Long Overdue.*

THE FACES OF WAR

OF WAR

JANE F. MCCARTHY

Publisher's Information

EBookBakery Books

Author contact: janefarrellmccarthy@gmail.com

ISBN 978-1-953080-23-3

Cover by Holley Flagg of Flagg Design Graphics

© 2024 by Jane F. McCarthy

ACKNOWLEDGMENTS

- I. Michael Grossman, my publisher, editor and friend for his unwavering support and encouragement for writing this novel.

- Holley Flagg for her impressive cover design.

- Georgette Taylor, editor extraordinaire, who focused on the chronology of the timeline which gave the novel clarity.

- Jeff Ayers for his editing via email and phone calls to change the novel to where it needed to go

- Martha Reynolds for line editing and suggestions for resources.

- Bob Steipock who stuck with me when I struggled with the writing. His knowledge of writing and WWll facts was an enormous asset.

- Dr, Stanley Carpenter for links to information on trop ships with passenger manifests, dates of arrivals and departures and war ship terminology

- Paul Rimovsky of Camp Cordia Museum for sending the book Camp Concordia: German POW's in the Midwest, 1943-1945.

- Barbara Reynolds, my friend, whose writing skills were an enormous benefit.

- The South County Writing Group, where I learned to hone my writing skills and accepted their critique of my novel with humility-most of the time. They are my mentors and friends.

- My husband, Gerry, a former Army officer and WWll aficionado, who kept me straight with dates, battles , geography, Army terminology, and decisions made prior to and during the war.

DEDICATION

To the men and women who risked their lives for freedom during World War II and to those who suffered enormous loss and hardship.

Chapter One

On December 7, 1941, in a surprise military strike on Pearl Harbor, Hawaii, Japan attacked the American naval fleet precipitating the entrance of the United States into a global conflict, World War II, which lasted until 1945.

In 1941, Robert Conway, the eldest son of Henry and Louise Conway, joined the Navy and was stationed in Pearl Harbor. His last letter to the family was dated November 30, 1941. Louise kept all Robert's letters, which she read when the uncertainty of war troubled her. After December 7, war became a reality and Louise's worry turned into fear. John watched his mother go through the mail and saw her shake her head when there was no news from Robert. Henry devoured the papers for news and listened to the radio every evening, chewing on his pipe.

John, their second son, kept his concern buried. Robert won't die, he told himself. He can't. Abby, their youngest, refused to go to school until John convinced her she must.

"Staying home won't change anything," he said.

On January 4, 1942, a telegram arrived informing the family that Robert was missing in action and presumed dead. Henry and Louise retreated into a sorrow that had no relief. Neighbors arrived bearing food, asking what they could do. When Robert left for the Navy, John and Abby never imagined that he might not come home.

In high school, John Conway was a star basketball player, math his favorite subject, and drama his favorite elective. He complimented his classmates, avoided rivalry, listened in class, and laughed at his own faux pas. After the loss of Robert, the brother he worshiped, John was left to tackle the world without the one person who paved a path before him. Henry returned to work and Louise performed all the myriad chores that made up her day. Abby and John went to school where Abby's friends surrounded her with attention, and John's friends, thinking they might be next, avoided discussion of Robert.

In America, war news was everywhere. Radio broadcasts, newspapers, and newsreels in movie theaters kept the grim updates at the forefront. Telegrams arrived with the dreaded news of soldiers missing in action or dead. The draft plucked thousands of young men from the workplace. Tears were shed for the war, for those already dead, and for those about to go. A man who was young during 1942 had uncertain chances of growing old. John Conway was one of them.

One afternoon, John shot hoops in the school gym with his friend, Harry Phillips. Harry was tall and slim with long arms that outshot John every time. Orphaned at ten, Harry lived with his Uncle Peter, a crotchety old man who refused to let Harry's friends visit under any circumstances and frowned on Harry visiting anyone. Despite these restrictions, Harry and John became best friends.

"How's it going?" asked Harry, dribbling the ball.

"After three months, it's still there. Our bedroom is full of his stuff. Can't throw it away. Mom takes care of us, but I hear her crying at night when she thinks no one is around, and Dad goes for long walks alone after supper. Abby seems to be coping best."

"I was a kid when my folks died and it was painful, but I had to move on. Uncle Peter was my father's brother and he lost a family, so we became one."

Harry tossed the ball to John, who shot a basket.

"We're graduating next week. Are you going to sign up?" asked Harry.

"No. I'll wait until they draft me."

"There's talk of lowering the draft to eighteen year olds. That means us in a couple of months."

"I'm scared of going. What if I die like Robert?"

"Soldiers stick up for each other. Robert didn't have a chance. We'll have to go, and we'll have to stay alive."

John and Harry joined the graduates of Central High to receive their diplomas. Several had received their draft orders. For many others, it was just a matter of time.

Uncle stood and yelled to Harry, who waved his diploma and grinned. Determined to lift her family out of the sadness that overwhelmed them since Robert's death, Louise invited them back to the house for a celebration. Friends filled the Conways' home, and for the first time since Robert's death, laughter echoed throughout the house.

The following afternoon, John sat on the front porch steps with his girlfriend, Lily, a slender blonde with freckles sprinkled across her nose. A sign of beauty, her father had said. Her mother admonished her for trying to hide them with face powder—God given she would say. Lily wanted to go to college, but there was no money for such a thing, her mother told her, especially for a girl. After applying for a job at a local bank, Lily was hired. "Good thing, we can use the money," was all her mother said.

"I'm going to save my money from my bank job and go to college. I can even go part time." Turning toward John, a smile stretched across her face, accentuating her high cheek bones.

John clenched his fist, raised his voice, and said, "Bully for you."

"Aren't you glad for me?"

"Sure, I'm glad. I'll think of you when I'm fighting the Germans."

Louise came out carrying two glasses of lemonade, set the glasses down, and wiped her face with the edge of her apron. Her hair was now completely gray. New lines appeared on her upper lip. "Thought you could use a cold drink. It's cooler inside if you care to come in."

John gulped his lemonade. "I'm going in, Lily. It's too hot." Hesitating, he cast a glance at the American flag hanging from a pole, it was still.

Taking a seat on the stairwell, he crossed his arms over his knees. Was he a coward for feeling terrified to fight for his country, or was he supposed to like going? These questions confused him. He was proud of the comradery of other recruits, but dread dragged that pride down.

"By the way. I'm not signing up, going to wait until I'm drafted."

"I'm glad. That will give us more time together," said Lily.

"Is that all you can think about? Suppose I get killed? Or the guy next to me gets killed and it's my fault."

"Not everyone who goes to war dies, and I only meant that we get to see each other longer. Is that so bad?"

John looked over Lily's head. "See you tomorrow." Lily shrugged and left.

Sleep eluded John that night. Everywhere he turned there were reminders of Robert—the empty twin bed, his high school graduation picture, his basketball trophies. He couldn't remove them, they were all he had of the brother he loved.

The next day, John waited outside the bank for Lily. He paced, rehearsing what he would say. Words stuck in his throat; nothing sounded right. He felt a tap on his shoulder and spun around.

"Hi, John."

"Lily, I'm sorry. It's just that I feel mad all the time."

"It's okay. I know it's hard to think about going."

"I can have the car tomorrow. Maybe we could do something. I finish work at five."

"Okay, see you then."

John watched Lily leave; his eye drifting over her body watching her hips sway. He felt an arousal that added to the pressure he felt.

The air was thick and humid. Sweat trickled down his neck as he stepped inside, grabbed a bottle of juice from the refrigerator, and took a long swallow. He called out to his mother.

"I'm going out with Lily, Mom. I won't be late." He kissed his mother's cheek.

"Drive safely," she said.

John and Lily ordered cones of chocolate at the ice cream parlor. Lily chatted about her job at the bank.

Lily looked at John out of the corner of her eye. "John."

"What?" he said, wiping his chin.

"Have you been listening?"

"Of course. Let's go to the lake."

Reaching the lake, they walked to a secluded area near the water's edge where a sultry summer breeze hovered over them.

They waded in, splashed water at each other, and walked onto the grass. He drew her in, inhaling her scent. She kissed his cheek. He turned toward her, kissed her lips, and lowered her to the ground.

Half-naked, they stayed entwined until John stirred and rolled over onto the grass. Lily pulled down her skirt and said, "I think we should get married before you leave."

"Married? I could get killed and all you can think about is marriage!" John stood, pulling up his trousers.

"I thought you loved me."

"What? We're just dating. How did you get that idea? I never said that!"

"But we just had sex!"

John shrugged.

"You used me," said Lily as she buttoned her blouse and straightened her skirt.

"I didn't use you. We both wanted to do it. I thought we were just having a good time. I'm going off to war. Don't you care?"

"How about me? What should I do?"

Irritated, John replied, "You're smart. Go to college."

"On what? My father's paycheck just about pays the rent and bills. And I'll never save enough to go to college."

"I'm not getting married. I'm taking you home."

"Just like that? You're despicable," Lily said.

"Look, I'm sorry, but I can't marry you or anyone. I'm only seventeen."

John drove her home and watched Lily run into the house. Gripping the steering wheel, he thought what a mess things were. I never should have done that to Lily. War reverberated through his head. It nipped at his heels.

He had to get a grip on things. He would call Lily and ask her to forgive him, but it would be years before he was able to do so.

Lily's world unraveled when what she thought was love was only fun for John Conway. It worsened when six weeks later, choking back sobs, she told her parents she thought she was pregnant but refused to tell them who the father was.

"Who is this despicable person that did this to you?" asked her mother.

"Does it matter, Mom?"

Her mother kept her suspicions to herself but kept on probing Lily, who refused to discuss the matter.

Her father's response was that after so much death in the war, every new life was important. "I can plan for you to go away to live with my cousins. They are childless and could raise the baby as their own."

"I'm not giving my baby to anyone."

Her mother pushed for marrying the father. Adamant, Lily stayed in her room—most days in tears. The Shays were devastated—their beautiful only child had been violated.

"You can't have a baby and not be married. It just isn't done," her mother said.

Lily left her room for meals only. One evening at the supper table, Lily's father asked her if she would like to meet a friend of his. Her mother sat in stony silence. Reluctantly, Lily agreed. That night, sitting on the edge of her bed, she felt like a cornered cat, wary and beaten. A week later, her father introduced her to his friend, Tom Brewster, a tall, muscular man with thick brown hair and a husky voice.

Two weeks later, they were married. Tom Brewster was forty years old and an affluent businessman.

They moved to Spring Hill Farm where Tom once tended the land which now belonged to him. Tom's heart was scarred by the loss of his first wife and baby during childbirth, but meeting Lily, he felt an instant feeling of attraction and powerful connection to her. He sat beside Lily, offering silent comfort when she confronted her circumstances and the tears flowed. With Tom, Lily knew what real love felt like—his understanding when she cried leaving home, the way he fixed her tea and toast to combat morning sickness, the way he made chicken soup, drove her to doctor's appointments, and cried when her baby was born.

As winter faded, the promise of spring and new beginnings lay ahead. On March 7, 1943, Lily gave birth to a baby girl, whom she and Tom named Eve.

"She's the most beautiful baby in the world," Tom told the household. "She has a tiny mouth and the bluest eyes I have ever seen."

He sat with Lily as she fed Eve, changed her diapers, and rocked her to sleep. Eve had the best buggy that money could buy and the best crib to sleep in, along with an array of figures dangling over her as she slept. Lily couldn't keep her eyes off her and swept her up in her arms the minute she woke or cried.

Chapter Two

Abby had a velvety-smooth voice and wavy auburn hair which she barely combed. As a teenager, she preferred sweaters to blouses and pants to skirts.

One Saturday morning, she watched through a window as her brother and a friend shot baskets. Must be Harry with the strange uncle, she thought. Watching him dribble the ball, she noticed his strong arms and long legs and how graceful his moves were. She stood back from the window and retrieved an apple from the bowl of fruit on the counter as the boys walked inside.

"Abby, this is Harry—my buddy. Harry, you've heard me talk about my sister, Abby."

Abby had bitten into the apple and, looking at Harry with his hands stuffed in his pockets and his damp hair falling over his forehead, felt an interruption of her breathing.

"Hi," he said.

The apple slid out of her grasp and landed on the floor. Harry picked it up, placed it on the table, and said, "I guess you'd like another." Abby felt a light static when his hand brushed against hers.

"Next time I come I'll bring you some," said Harry.

"That would be nice," she managed to say.

"Will you be around tomorrow?" he asked.

"Yes."

"Okay if I stop by?"

"That would be nice," she repeated.

Watching the scene unfold, John grinned. "At a loss for words, sis?"

"Of course not. Don't be silly."

"That would be nice," he mimicked.

Abby's eyes narrowed and she stomped out of the room.

The next day Harry arrived with a bag of apples and invited Abby to a movie. He suggested the latest Laurel and Hardy.

They sat shoulder to shoulder in the theater and laughed at the hilarious antics of the comedy duo. Abby had been on a few dates in the past, but she'd never felt an instant attraction until she met Harry, and the attraction intensified over the summer.

Most evenings, Harry and Abby sat on the front porch, a breath apart. People around them faded into the background. They swam in the lake, had picnic lunches, and listened to *The Pepsodent Show* with Bob Hope, but war news was never far away.

Sun filtered through trees that had started to shed their leaves. Harry and Abby walked along a path blanketed with asters. Sitting on a bench, Abby couldn't see his face but sensed his sudden stillness.

A hint of a frown creased Harry's brow. Taking Abby's hand in his, he said, "Abby…"

"Harry! What is it? Tell me."

"I've enlisted in the Army, and I leave in November." Her hands flew to her face.

In a hushed voice, he said, "Waiting for the draft was making me crazy. I wanted to get it over with."

Abby's world had become unpredictable, and her foreseeable future packed with uncertainty. She looked at Harry and thought how brave he was and how much she loved him.

"I love you, Harry," she whispered. "And come back to me."

"I love you, too, and I promise to come back. How could I not when I have you to come home to?" They sat there until dusk and walked back to the Conways' house, where Harry announced he had signed up.

Families with young men expected this news, but when it happened it was catastrophic. Neighbors leaned on each other for compassion and understanding.

Days turned into weeks. November arrived crisp and sunny. Harry's mood was somber. Watching Harry pack his duffel bag, Uncle Peter reached into his trouser pocket, pulled out a box, and handed it to Harry.

"What's this?"

"A Saint Christopher medal. He protects travelers. Your father gave it to me when I signed up for the war. He would be proud of you—as I am. Saint Christopher protected me, so I am passing it on to you."

Harry took out the medal, placed it around his neck, and hugged his uncle.

"I was too strict with you. I was afraid you would find someone else to live with," said his uncle, wiping his eyes with the back of his hand.

"It's okay. You took good care of me."

John appeared in the doorway. "All set?"

Harry patted the medal and said, "Yeah."

The family drove to the train station, thirty minutes away. The pre-morning fog was thick, and the car's headlights shone on empty streets.

Arriving at the station, clusters of families stood with their recruits.

Harry stepped out of the car, turning up the collar on his overcoat. "You okay, uncle?" he asked.

"I'm fine, son." Harry had gotten used to uncle calling him "son," in fact, he found it endearing—especially today.

Harry slipped his hand into Abby's.

Silently, the conductor checked his pocket watch.

"Okay, boys." The conductor blew a whistle and announced, "All aboard."

Abby felt a scream form in her throat. She placed her hand on Harry's left cheek and held it there as if trying to memorize his face.

Holding her tight, he gave her a last kiss. "Don't worry, I'll be all right. Write to me."

"I will, every day," she said, muffling her sobs.

"Meet you over there, Harry. My papers are probably in the mail," said John. "Be careful."

Harry hoisted his duffel bag over his shoulder and entered the train. The doors noisily slammed shut and a moment's silence was followed by the chugging of the train leaving the platform.

Harry leaned out of the train window. "Abby!"

Rooted to the pavement, she waved. John and Uncle Peter came to her side and linked hands until they could no longer see the train. The band of well-wishers vanished into the fog. Two weeks later, a letter from the president arrived, addressed to John Conway. Reluctant to open it, John stared at it until his mother said, "Let's see what the president wants."

John tore open the envelope. "He wants me, Mom. December 30, 1942."

The next morning, Henry and Louise dragged a Christmas tree home from the corner market and struggled to set it in the stand. By three o'clock, ornaments were hung from the tree and a string of lights were shining brightly. Satisfied, Louise wrapped the presents, set them under the tree, and while sipping tea, admired her work. With a look of approval on his face, Henry sipped brandy.

Abby and John brushed snow from their coats and were delighted to see the tree. They fussed over ornaments that had been in the family's box of treasures.

"Remember this one, John?" Abby held a soft Santa that John had made in second grade. Santa's felt coat was worn and an eye was missing.

"I do. It seemed to take ages to finish, and mine was the worst looking."

Pleased with the invitation to join the family for Christmas dinner, Uncle Peter arrived with a bottle of port wine.

Louise lifted the turkey from the oven. Henry did the carving, and they expressed their thanks for this day and each other.

Henry raised a glass of port and said, "To Harry and Robert and John."

It was a cold December morning when the family drove John to the train station that was packed with other recruits and their well-wishers. They waited in silence for the train to arrive.

The conductor picked up his light and said, "Boys, it's time to go." He waved it, and a bell on the front of the train clanged as the last hasty kisses were exchanged.

Henry wrapped both arms around John. "Take care of yourself. We're proud of you."

"I'll write every day," said Abby, hugging John.

Louise wrapped her arms around John and whispered, "Come back to us."

Silently, men boarded the train. A whistle pierced the air as the train pulled away in a cloud of steam. After the departures of both Harry and John, Abby woke each morning with a sluggish feeling. Most of her senior year was spent writing letters to Harry and John, leaving out her fear for their safety.

Chapter Three

John arrived at training camp in Fort Dix, New Jersey, in late December 1942. The line of recruits waiting to be processed for boot camp snaked around a corner. Rain drizzled without pause, intensifying the dismal atmosphere.

A wiry guy stuck extended out his hand. "Jeremiah Beauregard Adams."

John shook the hand. "John Conway."

The first thing Jeremiah told John was, "My daddy wanted me to be named Jeremiah. Momma hated it, so they compromised and called me Beau. Even Granddaddy was happy. Do your folks call you Johnny?"

"No, John."

"Okay, John. Daddy told me to keep my head down and shoot straight. Said he was proud of me for going, but Momma wasn't happy. She cried when I left. Hated seeing Momma cry. What about your folks?"

"It was tough for them. My brother was killed in Pearl Harbor, but they knew I had to serve." John wiped his rain-soaked face with his hand.

"My mom told me to come back safe."

"Sorry to hear about your brother. I'm all my daddy and momma have."

"Then you have to come back. And you have to obey your momma."

A subtle grin spread across John's face.

The line moved on. Hats, suits, and overcoats were exchanged for standard issue olive-drab uniforms. Each received a rifle and a chain from which hung a metal tag embossed with identification numbers. Heads were shaved and they were told what to do, what not to do, and when to do it. Eighty recruits ate and learned together. They endured endless push-ups, all-night marches, and cold showers. Hours of physical fitness, limitless inspections, and drills filled their time. John gained the ability to pay careful attention to detail, understanding that both his and his friends' lives depended on it. There was no time to think about what his life was like before. The young men began as strangers from different parts of the country but ended up working seamlessly together.

John hated the ceaseless drilling, the lack of a moment's privacy, the constant cold. He dreaded the exercises meant to prepare him for war but knew his chance of survival depended on them.

That night, John and Beau lay on their bunks.

"My folks have a horse farm in Kentucky. Kentucky folks like horses and bourbon. Every day at six o'clock, Daddy makes a mint julep for Momma. He and Granddaddy drink bourbon straight. The night before I left, they included me. Bourbon is smooth! Good stuff." Beau turned on his side to face John. "Didn't want to disappoint Daddy, but that was not my first drink of bourbon." Remembering, Beau laughed.

"Things changed at our house after my brother was killed. There was always that empty chair, his clothes in the closet."

"That's why you have to make it home."

"I intend to. I feel better prepared after boot camp, even though I hated it."

"If we're careful and watch out for each other, we'll make it home."

On the last day of boot camp, they received notice of a three-day pass before they shipped out.

John's world was upended by loss, war, and separation from family. In three days, he could return to Chicago and home, but the Army would find him. He erased negative thoughts from his mind and replaced them with thoughts about the courage of Robert and Harry, who set out to do their duty. He rolled his shoulders.

"Are you done thinking?" said Beau.

"I am. Let's go to New York City."

They stepped off a bus at the Port Authority terminal into a city where lively streets pulsed with energy. The whirring of buses, the beeping of taxis, and the crush of pedestrians competing for sidewalk space all added to the allure. Aromas of food drifted in the air.

"I swear the ground is vibrating," said Beau.

"Reminds me of Chicago," said John.

They stepped off a curb but were jolted by the shrill of a whistle.

A policeman waved them back. "Better watch where you're going." Noticing the uniforms, he said, "You on leave?"

"Yes, sir," said Beau.

"My boy's over there now. Been there seven months. Proud of him. If you need a place, there's a hotel three blocks that way. Turn right. Big sign, Lenox. Can't miss it. Good luck."

John nodded.

The manager took twenty dollars off the bill. They ate street food, visited several bars, saw the musical Oklahoma, took a run through Central Park, and laughed a lot. It would be the last time they would laugh.

Six o'clock had barely struck on the morning of March 29, 1943, when Beau woke.

"It's time, John. Ready? We're shipping out."

"I guess so."

Company C gathered outside and boarded a bus. John held his equipment in his lap; Beau sat silently next to him. Arriving at the pier, John stared out of the window. Lined up were imposing gray hulks of troopships. Men drove vehicles and lugged supplies onto the ships, and thousands of soldiers climbed gangplanks, entering the ships. Others stood on the pier waiting for orders.

"Quite a sight," said Beau.

"Impressive," said John.

Men stood at attention. An officer appeared in front of them and bellowed, "Company C, board the ship *Mexico*. The line is to your left. Maintain order. Move."

John and Beau boarded the *Mexico*. They found bunks and watched the shore disappear, wondering if they would see it again. Many wouldn't.

The crossing started out tedious. Life on the ship centered on food— what they would eat and when would they eat it. Soon the voyage turned stormy. John and Beau were ordered to stand watch. The sea lashed out; winds thundered. Waves splashed over the decks. They clung to the rail. Men huddled together on the bridge to wait out the storm. The ship heaved, rolled, and righted itself.

"Must be a test," Beau yelled.

"For what?" hollered John.

Hours later, the rain let up, the winds slowed, the sun set, and men stood upright as relief flooded over them. For the first time, many felt danger; it would not be the last time.

The next morning, the sun was bright and the wind was calm. The ship's navigating officer steered the ship, wary of German submarines and mindful of his responsibility for the safety of those on board.

"My first time away from home and I'm going to war," said John. "I'm scared, Beau. I think my heart is going to jump out of my chest."

"You're not the only one."

"Think we'll make it back?"

"We both will. We must watch out for each other. They taught us that in boot camp," said Beau.

"Yep. What we do affects our buddies."

"You'll come back. We both will."

John's nod was imperceptible.

In the darkness, John lay awake; someone coughed, someone hummed, and someone snored.

At 0600, a voice came over the intercom. "We will be arriving at the Port of Oran in Algeria at approximately 1300. Gather your gear and prepare for debarkation."

On April 11, 1943, the *Mexico* arrived at Oran. Weighted down with waterproof backpacks and rifles, soldiers climbed down a rope ladder. Wading to shore, dust clouded their vision. An atmosphere of chaos greeted them. Arriving soldiers were shoved by crowds. People shouted orders. Local Algerians, dirty and ragged, roamed the streets, sharing the port with horse-drawn carts and soldiers working on disabled vehicles. As the officials came closer, John noticed their weary faces.

Over a megaphone, a loud voice spoke. "Medical supplies are desperately needed for field hospitals and food for makeshift kitchens located 100 miles from port. Companies A, B, and C, unload vehicles from the troopship and fill them with supplies. Arab drivers will take you to your destination."

John's driver had thick, coarse hair and a bearded face; his smile revealed uneven, stained teeth. They bumped along cratered and debris strewn roads in a vehicle packed with supplies, leaving barely enough room for the driver and John.

John slept in a tent, swatted flies, ate unrecognizable food, and listened to a language he did not understand. Returning to port, John and Beau were assigned to do advanced training in the use of the M-4 Carbine assault rifle, a weapon used primarily for close-quarter combat marksmanship where light weight and quick action was required. It could save lives, their own and others. Receiving their own M-4s, they rose at dawn and practiced for hours until proficient.

On May 19, 1943, President Roosevelt sat in his wheelchair waiting for Prime Minister Churchill's train to arrive in Washington, D.C. The invasion of Italy was to be the topic. All principle personnel were in attendance. The conference ended after two weeks of discussion with a plan to invade Sicily first, then Salerno and Calabria, which would place the Allies on the mainland of occupied Europe.

Early one morning, a six-foot-tall officer with a commanding baritone voice gathered the companies together.

"As soon as Sicily is captured, preparation for the invasion of Salerno will begin. Salerno will be our first landing on the continent of Europe," the lieutenant announced. "It is imperative we take it. Our success depends on your courage and bravery. Remember, you are soldiers."

A priest gave them a blessing. Some shed tears; some cried openly; some threw up; and some were stoic. John and Beau sat next to each other, their eyes downcast, their fists wrapped around their rifles.

On July 8, 1943, an Allied armada of vessels left Oran for Sicily to launch one of the largest combined operations of WWII. Companies A, B, and C boarded the *USS Thomas Jefferson* at Oran, joining a sizable armada, and on July 10, they entered the gulf of Salerno.

"Good luck, John," said Beau. "Keep your head down."

"You, too."

Around midnight, the men climbed down cargo nets onto a Higgins landing craft. It was low tide and flares lit up the beaches. The Germans opened fire as soldiers jumped off the craft. A fusillade of bullets spattered the water, hissing and whining. Their landing craft sank. Intense enemy fire made radio communication difficult. The water turned red around floating bodies. Soldiers waded ashore, firing their rifles and tossing hand grenades. Slowly they advanced inland, squirming under barbed wire that marked enemy lines.

They trekked through woods, leaving a trail of bodies like footsteps across the land. Allied guns and tanks soon made their appearance and worked their way inland, knocking out German strongholds as they headed for their assembly point at a railway two miles away.

The Americans who survived advanced along with the British, passing dead bodies sprawled on the road and in the fields. Streets were sucked empty. John kept a watchful eye on Beau, who would raise his hand signaling John to follow. Untrimmed trees and weeds hid the fronts of houses that were vacant, their windows broken or boarded up, their roofs caved in. Papers and shredded cardboard clung to the steps. Further inland, doors and windows were shuttered, but laundry still flapped from iron balconies and geraniums spilled from window boxes. Dead dogs, their ribcages sticking out, lay in the street. Dead bodies lay like bloody throw rugs.

John and Beau mounted the steps of a church. As they pulled the door open, the smell of sickness and death hovered in the air. The church had been converted into a field hospital. The sick and dying were scattered everywhere—or what was left of them. Nurses bandaged wounds and offered sips of water. A priest laid his hands on the afflicted, prayed over bodies, shut the eyes of a young man, and covered him with a blanket. John and Beau knelt and bowed their heads. They moved on in silence.

Beau waved to John and pointed through hedgerows to jeeps in the road. John peered through trees just in time to see the lead jeep explode. They dove for cover. Crouching behind a stump, Beau spotted a machine gun muzzle under a mess of straw. He shoved John. They escaped the bullet that split the stump in two. Beau fired and the German was thrown back. John saluted Beau, but in the mayhem, they were separated from the rest of their unit.

The sun rose and set. Parched, John held his canteen to his mouth, licking the opening. Brambles tore their uniforms, but they plodded on. A bullet buzzed by John's ear, and he fired his M-4 into the direction of the bullet. The sound of gunfire and the explosion of bombs penetrated the air.

Beau heard a voice and turned. Facing them were three Germans with rifles raised. "Stillhalten!" one of them shouted.

John lowered his head. One of them bashed him with the butt of his rifle. He saw little in the dying light. The Germans snatched their rifles and pushed them onto a truck filled with captured American soldiers wearing torn uniforms, looking haggard with vacant eyes and sunken cheekbones. No one reacted to the newcomers.

They were driven for days with occasional stops on the side of the road to relieve themselves. Beau suggested they make a run for it during their next stop.

"It'll be suicide, Beau."

"We're going to a German camp, so we're dead anyway," Beau replied. John agreed.

While the Germans were smoking and adjusting their rifles, Beau whispered, "When I nod, run fast toward those dense bushes." John nodded. They heard guttural shouts and the clatter of boots on gravel around the trucks, but the Germans didn't come after them. John and Beau walked for days.

"Wonder who will find us," Beau mused. "Let's hope the Allies are making inroads."

"Maybe we should stay here…" John let the suggestion hang in the air.

He tapped Beau's arm, put his finger to his mouth. Leaning against a tree were two napping Germans, their packs beside them.

"Make it fast. I'll take the one on the right, you take the one on the left. Now!"

Leaping forward, they pounced. John wrapped his arm around one soldier's neck and squeezed until he stopped struggling. John let go of the body and gagged. Beau beat the other one unconscious and shot him with his own rifle. Breathing heavily, he wiped sweat from his face and turned away.

"They would have killed us. We were unarmed," said Beau.

"I know."

"Truth is, when you kill a man, it doesn't matter if he's your enemy and if he's trying to kill you. It's still hell and will stay with you," said Beau.

John wiped his mouth on his shirt and nodded.

With their backs to the dead Germans, John and Beau tore open their packs and found food and water, which they devoured. John and Beau moved on in shadows. Twice, they heard voices. They decided to move at night and hide in hedgerows during daylight.

Hypervigilance was wearing on them until John heard a click and froze. The first shot blew Beau's head off. A sniper!

A German rose in the bushes, aiming his rifle at John. John got off a shot that blasted the German in the chest—but not before a bullet hit John's leg.

Ignoring his wound, John cried out loud, "Beau, Beau!" Tears streamed down his face and blood oozed from his leg. He cradled what was left of Beau. "I couldn't save him," he cried.

He removed Beau's watch and placed it around his wrist. *That's all I have left of him.* He pulled himself to a tree and waited.

Hearing noises, he rolled over and lay still, face in the dirt, left leg twisted and throbbing with pain. He hid the rifle underneath his body. His helmet obscured his vision. The voices around him were German. A boot kicked his ribs. He took short breaths and clenched his teeth, willing himself to silence. John waited until he could no longer hear the thud of footsteps. He opened his mouth, sucked in air, and pulled himself up on one elbow. Adjusting his helmet, he took in the surroundings. Next to him lay the remnants of his buddy, Beau. Bile rose in his throat. Trembling, he dragged himself away from the carnage toward another tree. Leaning against it, he glanced to his left and saw the German soldier lying face up, a hole in the middle of his chest. John's blood wasted no time making its exit through his left pant leg. Placing a hand on his knee, he let out a moan into the silence.

His mind cleared as he drifted back to an earlier time. Come back to us, his mom had whispered when he left for the Army.

Shifting his position, he murmured, "I will. I will."

Chapter Four

Before the war, in the foothills of the Black Forest, the village of Weiss in southwest Germany attracted vacationers from Germany and France. After church, seventeen-year-old Karl and thirteen-year-old Hans spent the rest of the day in the woods, building lean-tos, climbing trees, and fishing for trout. Of medium height, Karl had a crumpled handsomeness and a mop of unkempt brown hair. Every day he walked to school with his friends and Hans. Their lives changed with the rise of Hitler. Food and fuel became scarce, and fear of Nazi reprisal was constant. Many German families left for Switzerland, leaving Weiss sparsely populated. But Weiss was home to Walter and Elsie Baum and their two sons. Generations before them had lived in the house, and they chose to stay.

The Baums' stone house had two stories. Curtains covered narrow windows on the second floor. On either side of the front entrance, wisteria sprawled, unplanned and slightly wild. A lean-to in the side yard held bundles of hay and stacked wood. A clothesline strung from two poles; laundry flapped in the breeze. They grew vegetables, their chickens provided fresh eggs, and Elsie sold her rye bread to neighbors. They gathered in beer gardens with friends to discuss the village's position on all matters. These conversations sometimes resulted in friends not speaking to each other until the next gathering, when all was forgotten, and new conversations ensued. With the rise of Hitler and battles being fought closer and closer to home, that all changed. Several villagers moved, and those who stayed kept to themselves.

Often Karl's good nature prevailed, but he was given to bouts of outspokenness when he saw wrongdoing—a trait not well-received by teachers who supported Hitler. This outspokenness was exacerbated by the rigidness of the Nazi school system, in which physical training outweighed academic work, and students saluted their teachers at the beginning of class. German Army officers routinely interrupted classes to announce the names of the boys who had to report for duty. Today, when Karl's name was called, his teacher, Herr Wienrath, quickly noted that Baum was excused because he worked on his father's farm to help feed the soldiers. Wienrath announced that tomorrow's class would be replaced by a discussion of military tactics.

Karl stood. "Another time when our schoolwork is neglected."

Furious, Wienrath strode toward Karl and shouted, "Sit down, Baum! Sit down!"

Karl sat but retorted, "Second time this week."

Enraged, Wienrath grabbed Karl's arm with two hands and pulled him from his seat. He dragged him to the front of the room and with one final twist, growled, "Another word and you will be reprimanded." After a moment, he shouted, "Class dismissed! Baum, get rid of that mop you call hair."

Karl left school, cradling his twisted arm. He attempted to join the other students, but they turned their backs on him. Karl wondered if some of them were afraid—afraid of being the next victim of tyranny. A boy from the neighborhood waited.

"Karl, you must be careful. Speaking out will cause trouble for you and your family."

"Why must it be this way?"

"It all comes from Hitler. He wants the best army, and we are his hope to win the war."

"Danka, Frederick, you better go along."

As he entered the house, Karl's mother looked up from wiping the table and saw him holding his twisted arm. "Mein Gott! What happened?"

Karl stepped inside. "I'm not going back."

"Not going back where?" she asked, tucking a few loose strands of blonde hair behind her ear.

"School, Mutter. I'm not learning anything. All we do is salute and praise Hitler. Half the class has joined the Army! My friend Willie left last week. Sixteen years old and I'm worried about Hans who has lived under Nazi rule most of his life."

"But soldiers will come for you!"

"They know I am needed here to help you feed them."

Walter, short and stocky with a heavily lined face, appeared in the doorway. His jaw, covered by thin whiskers, jutted out. "What happened to your arm?"

"The teacher twisted it. I am not going back, Papa."

"Can you use it?"

"Not yet, but I don't think it's dislocated."

"You will stay home with us. And Hans, too."

Karl walked outside, kicking dust where once their garden flourished. Living under a dictatorship, his youth had been snatched away; his education was fragmented, and his freedom was restricted.

Last winter, the electricity was off more than it was on. The only wood left to burn was green, and the village of Weiss smelled of wood smoke. His family had burned crates, papers, and furniture to keep warm. Down comforters kept them from freezing while they slept. Karl and his father trapped rabbits and hunted for mushrooms. He wondered who would rescue them from tyranny and how long his family could survive the life they were living.

British bombs rained on Saarbrucken, inflicting one staggering blow after another. The whistling of falling bombs accompanied by the banging of explosions terrified the people of Weiss. Troubled by what he was thinking and hearing, Karl wanted to rattle the bars of the prison he felt he was in. Weakened by a heaviness in his heart, he trudged back to the house.

Hearing the whinny of a horse, Karl pulled the curtain aside. Entering the village was a gaunt old man holding the reins of a horse pulling a cart, with a young woman sitting in back on a bed of hay, surrounded by their meager belongings. Her arm circled a baby sitting in her lap; nestled next to her was a young child.

"Papa, we have company."

Guided by the old man, the horse stopped at the Baum's gate. The old man climbed down, and with an outstretched hand approached Karl, who grasped it. Though thin and bony, he was surprised at its strength.

"Where are you headed?" asked Karl in German.

"The next village. We're staying with family until the war is over. All the young men are gone. There's only old men like me to take care of family. People rummaged through the debris of rubble-strewn cities where houses once stood and shops thrived, looking for pieces of a life once lived. They move in silence like ghosts."

He glanced at the woman, whose only sound was an occasional sniffle, which she wiped away with the back of her hand. "We have nothing, no shelter, and no food. Here is better. You have food and shelter."

"Stay with my family tonight. Tie up your horse. There is a pail for water inside the barn."

The man's eyes cast a glance at the woman. Her head turned slightly to the baby and a young boy. "Ja, just for tonight," he said.

The old man untied the reins of the horse and walked it to a barn. Karl reached out, lifted the young boy, and placed him on the ground. Holding the baby, the woman followed.

Walter stood in the doorway. "Welcome." Stepping out of the house he approached the cart. "Hallo!"

The old man tipped his cap. "It's good to be here, away from the madness."

"How bad is it?" asked Walter.

"You only see hazy smoke and hear the booming sound of bombs. We felt it. Bombs are dropped day and night with the force of an earthquake, killing thousands. Bombs flattened our houses and destroyed our buildings. There's no letup!"

"Terrible for our people. Come inside. We have food," said Walter. Karl held the boy's hand, and the old man held the woman's arm. Standing in the doorway, Elsie reached out and took the baby from the woman.

"Come, sit, you must be tired." Elsie placed her arm over the woman's shoulder and led her to a chair by the fire. "I'll bring you some tea." The woman squeezed Elsie's hand.

Elsie asked Karl and Hans to bring bowls, glasses, and plates.

Elsie poured milk, ladled out soup, and placed bread on the table.

When had they last eaten? Where had they slept? What had they seen?

Karl laid his hand on the young boy's head. His hair was greasy and his face dirty. Karl retrieved a washcloth, washed the boy's face, neck, and hands, and ran a comb through his hair. The boy ran to find his mother, who cupped his chin and smiled.

The woman fed the children first. Her shawl fell off her head, disheveled brown hair fell over her shoulders, but her youthful face revealed an astonishing beauty.

"Hitler scared us. We had no choice but to obey. If we refused to do what he said, we could have been sent off or shot. Now we hope for rescue," said the old man.

Karl's jaw clenched. He stood and pushed his chair back.

"Hans and I will sleep in the barn tonight. It will be better for you to sleep here."

Walter and Elsie agreed. The old man protested, but Elsie insisted. She took the child's hand and the woman's arm and led them upstairs. Walter followed. Karl lay blankets on the floor next to the cast-iron stove and gave the old man pillows from a chair.

"Danke. I was your age when the Great War ended. This time, things will be very bad for a long time. People have no confidence in Hitler. No one can stop him. Those who tried were killed. Some say he is mad."

"The Americans will stop him. It's our only hope."

The old man's eyes turned to the upstairs and said, "I need to stay alive for them."

"Stay with us."

"That's kind of you, but we must be with family."

"Before we sleep, I have something."

Karl went to the cupboard and found a bottle of Steinhäger and glasses.

The old man's eyes lit up. "Fill up a glass," he said.

Karl obliged and poured one for himself and Hans. They sat in silence, sipping their drinks.

Karl and Hans said goodnight to the old man, crossed the yard, and entered the barn.

"What do you think will happen to them?" asked Hans.

"They will find their family and wait until the war ends."

"What about us? No school, Mutti looks tired, Papa is scared, and our food is—"

"Hans, I will teach you what I know. Mutti and Papa are stronger than you think. We must be brave, take care of each other, and hope the war is over soon. Now, let us sleep."

Comforted by Karl's words, Hans wrapped himself in the blankets and fell asleep.

The next morning, Karl woke. The horse and cart were gone. He dashed to the house. The pillows were on the chair, the blankets neatly folded. He climbed the stairs.

"They're gone, Karl. Left before sunup. I watched the carriage leave," said Walter. "At least they had a warm place for a little while and some food. I'll wake Mutti to tell her."

Always fearful that a Burgermeister would arrive at their home to investigate Karl and Hans's absence from school, the family continued trapping rabbits and tending to their paltry crops.

"Karl, we must check our traps to see if there are rabbits and check for mushrooms. Hans, you stay with Mutti. It shouldn't take long."

"I'll make a stew," said Elsie. "Be careful."

Hans sat at the table slicing turnips. The door flew open. A grim looking soldier barged in. A mix of rancor and desire was on his face. Frightened, Elsie moved behind the table.

"Supper isn't ready, but I can give you bread and sausage."

"I'm not looking for food," he snarled.

Hans stood. The soldier backhanded him, knocking him to the floor.

"Hans!" Elsie cried out, reaching for him.

"Let him be," demanded the soldier.

Elsie recoiled.

The soldier's slick hair clung to his scalp. His dirty hands reached out for Elsie. She shrank back and folded her arms. Grabbing her shoulders, he attempted a kiss. His beard scratched her cheek; his rancid breath sickened her.

"No!" she screamed, pushing him away and turning her head. He pushed the table aside, shook her and started tearing off her clothes.

Abruptly, he stopped. His head jerked and he reached around to his back. Elsie recoiled as the soldier fell to the floor. Hans stared at Mutti, who focused on the knife handle sticking out of the soldier's back. Her hands flew to her mouth.

"I killed him," Hans cried.

Elsie gathered the sobbing boy in her arms.

"You did the right thing. Find Papa and Karl and bring them home."

The boy bolted toward the woods. Seeing his father and brother, he slowed and bent over, catching his breath. "Mutti was attacked by a soldier."

Noticing the boy's cheek, Walter placed his hands on Hans's shoulders and said, "What happened?"

"Papa, I killed him!" Tears streamed down the boy's cheeks. "I killed a soldier who was attacking Mutti."

Walter took Hans in his arms. "Karl!" he called out. "We must leave."

Karl appeared from behind the trees, carrying a satchel full of mushrooms.

"Hans! What happened to your face?"

"The soldier hit me."

"Let's go," said Walter, holding Hans's hand. "Papa, I was scared. He was mean."

"You saved Mutti. That's all that counts."

Elsie sat outside on the step, wrapped in her shawl, her blonde hair in disarray and her clothes askew.

Karl reached her first and sat beside her. "Mutti!"

"Where is Hans?" she asked.

"I'm here, Mutti."

"Are you all right?" she asked.

"Ja."

"Hans, you were very brave," said Karl.

Walter reached out his arms to Elsie and held her. "Hans, sit with Mutti. Karl, let's go inside," said Walter.

Karl stepped into the house and grimaced at the knife handle sticking out of the soldier. Blood pooled around his body. His eyes were open and staring. Gagging, Karl felt a hand at the back of his neck.

"Karl." Walter rubbed his son's neck. "We must do something, and quick. More soldiers could arrive any minute. Let's bury him, quick, but first the knife…" Walter yanked the knife out and tossed it aside. They dragged the soldier out of the house and deep into the woods.

They dug frantically, not stopping until the hole was deep enough to hide the body. Satisfied, they dumped the soldier into the hole and filled it in with dirt.

"They'll never find him. It's done, Papa. Let's go back to the house."

"Karl, what if—"

"No 'what ifs,' Papa. It's done. They won't find him."

"We're dead if they find the body."

Wiping his face with his shirtsleeve, Karl said, "We have to hope they won't."

"But what if they do?" Walter shouted.

Karl hurled the shovel. "Papa, stop!"

Walter weighed his son's advice, turned, and wandered into the house.

They scrubbed the floor, removing all traces of blood.

Walter made tea and gave a cup to Hans, who was wrapped in blankets and still shivering. Elsie sat next to him, her arm resting on his shoulder.

Karl remembered the smell of Elsie's stew, Papa's joy when he trapped rabbits for food, Hans following him around. His family mattered; he would give his life for them.

The incident with the soldier waned Karl's youthful enthusiasm, and fear became his constant companion.

One day while feeding the soldiers, the conversation turned to a missing soldier who had frequented the Baum house for supper.

"Have you seen Soldat Meissner?" asked the soldier in charge. "He was here several times, but he has disappeared."

"It's wartime. Anything could've happened to him," said Karl.

Elsie dropped a dish. It landed like an explosion amid the growing tension.

"Did I say something to upset you, Frau Baum?" the soldier asked, walking toward her.

"Nein, I am not feeling well today."

"War has everyone on edge," said Karl.

Clamping Elsie's arm with his large hand, the soldier said, "I hope you will be better soon."

Elsie flinched. Walter moved to Elsie's side and said, "I'm sure she will be."

By late summer, the war escalated, and soldiers no longer arrived for food.

The Baums' neighbor, Otto, had a shortwave radio. It was forbidden by the Nazis, but it was worth the risk since it enabled him to get information from Radio London. Otto had been orphaned during the Great War and had moved to Weiss to live with his mother's sister and her family, where they raised him as their own. His aunt and uncle had passed, and the family moved on, but Otto stayed in the only home he had ever known. Otto stroked the pipe that was a permanent fixture, either in his hand or between his teeth. Hearing the front door open, he was delighted to see his neighbor and friend.

"Just in time for a beer, Walter."

"Things are bad in the cities, Otto."

"Yes, they are." Otto handed Walter a beer and gestured for him to follow to the basement. "We have to be careful. Spies are everywhere."

"What is happening?" Walter asked.

"We must whisper. The latest information from my radio is that German troops in the Soviet Union are losing. The Americans and British are bombing our country day and night. No one dares speak the truth— that Germany may lose the war. We can only hope the Allies put an end to it soon before we are all dead from starvation or Nazi terror or bombs."

"That is what an old man told us about the bombing. So, it is true?"

"Yes. I saw him pull up in front of your house."

"Sad what is happening to our people." Walter finished his beer in silence. "I must go, Otto. You are a good friend. Be safe."

Walter ran back to the house and repeated what Otto said. The family's hope for an end to the war competed with their worries of worsening shortages. One morning, Elsie sat at the table, wondering if they would survive the war. She removed the worn ribbon that tied her blonde hair at the nape of her neck, ran her fingers through her hair, and refastened it. The memory of the day the soldier attacked her had receded, but not completely. The formidable enemy, war itself, lay in wait to rob her of what little hope she had left for peace. Opening the almost bare cupboard, she retrieved two turnips and several shriveled carrots. It was good that soldiers were no longer coming for food.

A fall chill was in the air. The leaves were starting to turn and the morning was crisp but not cold. A shortage of fuel kept their cast iron stove cold, and the family suffered from the universal scarcity of food. Elsie knitted socks for her family. During sparse meals, Walter told stories of Germany before Hitler and reminded the family that they were first and foremost Germans and not Nazis. Elsie reminded them to be grateful for what little they had.

"We can only hope for the end of the war—but for now I have something." Walter opened the door to a cupboard, reached inside, and retrieved a brown earthenware bottle. "Steinhäger," said Walter. "The best there is." He poured out four small glasses.

"Prost," Walter said and raised his glass.

Karl and Hans smiled knowingly. "Prost," they repeated.

Elsie placed her glass on the table and said, "I have a few turnips and carrots, and if you check the traps there may be some rabbits. There may be some mushrooms, too. I can make a stew."

"Hans, stay with Mutti," Walter said. He and Karl left, each with a satchel.

Chapter Five

Ameter of snow blanketed the mountains. Karl and Walter moved cautiously on and off the trails, always alert for mines.

"When will all this end? Half the people in the village have left and those who are here keep to themselves because they are afraid to be heard speaking out against the Nazis," Karl said.

"I understand, but Otto heard fighting in Leningrad during the winter was bad for the Wehrmacht. Very little food and severe cold."

"I hope it's over before we starve."

"We are a little late for mushrooms, but let's see what we can find. Look over there," said Walter, pointing to a cluster of button mushrooms.

Karl knelt, clipped off the tops, and filled his satchel. Walter checked the traps. Three rabbits.

"Karl, let's go home. Mutti will have her stew." Karl placed a hand on his father's arm. Frowning, Walter asked, "What is it?"

Karl withdrew his hand, brought a finger to his lips, and stood perfectly still. He heard a moan and beckoned his father to follow. Walter shook his head. They crept toward the sound, now easily heard.

"Our business is rabbits, that's all. Let's go." He put a hand on Karl's arm. "Don't go looking for trouble. Soldiers are moving through here. And the mines…"

Karl's curiosity outweighed his unease. He shook off his father's hand and headed in the direction of the sound. With a deep, plaintive sigh, Walter followed.

Approaching a clearing, they saw a soldier sitting up with his chin leaning on his chest, clutching a rifle, his pant leg soaked with blood. Next to him, two dead bodies lay sprawled in the dirt.

Walter grabbed Karl's arm. "Let's get out of here. This could be trouble for us. There is nothing we can do here. We must not get involved."

"Wait. He's breathing."

The soldier's breaths were shallow and rapid. He fumbled with his rifle, tried raising it and failing, slumped back against the tree.

Karl bent down. "What is your name?"

In a voice above a whisper, John replied, "Serial number … can't remember."

"He's American. We could be shot. Let's go," hissed Walter.

"We can't leave him here!"

"Yes, we can!" Walter paced, trying to avoid the scene they had come upon. He returned to Karl, stooped down, and said in a low menacing voice, "We've killed a German and now we are saving an American." He tugged Karl's arm. "If we help him, do you know what this means? What if we get caught?"

"He'll die if we leave him here, Papa. We must have to help him. Can't you see that?" The sight of the dead bodies was revolting for Karl. How many other young men had faced a violent death?

Walter's impatience with Karl's adolescent concern mixed with his own fear, and he shouted, "I see nothing, nothing except Mutter and Hans! We are putting them in danger, too."

"If they were here, they would help him. We're wasting time. Help me," Karl said as he placed one hand under the soldier's back and lifted the soldier's arm over his broad shoulder. Walter shook his head but did the same on the other side of the soldier's body. Karl slipped the soldier's rifle over his other shoulder along with the satchel. He noticed the gun was German, not American. The soldier's head bobbed above them as they started to drag him home.

"Wait, the rabbits!" said Walter.

"You get them. I'll hold the American. Hurry."

Walter returned with his satchel and flung it over his shoulder.

It was close to dusk. Elsie went to the front door, opening it a crack. Unable to see through the dense forest surrounding the house, she listened and heard the crunch of footsteps and the snap of twigs, but there was another sound: the distinct sound of something being dragged. She opened the door wider.

"What is it?" asked Hans.

Elsie wrapped a shawl around her shoulders and stepped out of the house. Hans stood slack-mouthed behind her. Elsie hesitated, looked at the dirt-caked face of the man they were supporting. His jet-black hair was pasted to his head. Eyes the color of ebony stared into Elsie's. Despite the grim set of his mouth, he had a nice face. Seeing the blood streaming down the man's leg into his boot, she shouted.

"Hans, get clean cloths from the closet and quilts from the bedroom! Boil water for tea and bring the iodine."

Karl and Walter dragged the man wearing a uniform Elsie did not recognize into the house and lowered him onto the floor. Karl tore the man's clothes to expose his bloody leg. A chain hung from the man's neck, nestling in the hollow below his Adam's apple.

"He's not German, is he?" Elsie asked.

Karl shook his head. "American."

For several seconds, silence hung around them.

"If soldiers come, we will all be shot," said Walter. "Maybe someone saw us and reported it."

"What would you suggest we do, Papa, bring him back to the woods?"

Words coming out of the American's mouth were masked by pain and a parched throat, but Karl heard, "Help me."

"Papa, we've come this far with him, let's do what we can. I'll get the Steinhäger."

Karl knelt beside the soldier, raised his head, and poured some Steinhäger into his mouth.

"You'll need this while Mutter fixes your leg."

Walter burst out, "If soldiers come, we'll all be shot."

"We have to help him, Papa."

Exasperated, Walter took a swallow of Steinhäger.

"Hold him down," said Elsie. Karl held the man's injured leg while Walter and Hans held the man's arms down. Elsie poured iodine over the wound. The man cried out, struggled to get free, and passed out.

The American's face was peaceful and slack under the numbing bliss of unconsciousness. Elsie packed the wound with torn strips of cloth and sprinkled yellow powder over it and wrapped his leg in layers of cloth.

"Karl, help me take off his uniform."

Karl touched the watch, but the soldier raised his hand and shook his head.

"Hans, find clothes." She turned to Walter. "Where did you find him?"

"In the southeast end of the logging trail. This is an American soldier, Elsie. You know what this means?"

"Ja. If we didn't help him, he would have died. Now we wait for him to get better. Staring at the soldier, she said, "He is not much older than Karl. Hard to tell. War ages people in different ways."

"His name is John Conway. I read his tags. Once he can walk, I will take him to Switzerland," said Karl.

"There are German soldiers everywhere. You will be caught and shot," said Walter.

Elsie wiped her brow with her apron and stood. "I'm weak from lack of food and angry from lack of basic comforts and fearful for lack of safety for my family. We will do what can for this young man," she said. "He's somebody's son and maybe somebody's brother."

"Come with me, Hans. We have just enough daylight left to skin and gut the rabbits and place them in brine," said Walter.

As Karl placed a blanket over John's body, he remembered the horror and wondered about the dead bodies at the scene. Pulling the blanket around John's neck, he felt pity for the wounded soldier. He sighed and joined the family for soup.

Elsie dipped a spoon into the pot of soup and tasted it. Glancing at the sleeping soldier, she knew their lives had changed, but they couldn't go back.

"How can we eat when at any moment soldiers could walk in and see our guest? These are dangerous times, and we may pay a big price for this."

"We would pay a bigger price if we did not help him. We must hide him." Ignoring his father's prophecy, Karl stood and, with determination, said, "We have to hide him."

Walter fidgeted. "Where?"

"Upstairs."

Karl leaned over John and said, "Can you hear me?" John opened his eyes and blinked.

"We are going to bring you upstairs, out of sight. You must remain quiet at all times, because if you are found, it could mean death for all of us."

John nodded.

"Let's go. Stand him up. Papa, get his left side. I'll take the right. Hans, you lift his rear going up the stairs."

Karl urged John, "Lift your good leg. We'll lift the wounded one."

John was barely conscious but did as he was told until they laid him on a bed.

"I'll burn the uniform and hide the boots and rifle in the morning. In the meantime, let us finish our soup," said Karl.

They ate in silence, listening for sounds. Their lives had changed in ways that were unimaginable.

"Thank you for the soup, Elsie. I'm going to bed—as if I could sleep with all this madness," Walter said as he stomped off.

That night, Karl lay awake listening to the sounds of his parents arguing in their room.

"He needs to leave, and soon."

"At least wait until he can walk again," said Elsie.

"It's enough that you stopped the bleeding. Karl and I can get him to Switzerland where he'll be safe."

"But he has to be able to walk."

"I know, Elsie—but if the Nazis find us with an American, we will be shot like dogs. Don't you wonder how he got the rifle we found on him? How do you think he got that? Karl and I can get him to Switzerland and leave him there."

"We haven't seen many soldiers the last couple of weeks. Give it time, Walter."

"Soldiers are retreating through these parts, Elsie!" He sat upright and leaned over her. "Who do you think shot him?"

Walter grabbed the bed covers and pulled them toward him. Turning on his side, he punched the pillow.

Taking the American into Switzerland would be difficult. There was dense forest, hilly terrain, and a stream crossing to manage. It was early October; soon trees would not give them cover. But Karl was familiar with the ground they would have to walk and was convinced he could do it.

Before the sun rose, Elsie rose, wrapped her green shawl around her shoulders, and went to check on the soldier. She wondered if he would die while everyone was out fetching mushrooms when he suddenly spoke. The words that came out of his mouth were masked by a parched throat, pain, and a language of which Elsie only knew very little. He tried to sit up but fell back on the bed. She patted his shoulder, made a shushing sound, and said, "Is good. Is okay."

Later that day, a young man limped to their front door and knocked. Elsie opened the door and looked around.

"Are you alone?" she asked.

"Yes. Please, do you have any food?"

He was a young man. His uniform threatened to engulf his lean body. Whiskers covered his jaw. A lace was missing from a boot.

"Come in."

Walter looked up from the table where he sat slicing turnips. A German soldier! Turnip pieces fell to the floor when he stood.

"My name is Schmid. Ben Schmid."

Elsie moved in front of Walter and said, "Come, sit. I will get you some tea and food."

The American's boots stood next to the fireplace. Walter seized them and tossed them behind a stack of wood, wiping his brow when finished.

"Welcome, soldier. Please, sit," he said, gesturing to the table. Stumbling over his words, Walter said, "Yes, yes, some food and hot tea. You must be hungry and thirsty." Walter glanced around the room wide eyed.

From upstairs, Karl overheard the conversation and flew down the steps, taking two at a time.

"Here's my son, Karl. He lives here. Upstairs—"

"Welcome. I'm afraid there's no fire. We are saving our wood for the winter months, but we have blankets. Papa would be glad to get you one." Karl squeezed Walter's arms.

"Of course, blankets." Walter hurried away.

Elsie brought milk, rabbit stew, and bread, which the soldier devoured, along with the last crumbs that clung to his whiskers.

In a low monotone voice, he said, "Hamburg has been bombed day and night. My mutter and schwester are there. Cities are deserted. Nothing left, yet they still continue to drop bombs. The worst was leaving soldiers behind who were too wounded to save and who begged to die."

Karl's jaw tightened.

Walter arrived with a blanket, which he wrapped around the soldier's thin shoulders. Hans moved closer to Elsie, who placed her arm around him. Fear spread its iciness over them.

"I don't know where I'm supposed to be anymore. We walk for days hearing bombs, but with no orders, it's confusing as to where the enemy is."

"When did you join up?" asked Karl.

"I didn't. They came to my house and got me. I had to leave my mutter and schwester."

Ben looked at Karl. "They didn't come for you?"

"No. I was needed to help here to feed the soldiers who came every day. But not so much now."

"You were lucky. War is hell. I must get back. Don't want to be called a deserter."

Karl shook Ben's hand and removed his sweater. "Take this."

Grateful, Ben pulled it over his head. "Danke. The sweater feels good. I'll remember all of you. The Nazis took my papa for speaking out. My family was left defenseless in Hamburg. I think of them all the time and will try to stay alive for them. It's good you are here with your family. You need each other."

"Maybe we'll see each other again," said Karl.

"Maybe."

"If you come this way again, stop and get some food."

"Danke."

Ben Schmid left the way he had come. Karl watched him walk toward the woods until he could no longer distinguish him from the black fringe of the forest. He walked back to the house, kicking dirt with his torn boot. He passed barren garden mounds.

Walter looked up as Karl entered the house. "Suppose he saw the boots and tells someone we have an American here?" Walter asked.

"He didn't see anything, and there were no sounds coming from the upstairs bedroom." Karl paused, stared at Papa, and said, "That soldier was too tired to notice anything except food. I'll take the American out as soon as possible."

"And you want to keep taking care of him," Walter raised his hand toward the bedroom. "So he can kill more Germans?"

"I understand, but he still needs us."

The next morning, John Conway opened his eyes and tried to move. Pain shot through his leg. His eyes darted around the room. *The rifle. My gear. What happened?* He fingered his dog tags as a young man walked into the room with a teapot and a cup.

John leaned on his elbow, scowled, and said, "Who are you? How did I get here?"

"My name is Karl. I live here with my family. My father and I found you in the woods. You have been here since yesterday. Now you have to get strong so we can take you back to where you were fighting. We have your rifle and boots. Your uniform was torn. We burned it."

John looked at the clothes he was wearing. He sat up, swung his good leg over the side of the bed, and glanced around the room. He lifted his hand and rubbed Beau's watch. The glass was cracked, and time had stopped.

"Where am I?"

"In Germany."

"Germany, what the hell…"

"It's all right. We are not Nazis."

"You speak English."

"Yes. I learned it in school."

"I must get back to my unit." John looked at his leg. It was twice the size and wrapped in cloth, his toes covered by a sock. He tried lifting it, but pain prevented him from doing so. Beads of sweat dotted his brow. "Where did you find me? Was I alone? Did you see—?"

"You were in the woods where Papa and I hunt, and yes, we did see an American soldier. He was dead. Sorry. Was he your friend?"

John squeezed his eyes shut and hung his head.

"Would you like some hot tea?"

"I want to go back to my unit."

"As soon as you can walk, I'll take you, but you must walk first."

John rubbed his bandaged leg. "Is that all you have—tea? I need more than that. Who else lives here?"

"Papa and Mutti and my brother, Hans."

"Sounds cozy. Any neighbors?"

"Yes."

"Great."

"No one knows you're here."

"That's what you say."

"I'll bring some stew up for you and some bread. It's dangerous for you to stay here—and dangerous for my family. It will take weeks for you to be able to walk, but when you can, I will take you to Switzerland."

"I'll walk soon, just you wait. And Switzerland! Nothing doing. I must get back to Italy to join my unit. Why do you wear that sling?"

"My arm got twisted, but it's better. I use the sling to rest it."

John stared at Karl, narrowing his eyes. "How come you're not in the Army?"

"I was needed here to feed the German soldiers, but they don't come as often anymore."

"This is where you fed them? In this house?"

"Yes."

"Will they be back?"

"No. We have little food, and they are needed elsewhere. I made tea."

Karl poured the tea into a cup and added milk. John sipped the tea until the cup was empty.

"How long have you been in the Army?" Karl asked.

"Signed up in December of last year. Went through boot camp in April. I was shipped to Oran in Algeria, then Italy, and waded into a war. My buddy and I got separated from our unit and got captured by the Germans. We managed to escape but got lost. You saw what was left of him when you found—"

"Yes, I did. Was he a good friend?"

"We were brothers in combat. We were taught to look after each other. I dropped the ball."

"It wasn't your fault. Looks like you were ambushed."

Silently, John waved his arm. "I heard your father telling you to leave me. Why did you rescue me?"

"Because you were badly wounded and would have died. Papa fears for us every day. He is afraid if the Nazis find you, it will mean death to all of us. You had best stay up here until you are well enough to leave."

"Just leave. I prefer to be alone."

"Are you feeling all right?"

"I don't feel anything." John rolled over and faced the wall.

He seems angry that we rescued him.

Karl turned and headed downstairs. "Mutti, he doesn't want anything."

"He is young, has a bad wound, has seen war, and now he is in a German home. He is afraid. Try to understand."

"But we saved him."

"Yes, from his wounds, but not from what he has seen."

John Conway's recovery was painfully slow. By incremental steps, he grew strong enough to sit in a chair. Constant pain intensified his anxiety. Fear of unwanted visitors hung over the house. John spent his days peering out of the bedroom window. When Walter and Karl left to find food and wood, John waited uneasily for them to return, listening for two sets of footsteps and not more. From a distance, he saw smoke curl into the sky and shuddered, hearing the whistle of bombs and the explosions that came after. He watched leaves fall from the trees and watched daylight disappear earlier each day. His sleep was disturbed by visions of the dead he had walked over, the German soldiers he and Beau had killed, the civilians with haunted looks—and his buddy, Beau.

John picked at his food. He was grateful for Elsie's care, but he couldn't talk to her. Her innate kindness reminded him of his mother, whom he sorely missed. He could talk with Karl, but even that was growing tedious. Karl's curiosity with everything American was grating. One day, Karl brought a map of North America and asked John to show him where he was born. John pointed to Chicago. Karl had many questions, and for a while John patiently answered. Eventually, irritation dampened his responses.

The next morning, Karl arrived with breakfast. Dark circles had formed under John's black eyes and his matted black hair gave him the look of a ghoul.

Karl set the tray on the bed. He had brought a cup of tea for himself. Sitting in the chair, John rubbed his throbbing leg and lifted it to place it on the bed, knocking the breakfast tray over, spilling the dishes and contents.

"Now look what you made me do!" John yelled.

Triggered by ingratitude, Karl fumed. "It's your clumsiness that did it." Regaining his composure, Karl picked up the dishes, wiped up the mess, and said, "I'll get you some more breakfast."

"You call that breakfast! Mashed turnip and carrots! Don't bother."

Karl was used to John's rudeness, but that didn't make it easier to accept. Hearing the noise, Elsie climbed the steps leading to the bedroom.

"Everything is okay?" she asked.

"Fine," John grunted.

Elsie glanced at the unkempt condition of the bandage, John's sunken face, and unfocused eyes. She spoke with a heavy accent, but in her effort to speak English, she spoke slowly to John, and he understood her.

Elsie placed her hand on John's forehead. "Hot. Karl, bring tea and clean cloths."

She unwrapped the bandage. The putrid odor made her stomach churn.

John looked at his swollen leg. Pus oozed from it.

"Shit. It's infected. I have to get out of here and get to a hospital," he said.

"Nein hospital. You will be arrested. I will clean it."

John sank back into his sullen mood. "If I don't make it home, no one will miss me."

Elsie was far too worried about John's leg to be concerned with his sulking. She said simply, "Your mutter will." Elsie tossed the bandages into a bucket and examined John's leg. "I will wrap leg, and you do as you are told. Is there a fräulein back home? She would miss you."

"There was, but we parted ways."

"Where does she live?"

"Chicago."

"We will get you home so you can talk to her."

"What makes you think I want to?"

Karl entered the room with a bottle of iodine.

"This will sting, but we have to pour over leg," said Elsie.

John fretted and writhed in pain. Embarrassed, he told Karl to leave. Elsie's voice and quiet way soothed him. She spoke slowly, describing what she was doing and the progress his leg would make.

After changing his bandages, Elsie sat on the chair next to John's bed. "Your leg will get better, but it will take time."

"How am I going to walk to Italy?"

"Karl will help you."

"With that arm? What about your husband?"

"Karl will do. His arm is better."

Three days later, Elsie and Karl climbed the stairs to the bedroom. "Okay, now we walk," said Elsie.

John was a head taller than Karl and thinner. Karl was strong, and with his broad shoulders and sturdy body, he lifted John to a standing position with no assistance from Elsie. Clinging to the chair, John took a step, grimaced, and took another. A week later, he was walking the perimeter of the room as often as possible.

After spending weeks in the room, the smell of iodine lingered in the room and John had enough of it. He opened the bedroom door and stood at the top of the stairs. Downstairs was unfamiliar territory. He took one step at a time and reached the bottom. He turned, looked around, and walked back up and down.

The front door blew open and cold air rushed in. Startled, Karl said, "What are you doing down here?"

"Got sick of the sights in the room and needed some exercise."

"You need a place to hide quickly if we have visitors."

"Find me a place. I'm coming down for meals from now on. I need the exercise."

John climbed the stairs to his room, sat on the bed, and was soon fast asleep.

Two hours later, he woke, lifted his uninjured leg, and swung it over the side of the bed—just as an explosion hit. The house shook, windows rattled, and he fell to the floor. Karl ran upstairs and reached for him.

"I can do it. Leave me alone." Immediately regretting his reaction, he said, "Thanks."

He clung to the bed frame, stood, and sat on the bed.

Surprised by the unexpected appreciation, Karl asked, "Who's Lily?"

"How do you know about her?"

"You yell in your sleep."

This was not the first time John's demons visited him in his sleep.

"She was my girlfriend. We dated over the summer before I left and we got carried away. Know what I mean?"

"Yes."

"She wanted to get married and had a fit when I said no. I was going to war. I drove her home and left her there. Never saw her again."

"You have regrets?"

Waving a hand, John said, "Is your arm the reason you're not in school?"

"Partly. Not enough academics, just rigorous physical training."

"But you can use it."

"Of course."

"What do you hear about the war?" asked John.

"The Americans and British have been bombing Germany with success, and the Luftwaffe is losing."

"If the Americans find me here, they will think I'm a traitor."

"They will take our word for what happened."

Karl's naiveté grated on John. "I need to get out of here as soon as possible to get back to my outfit."

"Will you tell them about Beau?"

"Beau was a hero. He died serving his country. Look at me, helpless and living with the enemy."

"We are not your enemy. Most Germans wait to be rescued by the Americans." Karl paused and said, "The walk to Switzerland is approximately five hundred kilometers. We must leave as soon as you are ready. We should leave before the snow falls, so keep exercising. It's a long journey, but I know the way."

"How far is Italy? Because that's where I need to go."

"Italy is farther. We may be able to find a place in Switzerland to rest first. Two hundred kilometers would be our limit."

John hobbled to the window and looked out into darkness. Leaves dropped and the ground outside hardened. John found himself alone.

I need to get out of here. He called down to Karl to bring up his rifle and boots.

Uneasiness swept over Karl. "Why the rifle?"

"Because it's mine."

Not wanting to question John further, Karl retrieved the boots and rifle and left them with John.

Later that day, John sat on the edge of the bed. He rubbed his whiskers, tucked his unruly hair under a cap, laced his Army boots, and waited for the call to supper. He wiped beads of sweat from his forehead and felt his heart hammer against his chest. His leg ached, but it was time to go. Limping to the bedroom door, he opened it a crack and peered through.

There were five steps leading to the living area. Wood was piled high on the left and a rack for clothes on the right. Straight ahead was a square table surrounded by four chairs. Elsie stirred the stew and called for John to come for supper. John let out a long sigh, lifted his duffel bag, stood at the top of the stairs, and positioned his rifle.

"No one move." John navigated the stairs and stood at the bottom, waving his rifle. "Thanks for your help. I'm leaving, and Karl is coming with me."

Elsie's hands flew to her face. Walter sprang to his feet shouting, "No! No! I will go."

"Karl is coming. He knows the way, and we are leaving now."

45

"Put that away," shouted Karl, pointing to the rifle.

"Nothing doing. Get your coat, pack a few things. You're coming with me."

Karl grabbed the satchel he and Hans used for hunting. He tossed in matches, socks, and gloves.

Trembling, Elsie handed bread and dried sausage to Karl. Hans wrapped his arms around Karl. An eternity of seconds passed. Walter took a step.

"Back off, old man."

Walter stood in place. We never should have rescued him.

John felt the urge to assuage Walter's obvious anguish. "Because of the war, there is a shortage of workers in England and America. If Karl gets captured, he could end up in one of those places. When he comes home, he can tell you about his travels."

Angered by the lame attempt to appease him, Walter glared at John and spit out, "Scheisser!" then turned his back.

John motioned Karl toward the front door. "Let's go."

Karl walked out into dusk and John limped along behind him. A chill wind blew.

Chapter Six

The ancient forest floor was nut-brown, and twigs crunched under the weight of the men's heavy steps. Branches creaked on aged trees, some rotting silently in the forest floor. A bitter, earthy scent filled the air as scurrying animals scampered away. The last of autumn's leaves had spiraled to earth. The darkness of night kept the men safe, but with daybreak there was a chance they could be discovered.

In an even voice, Karl said, "I'll get you to the Swiss border and then I am coming back. My family needs me."

John didn't acknowledge the statement. Italy was his destination. He waved the rifle and said, "Keep walking."

John's leg ached and he was startled by the slightest noise. "I'll shoot anything that comes near us!" He tightened his grip on the rifle.

"Shots will draw attention," Karl replied.

All night they walked silently, encumbered by thick brambles. The brisk air smelled of matted leaves. Trees groaned in the distance. The yellow moon sent shafts of light among distorted trunks. The sound of bombs, like harsh thunder, crashed in the distance. Smokey haze hung in the air. Their movements were deliberate, and the dampness and chill sharpened their minds. They walked from sunup to sundown, only stopping for a brief rest, water, and a bit of food.

John tripped over a downed limb, cursing his clumsiness. Karl looked back over his shoulder. "Are you okay?"

"Yeah, just fine." In fact, John was growing weaker and walking strained his good leg.

Karl's back was straight, his shoulders square, his eyes always looking ahead. John's eyes, sharp and suspicious, shifted reflexively from side to side.

Thunder cracked and jagged spears of lightning lit the sky. A wall of rain soaked their clothes. They retreated into the shelter of a pine tree and waited for the skies to clear. John used a stick to scrape off the caked mud covering his boots and tried to find a position to relieve his aching leg.

"What will you do when the war ends?" asked John.

"If the Allies are successful, I'll get my life back, finish school with Hans, and help my family get food."

"Seems simple."

"What will you do?"

John lowered his head. *Rid myself of nightmares*, he thought. "How far have we've come?"

"About two hundred and fifty kilometers. Then it's pretty much foot paths for a while," said Karl. He exhaled and watched his breath turn the cold morning air into a misty cloud.

"How do you know that?"

"This is my backyard."

"How much farther?"

"A little more than two hundred kilometers to Switzerland."

Weak from walking and fearful that he might not make it, John heard his mother's voice. *Come back safe.*

"Let's get going," said John, struggling to stand. "The rain has stopped."

Karl's eyes shifted to the rifle. He could be shot for aiding the enemy. He had to get John to Switzerland, and the border would have to do. Karl looked up at a starless sky and thought of his family.

They'd walked a fair distance when John's vision became distorted. He raised the rifle thinking he saw German soldiers. A chill ran through him. He rubbed his eyes, shook his head, and walked on. The air smelled like wet grain and hedge trimmings. Clouds parted, allowing a full moon to light their way.

The protection of night fell away, and dawn emerged, leaving them vulnerable. Karl brushed dirt from his clothes and kept his glances short when looking at John. Staring ahead, he called over his shoulder.

"Try to keep up. We have to move. We're in grave danger if a patrol catches us. They'll shoot us. And I must return home."

"Take it easy. I know it's hard for you, but I need you to help me," John said.

"Bad leg or not, we keep moving until we get to the border. By the way, how did you get a German rifle?"

"I killed for it. It was that or be killed. I saw things I wish I could forget, I but can't."

Karl sensed that John's resolve was cracking, yet he knew his support could be taken for sympathy. "I'm scared for my family. They might starve before the war ends. I must get home to help them. We saved your life in case you forgot. I'll get you to the Swiss border, and that will be the end of it."

Seeing John's difficulty walking, Karl slowed his pace.

John said, "Fine, just get me somewhere where I can rest." He pulled his jacket around his neck. "I had a brother. He joined the Navy a couple years ago and got blown up by the Japs. At least your brother is still alive."

"Sorry about your brother. Must have been hard."

"It was. I thought going to war I might get killed like my brother and Beau."

"You've seen a lot, but you're alive. You'll make it. I'll get you to Switzerland, and you can get to Italy from there."

The brush was thick, scratching their faces and necks. Every step required pushing away branches, struggling over felled trees, and plodding through water-filled ditches. By midmorning, they came to a road that was flanked on both sides by well-spaced trees and with no fallen limbs to impede their journey.

"Wait. I need to stop," implored John.

As anxious and exhausted as he was, Karl's frustration with John's grumbling spilled over. He spun around and yelled, "Stop complaining and keep up! Lean on me."

Karl placed his arm around John's waist and supported him for a good distance on flat ground, stopping briefly to catch his breath.

"Never thought I'd be in this mess."

"Neither did I," said Karl.

Karl removed his arm from around John's waist and they slid to the ground for a rest. Karl took a swig of water and passed the canteen to John.

"Is your family in Chicago?"

"Yes. Downers Grove, about twenty miles west of Chicago. Just my sister and mother and father now."

"And Lily?"

"I'm sure she found someone else. She was class president and smart. I told her she should go to college. 'How?' she said. 'My parents have no money.'"

Karl couldn't wait to get rid of John and return to his family. He filled the canteen from a clear, cold stream and upon returning said, "Come on, get up."

"Okay, okay."

Day after day, night after night, they struggled with only sunrises and sunsets offering them direction. Night became a new day, and the trail soon left the forest and trees dwindled to a few scraggly bushes. Their food was gone, their canteen was empty, and their spirits weakened, but they plodded on. John's wounded leg had healed to the point of being serviceable, but every step was painful.

They came to a creek, stooped down, and cupped their hands. They drank the ice-cold water and splashed it on their faces. Cautiously crossing, they collapsed on the other side. Rubbing their hands together, they pulled their caps lower over their ears. Everywhere they looked, the trees were black, wet, and lifeless. Their boots were encrusted with a watery gray ice.

Karl stood, looked east, and squinted at a body of water. "Must be the Rhine River."

"So what?"

"It flows north to south through Switzerland. If we follow it, we may see some farms. This is Alpine country, and the terrain is mountainous. But if we made it this far—"

"Wait, mountains?"

"Yes, the Swiss Alps."

"The Alps! I can't climb mountains. Why can't we find a road?"

"We need to stay away from roads where there is border control. Switzerland is surrounded by countries that are occupied by the Reich. There will be no defined trail from here on, so we cannot afford to make a mistake. If we stay close to the river, we'll be walking farther into Switzerland, where we will be safe."

Snow, silent and soft, began to fall.

"Are you sure."

"Yes. Follow me."

Karl tore two thick branches from a bare tree and handed one to John, who was still sitting.

"Let's go. Use this. It will help with the walking."

The snow became deep and dry and covered their boots. They silently followed the Rhine. Later that day, Karl heard the clank of bells and halted. Lowering his head, he listened. From a distance, he heard the mooing of cows and cow bells.

"We've arrived at a Swiss farm," he yelled. "There are Christmas candles in the windows!"

"Suppose they call the police."

"The Swiss are neutral." Karl eyed John's rifle, pointed to it and said, "That has to go."

"Are you crazy? Suppose they have guns?"

"Maybe, but they don't shoot people. Throw it away, now."

"And if I don't?"

"You go on alone."

Furious, John pointed the rifle at Karl, who started to walk toward the farm. Karl made a half-turn, and out of the corner of his eye saw the rifle hit the snow.

Looking out of the window, the farmer saw two men approaching the house. He called to his wife, "Elsbeth, we have company, much like the others that come. I'll see to them." He pulled on a jacket and cap and walked outside. "Hallo," he called out.

Karl waved and told John to do the same, which he did begrudgingly. Coming closer, the farmer saw their dirty faces, their torn clothes, and anxious looks. Having seen this before, he beckoned them to come.

Speaking in German, Karl said, "We got lost. Haven't eaten in a while. Do you have any food you can spare?"

Pointing to the barn, the farmer said, "Go there, I will bring food."

Covered in snow, they hobbled into the barn and fell upon stacked hay. The hems of their trousers were wet from snow, their socks damp, their faces stiff.

The farmer returned with two quilts, a plate of cheese, bread, meat, and a pitcher of milk. Karl's eyes widened and John's mouth hung open.

"My wife fixed food and sent these socks to keep you warm. Where are you headed?"

"Italy," said Karl.

Speaking in German, the farmer asked Karl if he was going to stay in Italy.

"Nein, I will return home once I get him to the border," Karl said, gesturing to John.

"I will take you close to the border in the morning."

"What did he say?" John asked.

"He will get us close to the border. There are border patrols everywhere. He has to be careful."

Sitting on a bed of hay, they devoured the food and drank the milk. Wrapped in the quilts, they fell into a deep sleep and did not wake until morning.

Sun beamed through the barn windows; a rooster crowed, and the cowbells clanged. The farmer opened the door of the barn, and they winced at the stream of daylight.

"Elsbeth is packing food. We leave soon."

"Thank her for us," Karl said. Glancing at John, he added, "We need a toilet."

The farmer pointed and said, "Over there, the field."

The snow had abated, making it easier for them to relieve themselves, and while John was in the field, the farmer spoke to Karl.

"I will drop you off as close as I can to the border. I cannot wait for you. It may look suspicious. Spies are everywhere. Follow the same way back I take you. Be careful. There is a town along the way. You will see the signpost. Tomorrow, I go to the feed store, and I will take you back to the farm, where you can rest before going back to where you came from."

Grateful, Karl pumped the farmer's hand. "I'll be there." He looked down at his clothes.

"Don't worry, refugees arrive there every day. You look better than most."

John joined them. "Looks like you two are buddies," he said.

Elsbeth arrived with food wrapped in a cloth. Her blonde plait hung over one shoulder. She handed them more thick socks. They kicked off their boots and pulled on the socks.

"Danke, danke."

John did not respond.

Karl retrieved the quilts from the barn, and they climbed onto the truck.

"I don't trust that guy," said John.

"What would you suggest? That we walk to Italy?"

Karl ate in silence and watched the direction the farmer was taking. The truck came to a halt. The farmer turned and said, "This is where I leave you. Head south, and just over the next hill you should cross the border into Italy. Viel gluck."

"Danke." Karl reached out his hand. The farmer shook it.

They waved as the farmer drove away, then continued to the hill. A steep incline covered with snow led into a village below. Karl knelt to hear what the voices were saying.

"From what I can hear, the British are rounding up German soldiers. This is where I leave you. You can make it from here. You'll be safe with the Brits," said Karl.

"I can't get down that slope."

"Just slide. Once they see you are an American, you'll be fine. It's not that steep. Listen, I need to leave."

"It's too steep." John's foot slipped in the snow and he tumbled down the slope.

"Are you all right?"

John moved slightly and lifted his snow-covered head. "I can't get up." Desperate, Karl cried out, "Try, try." He needed to leave before dark.

If he left now, he would make it. Someone would find John.

John pleaded, "Don't leave me."

"Can't you crawl? The village doesn't look too far from here." Frustrated and furious, Karl said, "I've done enough for you. I got you to Italy, put up with your whining. I left my family. I've had enough. I'm going home. Crawl to the village!" Karl plodded through the snow with one thought in mind—the feed store—until he heard John's voice.

"I'll freeze."

Karl stopped, wrapped his arms around his chest and blew his breath into the cold air. He turned and stumbled down the slope.

"Get up!" He grabbed John's arm and lifted him.

"Hold it!"

A soldier was aiming a rifle at them. Karl let go of John, who slid to the ground. Karl felt his heart knocking wildly against his chest.

"Get up. Let's go," snarled the soldier.

John raised himself up and clung to Karl, who stood rigidly next to him. John reached inside his jacket and, trembling, pulled out his dog tags. "I'm an American. Look!" he said, waving his dog tags and with a rise in the pitch of his voice, added, "I don't know who this guy is. He came from nowhere."

Karl felt a wave of outrage at what he heard. His eyes grew wide, and he tried to speak but was silenced by the guard.

"You German?"

Karl started to speak but was again silenced by the guard. "Over there." The soldier swung the rifle toward a footpath.

Karl heard the farmer's voice. *Be careful.* A sense of impending doom ran through him.

John blabbered about fighting in Italy for the Americans and how he got wounded.

"Quiet. Just move."

They entered the village and the soldier called out, "Look what I found! A Yank and a Kraut."

Sickened by the reference, Karl found his voice. "German."

"Bloody hell!" said an officer. "Where's your uniform?"

Trying to sound convincing, Karl said, "I didn't serve in the Army."

"You mean the Nazis didn't find you? Are you a deserter?"

"No, I am not."

John felt the ground beneath him give way and passed out. Blood oozed down his leg.

"Medics! Get this guy outta here."

Pointing to Karl, the officer said, "Okay, you, get your arse to the truck."

"Where am I going?"

"For a long ride."

Four soldiers arrived carrying a litter and placed John onto it. The movement woke him. Cold and pain swept through his body like an irreversible tide.

"Where am I going?"

"A collection station, to get a jeep. They travel better than ambulances over this terrain. We'll get you to a field hospital. From the looks of that leg, you'll probably be sent home."

Planes thundered overhead, artillery rumbled in the distance, and the cries of the wounded soldiers traveling with John pierced his ears.

Chapter Seven

Under the point of a rifle, walking toward the truck, Karl passed broken pieces of rock scattered in the road, empty buildings with cracked facades, and remains of exploded vehicles. Gunshots echoed in the distance and military trucks roared through the streets. Beyond, there was an eerie silence. He climbed aboard the truck, a tarpaulin covering its bed.

Prisoners were jammed in on metal seats that lined the sides. Karl stared at the faces of war with jutted-out collarbones, vacant eyes, and ragged uniforms that hung on bodies too thin to carry them. It was grim evidence of a war going badly for Germany. He lowered his eyes and stared at the floor. Thinking of his future was unbearable.

Two soldiers armed with rifles stood in the back. One of them rapped the side of the truck with the butt of his rifle and yelled to the driver, "Get this thing in gear, Crocker, and keep your foot on the goddamn pedal. Orders are to get these guys to Salerno. We've got a long drive."

Engines roared to life. The lead truck turned right onto a gravel road with the others following. They drove over rough fields and torn-up roads. The prisoners slept despite noise, despite cold, despite hunger as though desperate to stay detached from what was coming.

Later that day, the truck slowed and came to a jerking stop. The flap on the back of the truck opened and the gate was dropped down. A soldier climbed out and hollered, "Everyone out! Take a quick piss and get back on."

Grateful for the air, Karl bent over, inhaled deeply, and relieved himself.

The prisoners climbed out. One fell and remained on the ground, an arm trapped beneath him. Karl made a move toward him.

"Back off."

"But—"

"You heard me."

They stepped over the prisoner as if he were a fallen log. Once all the prisoners had boarded, the truck sputtered to life, putting more and more distance between Karl and his family. He stared out the back of the truck and watched the motionless body of the young soldier on the ground.

"They don't care," said a man to no one in particular.

Bent over, Karl held his head in his hands. "Where are they taking us?"

"Salerno, to board a ship."

Karl looked up. "A ship!"

"Yes. It looks like we will be crossing the Atlantic."

"The ocean?"

"What else?"

Daylight gave way to darkness. The life Karl had left behind was as distant and out of reach as ever. *How will I get back?*

Chapter Eight

Bumpy roads jostled the prisoners. Wondering what fate awaited him, Karl felt a rush of anger and regret for rescuing John Conway. The truck made a turn, its brake squealed, jarring the prisoners.

More orders were shouted. "Everyone out!" They stepped onto frozen ground and cold air swept through them. "Strip and toss your clothes in a heap and keep your boots. Go through the front door of the building, one at a time. Move it!"

Karl's fist tightened. No one came back after entering.

Assorted trousers, shirts, jackets, and caps were piled on a table. "Take your pick and line up."

Karl reached for the clothing, pulling on trousers that were too long, a shirt that was too tight, and a jacket that fit. Walking out the back door, he saw the scorched earth of Salerno. The air was full of smoke and dust. Houses sliced in half were left with charred window frames and shattered glass. A man slumped over a table was sleeping on his ear. A dark maroon stain made its mark and spoke volumes about his story. Scattered survivors clung to each other like magnets as they threaded their way through the ruins. Furniture was scattered across the road. Shells of windowless buildings stood silent. Women and children emerged from their hiding places to find food overlooked by pillagers and picked through the rubble. An old woman removed stones with withered hands that appeared ancient. The living searched for the dead. Children, too thin and listless to move, sat on piles of rocks. Laundry flapped from iron balconies, but every door and window remained closed.

"Let's go, blokes. Get your arses going. Follow me."

Following those ahead of him, Karl walked over a makeshift dock and stepped on the bottom rung of a rope ladder. He advanced to the top of the ship where he felt a hand squeeze his arm. He tried to pull away, but the hand squeezed tighter.

A gruff voice said, "You didn't serve our country."

Karl boarded the ship and snapped, "Let go of me."

"Maybe you are a spy."

The man struck Karl in the stomach. He doubled over but managed to push his foot against the man's shoe, loosening his grip and causing him to slip, giving Karl just enough time to shove him away. The man had an ordinary face, but the broken zipper-like scar cutting its way across his cheek made him memorable.

Grabbing the man by his shirt and staring into his cold eyes, Karl said in a terse voice, "I am as good a German as you are. The next time you lay your hands on me, I'll break your fingers." He pushed the man aside. Trembling, he walked over to the rail and looked down at the sun-speckled sea. Waves of uncertainty washed over him. Doubt curdled his thoughts. Who could he trust? Where was he going? Would he ever get home?

"Hey, you! Move!" yelled a soldier whose formidable stance deterred any thoughts of resistance.

"Where are we going?" asked Karl.

Hearing the break in Karl's voice, the soldier looked at Karl with narrowed eyes. "What difference does it make?"

"It makes a difference to me."

"Guess, you lucky bastard. Now, move."

The undertow of fear pulled hard against the current of disbelief. Ignoring others rushing around him, Karl watched the line of prisoners disappear into the ship. John had mentioned Chicago, but he didn't really know where that was. Karl was adrift and lonely. Nothing would wash away the yearning for his past as his future stretched before him. He climbed through an opening in the ship and followed the crowd through a maze of hallways until he reached a room with filled bunks on either side, so close together that walking was impossible. Fear permeated everything. A pall of silence prevailed. Karl squeezed by as unobtrusively as possible until he found an empty bunk. Relieved, he slid in. A prisoner a foot away from Karl turned and said, "Willkommen, namen Eric."

"Danke, Karl Baum."

A head popped up from another bunk and said, "Karl Baum, is that you?"

Karl turned his head. "Ben Schmid!"

"Never thought I'd see you here," Ben said, leaning over his bunk. They grasped hands, each grateful to see a familiar face. Disgruntled prisoners demanded they lower their voices.

Speaking quietly, Ben said, "Got captured a few weeks after I left your place." He opened his thin jacket and rubbed his sweater. "Still have it. What happened to you?"

"We hid a wounded American."

"Yes, I know."

"You knew?"

"Saw the boots."

"Papa was so worried that you would report us."

"What I see I keep to myself."

"Mutter healed his leg as best as she could, and I got him to Italy where the British picked us up. The American was in bad shape. He was taken away by ambulance, and I was sent to board this ship."

"So you rescued an American and got captured by the British. There must be more to that story."

"Yes, there is, but I'm trying to forget it."

"What about your family?"

"They are probably still waiting for me to return."

"They'll be safe where they are. I ended up in Naples. It was brutal. Constant attacks, but at least I'm alive."

"Yes, I saw the effects of war in Salerno and that was enough," said Karl, tipping his head toward Eric. "Meet Eric. This is Ben. He was at my house in Germany."

"Willkomen."

"Danke."

Sitting on the edge of his bunk, Eric said, "I saw what that guy did to you boarding the ship. I don't care if you weren't in the Wehrmacht, but there may be others that do."

Grateful for Eric's thought, Karl said, "Thanks for the warning."

Soon the room was full. Engines turned, the ship shuddered and gave life to cold steel as they left Salerno for the Atlantic Ocean. Swells began to form and indicated the ocean's unease. Prisoners were ordered to stay in their bunks.

Outside, waves rose to ten feet and higher, which caused the ship to sway. Waves crashed against the hull. The ship heaved upward and slammed down into the troughs. Water flowed down the steps of the ship. Furniture was airborne. In the bunks, prisoners began to retch and left vomit in their wake on the way to the latrine. Seasickness spread like a contagion. Those who made it on deck slipped in the slime left by men who had emptied their stomachs before they reached the rail. Some hung their heads over the side of the ship, moaning softly, as if it were a secret shame. The ship stank with the odor of vomit. Mops and buckets were given to those who were able to clean up the mess. Seasickness and dread vied for dominance.

Three days later, the storm abated but the smell lingered. Men were allowed up on deck twice a day to alleviate their nausea. Prisoners queued up for meals, for the use of latrines, and for time on deck, where the air was fresh. Crowding and boredom aggravated anxiety, and tempers flared. Not knowing their destination, the prisoners were on edge. Skirmishes broke out but were quickly halted by guards, vigilant about problems.

Eric burst into the room. "Heard talk on deck. We're heading for America, where there is no war and no bombs. So, brush up on your English."

"It will be better than Germany. At least there will be food and a bed," said Ben.

Karl turned toward the wall and, for the first time, prayed to a God he wasn't sure existed. Between the arduous routine of a troopship at sea and the sheer boredom of having only the ocean to look at, the minutes passed like hours. There was nothing to remind him of home, only memories.

Baseless rumors of harsh treatment of the Americans caused unease among the prisoners. The guards remained vigilant to uphold order but demonstrated restraint and fairness. Eventually, the prisoners came to terms with their situation.

Early morning announcements included the day of the week, the number of days away from the port of entry, and reports of Allied advances in Europe and the Pacific. The German translation was, to be expected, brief and perfunctory. Karl translated for prisoners. Hardline Nazis, who remained hopeful that Germany could counterattack, shouted expletives.

One morning a voice echoed through the main circuit: "Attention! Attention! Arrival at New York Port will be at approximately 0900 hours. Obey orders and stay in line."

A new part of their journey began.

Karl stood on deck in the slanted light of early morning, his hands thrust into the pockets of his trousers. The bitter cold sharpened his senses. Memories of his family were so vivid they appeared in the air before him. They became the thread he would cling to when he was lonely.

Determined to see the sights, he stood shivering until the Statue of Liberty, reaching powerfully to the sky, soared into view. Awestruck by her magnificence, he wondered how many immigrants from other countries she had greeted. The ship moved closer, and coming into view were buildings with floor-to-ceiling windows like curtains of glass mirroring others.

Coming alongside Karl, Ben said, "Quite a sight."

"No shattered buildings," Karl said. "German propaganda had depicted the United States as war torn."

As they made their way to their bunks, orders were shouted from the loudspeaker: "Prepare to go ashore. Remain silent."

The ship hugged the dock and came to a stop with a soft thud against the pilings. A well-ordered human chain wound around the steps and prepared to go ashore. Fidgety soldiers, acting as armed guards, lined the gangway to prevent escape, their eyes darting from one prisoner to the next. At the end of the gangway, the prisoners stepped on the shores of America and entered the reception area inside an enormous tin-covered warehouse on the docks. Prisoners were fingerprinted and given identification cards. The line rushed through without an incident. Open-door buses were at the curb, waiting to take them to the train station.

Karl's eyes were fixed on the sights through the bus window. Buildings were intact; people walked freely, carrying bundles, dressed in warm clothes, chatting with each other. Beeps and blasts from car horns filled the air. A line formed at an open window on the side of a truck with the words "HOT DOGS" written on it. Karl wondered what a "HOT DOG" was. Astonished by what he saw, he momentarily forgot how he arrived at this place.

The bus pulled up to the train station, where throngs of people were entering. The soldier who had ridden with the prisoners stood. "Follow me, stay in line."

The men trudged downstairs to the platform to await the train that would transport them to the last stop on their journey.

Chapter Nine

Karl Baum stood among the German POWs at the end of the platform under the watchful eyes of two guards. Anticipating the train's arrival, crowds jostled for position to find suitable seats. The train pulled into the station with the high-pitched squeak of brakes and a great gust of smoke and shuddered to a stop. The prisoners were unnoticed by the crowd. Two portly conductors stepped onto the platform. One pulled his black vest aside, glanced at his pocket watch, and headed toward the prisoners assembled at the other end.

Karl shifted his weight, fisted his hands, and listened as the conductor spoke to a guard. "Have them enter the last two cars when the platform is empty."

"Where are they headed?"

"Chicago. Camp Grant," said the guard.

"That's the reactivated one?"

"Yes, all the comforts of home."

The conductor shook his head and walked away. Exiting passengers hurried off while others stood ready to board. Men in felt hats, suits, and topcoats held briefcases and folded up newspapers as they extinguished their cigarettes with the tips of their shoes. Women adjusted their shopping bags while keeping an eye on their boisterous children. Soon the platform was empty. The last two car doors opened.

The sound of the guards' boots created an echo. One of them shouted, "Columns of two. No talking. Enter the last two cars. March!"

Lining up, Karl, Ben, and Eric managed to stay close to one another. Fortune favored them as Karl hustled to a window seat, yanking Ben down beside him. Eric out muscled a guy for a seat across the aisle.

"Upholstered seats," said Ben, settling in his backside. "In Germany, we were transported jammed inside baggage cars and sat on damp, cold floors. Some soldiers were sick, some fell getting off. We had to help them, or they would have been left behind."

The conductor stood by as the last man entered. "All aboard!" The train pulled out of the station in a cloud of steam, its destination—Chicago, home to John Conway.

I need to settle a score with him someday, Karl thought.

The train sped through the peaceful countryside with gently rolling hills, magnificent mountains, and long, meandering rivers. There was no sign of the war that raged overseas.

Karl nudged Ben. "What a beautiful country."

Leaning across the aisle, Eric said, "We were told the Luftwaffe had bombed major American cities. Doesn't look like that from what we've seen."

"I saw shells of houses and what was left of chimneys. Made me wonder where the people went until I saw kids, scrawny as alley cats, skittering over the ruins like crickets, following women with kerchiefs covering their mouths against a thick haze of dust while rummaging through debris. There was no food in sight. War obliterated their landscapes and stole their youth," said Ben.

Looking out of the train window, Karl said, "Someday Germany will look like this."

"It will take a miracle. I just hope my mother and sister survive," said Ben. He scratched his whiskers and added, "Right now, I could use a good wash-up and a shave. What do you think they will do with us?"

Leaning across the aisle, Eric said, "Put us to work, I hope. I could learn a trade. As far as Germany is concerned, I'm never going back." In a hushed voice, he said to Ben, "Papa is a Nazi sympathizer. If I went back, I could be shot by Hitler's enemies." Eric rested his broad shoulders against the back of his seat and threaded his hand through his blond hair.

"What about your mutter?"

"When she left, I left. She told me to go because she was leaving Germany with her boyfriend."

Ben's eyes widened. "Did she say where they were going?"

"Nein. Just left."

"My papa was a schoolteacher," said Ben. "He spoke his mind against Hitler wanting more physical exercise than academics. One day, he went to school and never came back. When I left for the Army, my mother and sister stood in the yard crying. I'll go back to find them."

"My family endured Nazi brutality," said Karl. "Soldiers arriving regularly, demanding to be fed, laughing when one of them called my papa a stupid old man and made lewd remarks to my mother. I was kept out of the Army to help feed the soldiers—and for this they called me 'Katrina.'"

Daylight ebbed to darkness. The only lights were from cars on a nearby road. Karl closed his eyes, wondering about his family and home. The rhythmic sounds of the train wheels calmed him as he drifted into a state between sleep and consciousness.

He was riding a bicycle. He felt a hand on the small of his back. A familiar voice said he could go a little farther. He kept pedaling. The hand disappeared.

Hours later, he woke and watched the sun rise. The passing landscape lulled him as he reminisced about his family, his proud father, his stoic mother, and his fearless brother. The road ahead seemed long but hope swelled that he would return to them. Karl looked out the window for a closer look as the train continued to chug along. It came to a halt, but the prisoners' car doors remained closed. It didn't matter to the occupants. Their freedom was gone, their homeland destroyed, their futures unknown. A whistle blew and the train lurched forward. Guards passed out small paper bags. Each contained an apple, a hard-boiled egg, and a ham sandwich.

"I could eat three of these," said Karl.

"Easily," Ben exclaimed through a mouthful of a hard-boiled egg.

The following day at LaSalle Station in Chicago, the train braked to a stop amidst white hissing clouds. Two soldiers with sidearms in holsters stood on the platform. A conductor with a bulky frame barked, "Follow me! Stay in line! No talking!"

The car door slid open. The scruffy young men stumbled off the train and climbed the stairs to the city. Parked at the curb were four buses. One of the drivers stood outside smoking a cigarette, sipping hot coffee.

"Where are you taking us?" Karl asked.

The driver blew smoke out of his mouth, coughed, and said, "Camp Grant, an hour from here."

"Do you know anything about it?"

"The wife works there two days a week. She keeps track of the prisoners' paperwork. Government requires it. She says they're good to the prisoners. Feed them well and give them work to do."

"Get on. Get on. Move," commanded the guard.

The last prisoner entered, the doors closed, and the driver shifted gears and merged onto a smooth two-lane road. Above was an endless clear sky. Rolling hills stretched to a river which flowed silently to its destination. They passed parks where women wearing long coats and hats and gloves watched children play while others steered baby carriages. Well-kept triple-decker houses and apartment buildings surrounded the park. Karl imagined families sharing meals and telling stories.

They hadn't bathed in weeks. Ben's brown hair was a shade darker from grime and dirt. Karl stank of body odor and sweat—or perhaps it was his skin or hair. Dirt covered Eric's hands and face. They were so dirty they didn't look human.

The buses turned off onto a treeless dirt road and drove through a gate where a large sign greeted them, displaying Camp Grant in large black-and-white letters. A guard waved the buses through toward a building where the driver pulled a lever and stepped off. The prisoners sat motionless until a guard caught their attention with his booming voice and ordered them off.

His stern face was transformed when he smiled and said, "I'm Corporal Chase. Form a line outside the processing center."

Shivering, they stepped onto frozen ground. The perimeter of the camp was clearly defined, with tall watchtowers manned by guards with rifles. The camp contained wooden barracks lined up like sentries, a mess hall, an infirmary, an administration building, an office, and a processing center for new arrivals. Adjacent to the camp was a large field. Prisoners entered a confusing maze of registration procedures. They were assigned numbers, fingerprinted, photographed, given swift physical examinations, interrogated for military information, and told to wait for further instructions.

Karl leaned in toward Ben. "The guards have rifles."

"I noticed. Wonder how many there are."

"Enough to keep us from escaping."

"Where would we go?"

"Quiet, you two!" shouted a guard.

Remembering his experience with German soldiers, Karl stiffened. Would they snatch him out of the line and reprimand him, or worse?

He had much to learn from his new life of imprisonment.

Chapter Ten

A tall, broad-shouldered man stood before the newly arrived prisoners. His left arm ended abruptly at the elbow. Sergeant Jackson had lost it in Tunisia when the vehicle in which he was riding was strafed by fighter bombers. He had grown war-weary and tired and had witnessed one surreal moment after another until nothing seemed real anymore. To him, war was chaos and fear. Bravery mixed with panic and anger—sadness for those who had fallen and guilt for being alive. Sergeant Jackson had been sent to Camp Grant with a mission: to maintain order and treat prisoners in accordance with the Geneva Conventions. Remembering the men lost in Europe fighting a madman, being a caretaker for German POWs left him permanently bad-tempered.

"I'm Sergeant Jackson, in charge of Camp Grant. Rules will be obeyed. Disruptions will not be tolerated. Lights out at 2200 hours. You will be awakened by a siren call at 0600 hours. Meals are served in the mess hall at the back of the camp. All buildings are marked. Mealtimes are posted, be prompt. You have each been assigned to a barracks and a work detail. Some of you will work here; others may be transported to sites outside the camp. Corporal Chase, to my right, has the list. You are a sorry-looking batch, but we'll have you in shape in no time."

He waited while his words were translated into German. Hearing their native language, prisoners' spines straightened. Sergeant Jackson introduced Corporal Chase and exited the room.

Corporal Chase's maternal grandmother had left Germany at the end of the first World War. For as long as Chase could remember, she had always lived with the family, and he had grown up listening to the German language. He was sent to Belfast in 1942. His cousins were fighting for Hitler. His grandmother was inconsolable.

To avoid incidents at the camps, soldiers with an understanding of the German language were sought to monitor mail and listen to conversations between POWs. Four months after his arrival in Belfast, Corporal Chase was brought back home and sent to Camp Grant.

Looking over the prisoners, he addressed them in German. "Strip and toss every bit of clothing in the barrels. Showers are on either side. Plenty of hot water. Towels and soap are provided. By the looks of you, you will need plenty of soap," he said. "A raincoat, an overcoat, belt, gloves, underwear, socks, summer and winter pants, and shirts are provided. Choose a size. The letters POW are on every sleeve and pant leg. In English, that stands for prisoner of war, so you won't forget who you are. Get cleaned up, dress, and report back here."

The men washed away accumulated dirt and grime with soap and plenty of hot water. The runoff from the showers turned murky gray. They dried with large soft towels, agreeing in German that America was the land of plenty.

They pulled on new shorts and tee shirts and delved into the piles of clothing for sizes. Ben was pleased that he found a size to fit his small frame.

Karl looked into a small mirror and buttoned his shirt. The "POW" on his sleeve branded him, but his soul remained German.

After dressing, they rushed back and stood at attention. A bag containing toothpaste, a toothbrush, soap, shaving cream, and other amenities was given to all POWs. Two barbers stood by their chairs with scissors, a comb, and a razor.

Ben rubbed his whisker-free chin. Eric ran a comb through his close-cropped hair. Karl brushed his hair, which defied taming.

Chapter Eleven

A t the field hospital, a doctor examined John, probed his leg, and packed it with sulfa while John writhed in pain.

"You've got a nasty wound, soldier. May take weeks to heal. But your leg is salvageable. You can't go back into battle. You'll be going home."

"Where's Karl?"

"I think that's the German they found with him," said the medic.

"What happened to him?" the doctor asked.

"They arrested him. Probably sent to the states, to one of those camps."

The doctor snapped off his gloves and moved to the next patient. John felt the blood drain from his face. Karl!

Unceremoniously, the medic wrapped John's leg in bandages. "We've done what we can for you, soldier, but we're not sending you back out there. Your leg may require surgery, but whoever took care of it saved it. You'll be on the next hospital ship going back to the states. Good luck."

Two and a half weeks later, John was carried off the hospital ship on Staten Island and boarded a hospital train to Chicago, where ambulances waited to transport the wounded.

"No room at the VA. He's going to Mercy, close to his home." The ambulance driver signed the release form and, with sirens blasting, drove away.

In the Conway's kitchen, the telephone rang. After wiping her hands on an apron, Louise answered. Responding to the caller she said, "Yes, this is Louise Conway...When will he arrive, Sergeant? ...You say later today at Mercy Hospital, and he has a leg wound but otherwise seems okay...Thank you, Sergeant."

Louise clutched the telephone, her heart raced. She tossed the apron, found her coat, left a note for Henry and Abby, and left.

"We do not have a John Conway here," said the woman behind the desk at the hospital.

Twisting the handle on her purse, Louise shouted, "My son is coming by ambulance from the war! I got a call from a sergeant today."

"Have a seat, I'll see what I can find out."

Louise paced, her eyes darting around the room. After an eternity of minutes, the woman called Louise.

"Your son will be arriving in an hour, but it will take some time to get him admitted. Would you like to go home, and we'll call you—"

"I'll stay right here, thank you."

Louise sat in the last empty seat in the waiting area, tucked one foot behind the other, and placed her hands over her purse. Amid utter confusion, she remained focused and began the wait for her soldier son to arrive.

Henry and Abby arrived, looking for Louise in the crowded emergency room.

"Dad, there she is!" said Abby.

Louise reached out and grasped their hands.

"Are you okay?"

"Has he arrived?"

"How bad are his injuries?"

"I'm fine and no, he hasn't arrived, and he has a leg wound."

Hearing her name, Louise's eyes widened as she stepped up to the desk. Harry and Abby were close behind.

"You have news for me?"

"Your son has arrived in room six. It's the third room on the left. You can go in for a short visit."

Overjoyed and apprehensive, they stood next to the gurney. Tattered clothes covered John's gaunt body. They saw a shadow of who he used to be, but he was alive and home.

"John, we're all here," said Louise.

"Am I home?"

"Yes, you are. You're in Mercy Hospital, not far from us."

John saw joy, relief, and sadness in their faces and wondered if he would ever be the same again.

Leaning over the gurney, Henry kissed John's forehead and said, "Welcome home, son."

Squeezing John's hand, Abby said, "You're back with us."

She noticed he wasn't in uniform and what he wore was unfamiliar. She wondered where he had been and what he had seen.

A doctor entered the room. "Sorry to interrupt, I'm Doctor Jackson, and I've got to examine him. When I'm finished, I'll tell you what needs to be done. Have a seat in the waiting room. This won't take long."

"How are you doing, soldier?"

John shrugged his shoulders.

"Proud of you for what you did over there," the doctor said, moving his hands over John's leg, pressing his fingers around the wound. He then examined the rest of John, asking him if he had any pain other than the leg.

"No," John said.

"Your wound still has signs of infection, and you are getting antibiotics, but I'll need to clean out some dead tissue. We'll put you to sleep for that. First thing is an X-ray to determine the extent of your injuries and the condition of your bones. Once we establish that, I'll schedule you for surgery. You will be here for a week in the meantime so we can manage your pain and monitor your progress. I'll tell your family."

John saw the doctor through unfocused eyes with minimal awareness of what he said.

The family reentered the room with high hopes of recovery for John, but for John, recovery would baffle him.

Each evening, Henry Conway ate his supper and retreated to the front porch until bedtime. Abby sat next to him and tried to distract him for a few moments.

"Dad, John will be all right. You'll see."

"I wonder what he saw over there. How did he get wounded?"

Henry knew of stories his friends told of relatives coming back and all had changed.

"It will take a while, Dad, but with time he should be okay."

"He's home. That's all that matters."

"Yes, Dad, that's all that matters. Have your coffee. I'll be back soon."
Abby called out to her mother, "Mom? I'm going to see John."

Louise stepped out onto the porch. "No word from Harry?"

Abby shook her head.

"He'll come home. You'll see," said Louise.

"Tell John that Dad and I will be there tomorrow."

Chapter Twelve

Abby stared through the window of the bus. A light snow began to fall. She stepped off the bus, adjusted her red hat, and crossed the street to Mercy Hospital where John teetered between lucidity and confusion.

Entering John's room, she placed her hat and coat across the only chair, next to her brother's bed.

"Hi John, it's me, Abby."

John Conway drifted in and out of a drug-induced sleep. His leg, wrapped in bandages from thigh to ankle, was propped on a pillow, five toes with blue-tinged nails were visible. He was plied with painkillers, and for two days after surgery was rarely awake. With unhurried efficiency, staff moved in and out of John's room. He listened to the intermittent alert system over the public address system, hoping it would not be for him. White walls deeply scored by metal-framed stretchers being pushed about surrounded the room. Fluids in marked bottles ran through tubing taped to his arm, which was cradled in a half-cast and wrapped with layers of gauze. An over-bed table reached across the side rail, upon which lay a menu, a short pencil, a box of tissues, and a glass of ice chips slowly turning to water. The smell of bleach filled the air. A curtain was drawn between John's bed and the bed next to him which, for the moment, was unoccupied.

John's eyes rested on his sister's face and he took her hand. Lifting his head, he said, "Abby, where's Karl? What happened to him?"

"Who is Karl? Someone you met in the war?"

"He saved me, and I…" His head dropped to the pillow, and he closed his eyes.

Leaning over the bed, Abby said, "John, you're home in Chicago and your surgery is finished. The doctor says you did fine, and your leg will heal."

Grabbing the side rails and in a curt voice, John said, "I have to find him."

"Who do you have to find, John?"

He flashed a look at Abby.

"Is it Karl?" she asked, her voice ringed with concern.

Clutching his chest, John's eyes narrowed. "Yes," he whispered.

Someone appeared in the doorway to John's room. Abbey's eyes shifted to the newcomer.

"Harry!" she screamed. She ran to him, wrapping her arms around him.

"Abby, it's been so long." He lifted her chin and planted kisses all over her face.

She pulled her head back. "Did you get my letters? When did you come home? I thought of you every day. Are you all right? News of the war has been awful, and I was so afraid … I saved all your letters. I was afraid that was all I had left of you."

"Yes, I did get your letters. I arrived last night. Lost the hearing in my right ear. They sent me home."

"What happened?"

"Constant exposure to loud noises. Couldn't hear orders, too dangerous for me to stay."

She wrapped her arms around him again. "Oh, Harry."

"My uncle told me about John. I called your folks, and they told me you were here."

"I'm so glad you came. The doctor called this morning and said the surgery went well. They closed the wound, and he'll be here a week. The injury was bad, but they did the best they could over there. Let him know you're here."

Harry moved closer to John. "Hey, buddy. It's me, Harry. I just got home. Looks like you got banged up. How're you doing?"

John lifted his eyelids and brightened. "Harry, you're back!"

"Just got back today. I came as soon as I heard."

John reached for Harry's hand. Harry grasped it, leaned over the bed, and whispered, "We made it back."

Abby moved closer to Harry and led him away from John's bed to the window, where they looked out at the streets below. The sun dipped below the horizon, leaving a vibrant deep shade of blue over the city with just enough daylight to illuminate details of the surrounding buildings. Harry's shoulders sagged. Deep sobs prevented him from speaking.

"It was hell over there." He blew his nose. "I worried every day that I would not live to come home to you."

They clung to each other until the moment passed. "Abby, would you pass me my water?" asked John.

Releasing Harry, she gave John his water.

He took a long drink. "Harry, come see me again. I'm going to take a nap."

"We'll get you better, buddy. See you tomorrow," said Harry.

Abby kissed John's forehead. John closed his eyes. Damaged bodies flashed before him; he opened his eyes, wet his lips, and reached for the call bell.

A nurse arrived at the door of his room. "Can I help you?"

"I need a pain pill." *I need to forget Beau, to forget Karl, and forget Lily.*

She returned with a paper cup and handed it to John, who swallowed the pill, refusing the water she offered.

Driving home, Harry asked, "What happened with John and Lily? Maybe she could visit him."

"I don't think so. They stopped seeing each other the summer after graduation. She disappeared. He won't talk about it. Rumor has it that she married a friend of her father's."

"She got married!"

"It's only a rumor, but no one has seen her around. Harry, all that matters right now is that you and John made it home."

Chapter Thirteen

The next morning, a nurse walked into John's room and pulled the curtain back around his bed, allowing sun to shine over his face. John covered his eyes.

"What the hell—?"

Noticing the scowl on his face, the nurse approached the bed and said, "Good morning, John. My name is Emma, and I will be taking care of you today. How are you feeling?"

"Pretty banged up."

"The worst is over, and your surgery went well." She removed his breakfast tray, placed it on a cart, and pulled the over-bed table away from him. Her nearness made John's pulse quicken. For a moment, they stared at each other.

John took a closer look at Emma, whose face was a confluence of circles: round eyes, round mouth, and a head full of dark curls. Pushing the sheet aside, she examined his toes and his leg.

"Dressing on your leg looks good. Can you wiggle your toes?"

John responded.

"Today, you will be getting out of bed." She paused, waiting for his reaction.

"I don't think—"

"It's only a stand up and sit in a chair. Come on, soldier, we'll do this together." She helped John to a sitting position on the side of the bed. "Ready to stand?" she asked.

"Yeah."

Emma wrapped her arm around John's waist, and he put a hand on her shoulder.

"You can lean on me," she said, guiding him to a standing position. The top of her head came to his shoulder. "Are you okay?" she asked.

His hand tightened on her shoulder. "A little wobbly, but I like standing."

There was a slight upturn in the corners of her mouth.

"The chair is right behind you," she said as she eased away from him, allowing him to sit.

John lowered himself into the chair and slid his hand down Emma's arm.

Emma stepped back. "I have crutches for you."

"I don't need them."

"You'll need them when you begin walking."

She pulled a chair over, placed a pillow on it, and lifted John leg. "Leg elevated when sitting. Doctor's orders."

Emma was familiar with the scars of war that left their mark inside and outside on returning soldiers. She respected their walls of silence and grieved with the families who wept at the bedside hoping for a miracle.

"Want to tell me what went on over there?"

"Got captured by the Germans."

"Then what happened?"

"I escaped but got lost. I'll tell you the rest some other time."

"Whenever you're ready. I must see other patients."

"Will you be back?" John asked.

"Yes."

"When you come back, will you bring me a pain pill?"

"I will if it's time." Emma turned to leave.

"Emma."

"Yes?"

"Thank you."

"Don't mention it."

John's dreams dissolved before he could reach them. In his waking state, he stared into space. Noises startled him. The quiet presence of Emma soothed him, and the pain pills kept him from facing reality. With Emma's encouragement, John used his crutches to walk around the room, three times a day, refusing to walk in the corridor.

"I can't face people. What if I fall?"

"You get up."

John stared at the ceiling. "They see the outside, not the inside. I'm just not ready."

"Let's give it a try."

John hobbled into the corridor, dismayed by what he saw. Sitting in a wheelchair at the nurses' station was a man with one bandaged leg elevated, the other a stump. Two men sat opposite him, one whose arms were swathed in bandages, the other had one eye covered. One of John's crutches slid out from under him. Emma placed her arm around his waist, preventing a fall.

With a look of concern, the man in the wheelchair said, "Be careful, buddy."

John hobbled back to his room.

Emma said, "You're going to have to face people at some point."

"Where is my pain pill?"

"It isn't time."

"Make it time. My leg is killing me."

Emma frowned. "You know I can't do that."

"What am I supposed to do?"

"Get your mind off things…"

"I can't. I did my job like everyone else, but I couldn't save Beau. I couldn't save Beau."

"It wasn't your fault."

"How will I face people after what I've done?"

He felt distant from those around him. He needed escape from the conflict inside of him and the war's grasp before he could reach out for help. The pills provided this escape.

Dr. Jackson knocked and entered the room.

"Good morning, John. How are you today? I see you have been using your crutches. Good. Let's have a look at your leg."

Unwrapping John's leg, he said, "Leg wound is healing fine, but you will need to use crutches until your leg is strong enough to carry you. A couple more days of antibiotics and using your crutches and you should be able to be discharged. Let's see you walk."

Using the crutches, John walked across the room, but dread mounted with every step.

"Well done. Keep up the good work. I'll check in with you tomorrow. Is there anything more I can do for you?"

Physically and mentally tired, John was unable to reach out. "No, I'm fine."

Moonlight spilled over John's room, making the floor shine. Hobbling to the window and with his hands resting on the sill, he looked out; a curtain of darkness obscured his vision. He hung his head and wondered how he was going to face people. He turned, pressed the call button, and asked for a pain pill. A voice said it wasn't time. He sat and, with curled fists, waited until a nurse entered with a paper cup.

"Here's your pain—"

John grabbed the cup and swallowed the pill.

"Are you all right?" she asked.

"Fine."

The next morning, the door to his room opened. "Good morning, John. How are you?" asked Dr. Jackson.

Some soldiers shared their anxieties about going back into the community with Dr. Jackson; John was not one of them.

"I'm fine." He compressed his lips and looked away from Dr. Jackson's stare.

"Living at home may be hard at first. Plan to see friends. I know your family doctor. He's a good man. Talk to him. Talking about your war experience makes it easier."

John remained tight lipped.

Dr. Jackson reached out and took John's hand. "Thanks for your service to our country, and good luck back home. Here's a prescription for a week of pain pills with instructions."

Giving Dr. Jackson a small smile, John managed to thank him. He drank his coffee and left his eggs and toast untouched.

"John." He turned to see Emma holding papers. "Well, soldier, are you ready?"

With a wistful smile, John asked, "Will you miss me?"

"Yes, I will, but you'll be better off at home. Get a routine going. See your friends. The rest is up to you." She added, "If you need to talk to someone, call the Veterans Hospital. Here's the number. There are people there who can help."

Entering the room, Abby said, "Big day, John. Mom and Dad are getting the place ready. Meatloaf for supper, your favorite. I've got Dad's car outside."

"Let's go," said John gruffly.

Emma stood in the doorway, watching them leave. She walked down the corridor to her next patient, a soldier who was sightless.

John stood outside the door of his home a changed man. His father stood in the doorway and, with an outstretched hand, helped John across the threshold.

"Welcome home, son. Louise, John's here."

The drapes on a cluster of windows were pulled back, allowing sun to filter through sheer curtains. Two brown overstuffed easy chairs with lace doilies were opposite each other, with a table in between, upon which was a radio. A tall lamp with a fringed shade stood between an easy chair and the sofa. The dark wood floor was partially covered with a rug of deep reds, blues, and greens. John sank into the sofa.

Louise came from the kitchen, sat down next to him, and kissed his cheek. "You're home with us now. I made meatloaf. A special occasion."

"Thanks, Mom. My favorite."

"Can I fix you something else?"

"Not right now. Just let me rest, Mom."

"Let him be, Louise." Henry turned to John. "You made it home, son. That's all that counts."

"Yeah, useless."

"Not so," said Henry. "Your leg will heal. You'll see. Harry has called twice to see if you were home."

"I think I'll take a snooze. Abby, can you take my prescription to the drugstore?"

"Okay."

John climbed the stairs to his bedroom and closed the door. Images of war haunted him. Images of Karl taunted him. Images of his damaged leg petrified him. Images of Beau saddened him.

Harry climbed the steps to the Conway house.

"Harry, just in time," said Abby. "I'm going to get John's pills. He's upstairs. Go see him."

Harry knocked on the bedroom door and turned the knob. "Hey, you're home."

"Yeah, I'm home."

"Abby and I are going to Duffy's Pub this weekend. People are asking for you. Come with us."

"I don't know about that…"

"Sure you do. Today's Tuesday. Get three days of your mom's cooking and rest. I'll be back on Saturday. Abby and I won't take no for an answer."

At supper that evening, John was silent until he tasted his mother's meatloaf, mashed potatoes with gravy, and peas.

When his plate was clean, he said, "It's good to be home."

Chapter Fourteen

Three days later, Abby greeted Harry at the door. "I'm so glad you're here.

"What is it, what's happened?"

"John stays in his room most of the time. He yells at me when I ask him to join us for supper. Even when I offer to bring him a ham sandwich, he tells me to go away."

"Let me see what I can do."

Harry climbed the stairs, tapped on the door, and turned the knob. The shades were drawn, and clothes littered the floor. The room smelled of damp socks and dirty underwear. Harry lifted the shades, opened the window, and turned on the light. John was stretched out on rumpled sheets.

"What the hell?" John covered his eyes.

"When are you getting up? It's five o'clock."

"Soon."

Noticing a half-empty pill bottle on the nightstand, Harry picked it up. "What's this?"

"None of your business."

"I'm making it my business." He tossed the container into the trash.

"Hey, those are my pills."

Harry kicked the trash can aside. "You don't need those. Get up."

"I can't, my leg."

Harry rifled through the closet and chest of drawers. He threw clean clothes on the bed, pulled a chair next to it, and sat. "Look, it was pure hell over there. But think about those who didn't make it back. We both did, and we must be grateful for that. I still have nightmares and have trouble concentrating, but I go to my job, spend time with Abby—"

Turning away from Harry, John mumbled, "I can't."

"Look, at least come out with us tonight. Try it. C'mon, get up. I'll wait for you downstairs."

Seeing bodies litter the road and seeing his friend, Beau, get his head blown off spurred a moroseness in John that he was unable to overcome. There were daily reminders that in the war he could have died in the next hour, the next day, or the next week. Beau, Karl, and Lily took up residence inside John's head and haunted him like ghosts in an attic. John retrieved the bottle from the trash and swallowed a pill.

Knowing Harry would return if he didn't go downstairs, John shaved, brushed his hair, and limped into the living room. His right hand was in his trouser pocket with his fingers wrapped around the pill bottle.

Harry's apprehension was eased when John said, "I guess I'm ready."

Duffy's Pub was unpretentious, a haven for the locals. An American flag stood in the corner. A large poster of Uncle Sam hung on the wall in the back of the bar, stern-faced, pointing his finger straight ahead, above the words

I WANT YOU FOR THE U.S. ARMY

Behind the bar, Duffy wiped the counter with a white cloth. Customers sat on four-legged stools, shoulder to shoulder, drinking beer or sipping whiskey. Two men were seated at a side table, playing cards. One held up two fingers, signaling for more drinks. The low hum of voices mingled with the sound of clattering plates and glasses. "In the Mood" by Glenn Miller played on the jukebox.

John, Harry, and Abby slid into a wooden booth. Expecting to see a waitress, John was surprised to see Emma walking toward them. "I saw you come in. Nice to see you out and about. How are you doing?" she asked.

Rubbing his chin, he said, "I'm okay."

"You're Emma, the nurse from the hospital," said Abby.

"Yes."

"Care to join us?" asked Harry.

"Yes, I would—that is, if John doesn't mind."

John looked up at Emma. "No, I don't mind," he said, and returned to reading his menu.

"Have you seen any of your friends?" Emma asked John.

"Just Harry. That's enough."

"What do you do with yourself?"

"I drink beer, limp around the house, and listen to ball games."

"Doesn't sound very exciting."

Duffy's voice interrupted the musing. "Come on. Next round is on the house. Here's to our boys!" He dropped nickels into the slot of the jukebox and pressed buttons for "The Trolley Song" and "Swinging on a Star."

John thought of the kindness of Karl's family. The memory of his betrayal of Karl played over in his mind. Abruptly, he stood, wavering, and said, "I have to go."

"John, we haven't ordered," declared Abby.

Emma reached for a napkin, wrote something on it, and handed it to John.

Chapter Fifteen

Louise closed the oven door on her biscuits, noted the time, dipped a spoon into the stew simmering on the stove, and tasted it. Satisfied, she replaced the lid and joined John in the living room, where he was listening to the radio and drinking a can of beer with his leg stretched out on the hassock. His sweatpants were stained, and his tee shirt had a hole on one shoulder. Whiskers covered his jaw. Hair hung down the back of his neck.

"When's the last time you shaved and got cleaned up?"

"For what, Mom, to sit around the house?"

"For yourself. Have a look in the mirror. Maybe this will help." Louise placed a napkin on the table next to his beer can.

"What's that?" he asked.

"I found it in your trouser pocket. I almost washed it with the laundry. There's a number written on it, and I thought you might need it."

Staring at the crumpled napkin, John took a deep swig that emptied his can of beer.

"I messed up. She asked me how I was." He turned to his mother and continued. "I said, 'I limp around the house, drink beer, and listen to ball games.' Then I walked out."

"I am sure she understands, but you can change that."

John took in a long breath, let out an audible sigh, and mumbled, "No one understands."

"Give her a call. It sounds as if she's interested."

"In what, a drunken cripple?"

"The doctor gave you a clean bill of health, so you're not a cripple, just stubborn."

John's inability to share the inner turmoil of his choices and the war, either from shame or guilt or horror, held him captive.

Harry rapped twice and opened the door. "Hello," he called.

"Harry! Come in. Abby is going to be a little late," said Louise.

"Yes, I know. I came early to talk to John."

"What about?" asked John.

"My night-school teacher owns an accounting agency in town and is looking for help. He's willing to give you an interview."

"Not interested."

"Why not? You're good at math."

"Because when I'm ready, I'll get my own job. Now leave me alone."

"Just go for the interview. You don't have to take the job. It'll be good experience."

"Like running into the nurse, Emma, last night at Duffy's? I couldn't even talk to her. She must think I'm a jerk."

"You're just out of practice. This will be a start," pleaded Harry.

"Harry's right," said Louise.

"I'll think about it."

Sensing a change in John's attitude, Harry persisted. "Good. I ran into Billy Jackson yesterday. You remember him? He coaches basketball. He knows you're back and asked if you'd be interested in coaching. His son, Buck, is home from the war and is helping him. February is a tough time for the kids. Some have fathers still in the war and others have lost them. They've been playing on Saturdays at the boys' club. A couple of guys had to quit, and he could use some help."

John shifted his leg. "Yeah, I remember Billy. Buck was in our class. We played ball with him."

"We did."

Abby arrived home. Harry's face brightened.

"Sorry I'm late. Have you been here long?"

"Long enough to get me a job and volunteer for coaching some kids," John said.

"Harry has suggestions for a job, and thought he might help out Billy Jackson," said Louise.

"Great!" said Abby. "We'll have to do some shopping first." Eyeing her brother, she added, "Quite a bit of shopping, by the looks of things."

"I haven't agreed to anything. Let me listen to the radio, will ya?"

"Okay, okay. You don't have to shout," said Abby.

Abby was used to John's abruptness but wished their relationship could be what it was before the war when there were no scars. He was drifting away from her, but she knew their bond after Robert's death could never be broken, and she loved him.

"I'll just be a minute, Harry."

The constant vigilant state John maintained during the war was out of sync with life at home, which was predictable and docile.

"I'm going to take a nap. Call me when supper is ready, Mom."

He went upstairs and put the napkin in his bureau drawer. He looked at his image in the mirror and was repulsed by what he saw. He passed a hand over his sallow face and blinked, trying to bring life into his dark eyes. Pictures of Robert in the room stared back at him. I should have died along with Beau. I'm useless. He opened the pill bottle; three left. A voice in his head said, *Coward. Robert was brave. Beau was brave; Karl was brave.* He recapped the bottle and laid down.

"Harry's taking me for Chinese food, Mom. It's the new place on Baker Street."

She asked Harry if she had enough time to change.

"No, you're perfect just the way you are."

Abby smiled, took Harry's hand, and kissed him. "You always say the right thing," she said in a hushed tone.

Under the China Doll restaurant sign was a picture of a Chinese woman wearing a long, sleeveless, high neck red dress. The restaurant was crowded but diminished voices and soft lighting lowered the noise level.

A man approached and said, "May I take your coats?" Abbey slipped out of hers. Fumbling, Harry removed his.

They were seated at a table for two and handed menus. A woman placed a pot of tea on the table, along with two small cups, absent handles.

Abby looked over the menu. "Harry, I have no idea what to order. Do you?"

"Do I what?"

"Harry, are you listening?"

"No."

Abby put aside her menu.

"We've been seeing each other a while and I was wondering—" Harry stammered.

"Wondering what?"

"You know I love you."

Abby smiled. "Of course I do."

"Well … that is … will you …" Harry reached into his pocket and retrieved a small box.

"Open it."

"Harry, it's beautiful! I love you! Should I put it on? Maybe you should. Be careful."

Harry's hand shook removing the ring, but he reached over and slipped it onto Abby's finger. Abby wrapped her arms around Harry's neck. The ring sparkled on her finger, and for the moment, all that mattered was each other.

On the drive home, Abby glances at the simple solitaire ring on her finger. The warmth of Harry's shoulder against hers enveloped her in a sense of love and hope for their future.

"I showed uncle the ring and he was so happy—we actually hugged. Let's stop by, he would love to see you."

"I'd love to."

Hearing the door open, uncle stood and was greeted by the two people he loved most and knew they were made for each other.

After a short visit with uncle, Harry drive Abby home. Pulling in front of the Conways' house, Abby jumped out of the car, followed by Harry.

"Mom, look!"

Louise wrapped her hand around Abby's. "It's beautiful and so are the both of you."

Grinning, Henry said, "What took you so long?" and hugged them. "Welcome to the family."

Hearing the commotion, John came downstairs and joined in the celebration of his two favorite people, who were now engaged.

Chapter Sixteen

Dr. Burns examined John's leg and said, "Leg looks good, healing well. How's the walking?"

"Still have a limp but it's better. And still have pain."

"Have you any pain pills left?"

"I ran out."

"I'll give you a refill for seven days and I'll see you back in the office then."

Three days later, John entered the gym, walking with a slight limp. Boys shouted, their sneakers squeaking on the floor as they bounced the balls. Coaches looked at their clipboards, seemingly oblivious to the raucous noise. Whistles hung from their necks.

Why did I agree to do this? It's chaos.

One of the coaches saw John and with an outstretched hand said, "You must be John. Glad to meet you. Bob Martin. Thanks for coming."

John shook hands and looked away. Coach Martin's eyes narrowed. "We let them loose for an hour, then they choose teams, and we have a game. Nothing serious. I do the coaching," he said.

"What will I be doing?"

"You keep track of the score, hand out cold drinks and towels. Everything's on the bench."

John found the scorecards and sorted through the towels and cold drinks.

"Hey Bob," Harry called out. "I see you've met John. How's it going?"

"He seems a little distracted."

"He'll be okay. He's had a rough time of things."

Harry waved to John and took a seat in the bleachers.

Coach Martin called out to the players, "Let's play ball!"

The players chose sides, lined up, and the game began. The first ball went wild, knocking the scorecard out of John's hand. The play and the yelling continued, but the coach's eyes were on John, sitting on the bench staring at the scattered scorecards.

Harry climbed over the bleachers. "Are you okay?"

John quickly looked away.

"Come on, let's go."

Harry called the coach, who was gathering up the scorecards. "We're leaving. Sorry, but thanks."

Arriving at home, John went upstairs, swallowed two pills, pulled down the shades, and waited to sleep.

"How did it go?" asked Louise.

"Not well. But he tried," said Harry.

Harry sat with Louise. "It might have been too much right now. He should take it easy over the weekend. He's got that job interview on Monday."

"I'll see that he gets rested and fed. Thanks, Harry."

John woke with a throbbing headache. Pulling on a wool sweater and black trousers, he snatched a jacket from a hook by the door and headed outside into the crisp air, hoping it would clear the torment he felt. His mind was a tangled web of self-loathing; pills were his escape. Tightening his grip around the pill container, he breathed in the air thinking he'd find a way out of the turmoil without pills.

When he arrived home, his mother met him at the door and asked where he was and if he was okay.

"I needed to walk, Mom."

"Is your leg okay?"

"A little sore. I'm going to take a bath."

"I'll fix you something." She kissed his cheek and watched him climb the stairs. He filled the tub, took a pill, and soaked for an hour.

The following Monday, John stood outside an office with the words

MERIWETHER ACCOUNTING

etched in black letters on the window. Trying to move air into his chest, he pulled at his shirt collar. He opened the door, removing his hat.

A woman looked up from her desk. "May I help you?" She appeared to be in her late forties, with tightly bound hair and a compressed mouth. She was dressed in brown, brown blouse, brown skirt, and brown shoes.

"I have an appointment with Mr. Meriwether."

"Your name?" she asked.

"John. John Conway."

She glanced at her calendar and said, "Have a seat. I'll tell him you're here."

Mr. Meriwether arrived at the office every day at seven-thirty dressed in a shirt, tie, vest, and suit, carrying a briefcase. A rim of gray hair circled his head. His sharp blue eyes identified an incorrect invoice immediately. He seldom pointed out flaws, but, when necessary, he was direct and honest. Due to its reputation for integrity and reliability, the company managed twenty accounts, but they were turning away new customers until they could hire more bookkeepers. Mr. Meriwether looked forward to meeting Harry's friend.

Located behind the receptionist's desk were three desks. Sitting at one, a young woman entered information from papers stacked neatly to her left into a machine in front of her. Occasionally, she would glance at the paper roll emerging from the top of the machine. The other two desks were occupied by middle-aged men who, hunched over their desks, entered information into loose-leaf binders, their shirtsleeves rolled to their elbows, their ties loose.

"Mr. Meriwether will see you now. Right this way."

John sat motionless, his hands gripping the arms of the chair. The woman's voice was distant and muffled.

"Sir?" She removed her glasses. "Mr. Meriwether is waiting." John stood and followed the woman.

"Come in. You must be John Conway." Meriwether extended a hand and John shook it. "Philip Meriwether. Have a seat." He motioned to a chair in front of his desk and opened a folder.

"I have your high school academic record. Impressive. Your teachers speak highly of you. What have you been doing since coming home from the war?"

"I got wounded and spent time in the hospital."

Meriwether fell silent. He leaned forward, elbows on his desk. "Well, at least you made it home, and I'm glad you did. The wounds of war are everywhere. But we who are here must make the best of things."

John pushed the chair back and started to rise. "Maybe I should come back."

"Please, sit. How are you now?"

"I'm okay."

Looking at John's high school record, Mr. Meriwether said, "Your math marks are excellent. It seems like that is where your talent lies."

"Yes, but maybe you want someone else. Someone—"

"I think you'll do fine. Your skills are what I need. I can use a bright young man, and if you're willing, I'll have you train with Alex. Once that is complete, you will have your own accounts using a ledger, posting debits and credits. To start, you will be keeping the financial records of two companies. Is that agreeable?"

"Yes, yes. That's fine."

"You can start tomorrow. I'll tell Alex. Eight o'clock. I do insist on punctuality." Mr. Meriwether thrust out his hand and John shook it.

At the end of the first week, John stood and stretched his arms. Attempting to tidy up the mess on his desk, he knocked over his coffee cup, spilling the contents. Alex handed him a roll of paper towels.

"Keep a roll handy, it happens. You managed to get through your first week. Good job," said Alex.

"Thanks for your help."

As he left, John nodded to the secretary.

Returning home, his tie hung loose and his shirt lay open at the collar. He hauled himself up the steps of his house. Each figure, each calculation must be accurate. It was other people's money and had to be flawless.

He ate little and spoke little to his family at supper, saying he was tired and going to bed early. Waiting for sleep to come, he overheard his parents talking in the living room.

"He'll be all right, Henry. He just needs rest."

"He needs more than that. He seems troubled, distant." Henry bent an ear to the radio, then straightened and said, "I feel I can't reach him. I can't lose another son."

"We won't, Henry. We won't," said Louise.

When John fell asleep, faceless creatures floated above his head. He reached into the air to touch one, but his hand slipped through the image.

John woke, sweat trickling down his neck. His heart raced. Stifling a scream, he dragged himself to the bathroom and turned on the water for a bath. He scrubbed his body, then washed his hair and rinsed it. Laying in the tub, he stared into the middle distance and punched the water. He slid under the water until he had to come up for air.

As he entered the kitchen the next morning, his mother asked him if he wanted breakfast.

Refusing, he poured coffee and looked out the window. "Mom, I hope I can do this. Suppose I mess up?"

She motioned John to sit. "None of us are perfect. If you have questions, ask the man that trained you. People are willing to help if you ask."

Later that morning, lying on the couch, John opened his eyes and stared at the ceiling. He hadn't eaten but wasn't hungry. His mouth was parched, and his muscles ached.

"John."

Louise brought a ham sandwich, a brownie, and a cup of steaming coffee, placed it on the table and sat in a chair across from him.

"Maybe you should talk to someone."

"Who? All I need is rest."

"You need that too, but the Veterans Administration has clinics for veterans coming home from the war."

"You mean the crazy ones like me."

"You're not crazy. I'll make an appointment for you. Dad and I or Harry and Abby will go with you."

John sipped the coffee and bit off a piece of the sandwich. "Thanks, Mom. I don't need a clinic. I'll go to see Doctor Burns again."

"Well, that's good. Ask him about the clinic. See what he has to say. We all care about you."

"I know, Mom."

John went upstairs and fished around in his nightstand drawer. He found the empty pill bottle with Dr. Burns' name and telephone number. He dialed the number and the receptionist said Dr. Burns would see him in an hour. Seated on the examining table, he looked up as Dr. Burns, who had white hair, a rosy complexion, and a kind smile, walked in.

"Hello, John. What's going on?"

"Pain and I can't sleep. You gotta help me."

"You have to be careful with them."

"I have a job now, and if I can't sleep, I am afraid I'll get fired. My friend recommended me for the job, and I can't let him down."

"I'll give you one more refill of seven pills if you assure me you'll come back in a week."

"Sure."

†

The American home front changed in many ways during World War II. Citizens endured rationing of items ranging from sugar to gasoline, along with heartache for loved ones fighting overseas. The military draft was a constant drain on manpower. Despite every effort to enlist citizens in the gathering and canning effort, acres of harvest went unpicked, and tomatoes rotted on canning company platforms. Many women went to work and filled in for men who were serving their country overseas. They worked in factories building ships and planes. They were air-raid wardens, fire officers, and evacuation officers. It was not enough.

As the war raged in Europe, Great Britain requested help with the housing of POWs due to a shortage of space in Britain. The American government feared the presence of Germans on US soil would create a security problem and raise fear among citizens. Many Americans lost loved ones in the war and hated the Germans. Given wartime labor shortages, especially in food production and agriculture, the US government agreed to accept German POWs. Army officials met with local officials, reporters, and civic groups to assure them of security safeguards. There would be a boost in the economy for local builders to build prison compounds. POWs could provide much-needed labor on farms and factories, which proved attractive to farmers and businessmen. Following the requirements of the Geneva Conventions, the US would provide living quarters like those of its own military, with the inclusion of barbed wire and watchtowers. This addition reassured the opponents.

From 1942 through 1945, more than 400,000 German prisoners were shipped to the US on Liberty ships and detained in camps across the country. Thousands of Italian and German prisoners were captured in the Tunisian campaign, and it was here that President Roosevelt looked for manpower. Trains arrived from the East Coast carrying hordes of enemy soldiers into neighborhoods in the United States. Signs that read,

GERMAN POWS COMING
SOON TO A TOWN NEAR YOU

were posted in various communities. Farmers were encouraged to contract for prisoner labor. POWs dug peanuts in Georgia, picked potatoes in Maine, tomatoes in Indiana, cotton in Texas, and harvested sugarcane in Louisiana. They shoveled snow, worked in food processing plants, on flood-control projects, and on road construction. For this they were paid eighty cents a day. They were fed properly, slept in comfortable beds, and were warm. They were hard-working, thorough, diligent, and they were essential.

GIs who spoke German and others who were wounded in battle or ineligible for the draft by reasons of health, lack of training, or psychological makeup were sent to work at managing the camps.

Chapter Seventeen

The loudspeaker squawked. "Attention. All new arrivals report to the office." The men raced across the yard and fell in line.

Corporal Chase stepped up. "List of barracks numbers and jobs are posted outside the mess hall. Find your name and report to your barracks." He glanced at his watch. "It is 1500. Supper is at 1800 in the mess hall. Dismissed."

Shoving, pushing, and neck-stretching followed as everyone tried to learn their fate. Karl eyed the roster and saw his name followed by Ben's and Eric's.

Karl Baum—prepare a bed for a garden. Barracks Ten. Ben Schmid—prepare a bed for a garden. Barracks Ten. Eric Hoffman—cook's helper. Barracks Ten.

"Cook's helper? I can't even boil an egg. We never had enough food to eat, never mind cook."

"You'll have to learn," said Karl.

"Garden what? It's early March and the ground is still frozen," said Ben.

"Spring thaw will come," said Karl.

"What do we do in the meantime?"

"Eat Eric's food," Karl replied. He bent down to retie one of his shoes. Suddenly, a foot came into his line of sight and stomped on his new shoes, crushing the top. Karl looked up and saw the prisoner with the scar on his cheek.

Karl gave him a hard stare and growled, "I told you if you ever touched me again, I would break your finger." He grabbed the man's wrist with one hand and bent his middle finger back as far as he could. The man's scream pierced the air.

A guard stepped in, separated them, grabbed Karl by his shirt collar, and pushed him away. He turned to the injured prisoner and shouted, "Quit yer bellyaching!"

"Get them out of here!" hollered Corporal Chase. Two guards jostled Karl and the wounded man, cradling his finger, into Sergeant Jackson's office. Jackson looked up from his desk. "Why are you hauling these wretches in here?"

"They were fighting. One of them needs medical attention. His finger may be broken."

"I thought I made myself clear, No disruptions! Take Scarface to the infirmary. And you," He pointed at Karl. "If I see you here again, drastic measures will be taken, ones you will not forget. Do I make myself clear?"

"Yes, sir," Karl muttered. He hurried to the barracks and sat on the edge of his bunk, his mind a tempest of unrest.

Ben glanced down from his top bunk. "You made a grand entrance."

"My new shoes! I thought I was done with that Nazi."

"You remember what life was like under the Nazis. All it took was a word or a glance to get you into trouble or worse. Scarface thinks the rules of camp do not apply to him. He has Nazi mentality. Stay away from him."

"Thanks for the advice. We're not free here, and that is a threat because of Scarface."

"That way of thinking could get you in trouble. We're safe here."

"We'll see," said Karl.

"I've had enough of this talk. I'm going to the mess hall."

Tight-lipped, Karl followed close behind.

Wide wooden stairs led to double doors. Stepping inside, a blast of warm air greeted them and the aroma of food comforted them. A stack of trays was at the beginning behind the counter. The staff piled plates with meatloaf, gravy, mashed potatoes, carrots, and peas. Each prisoner took a tray, grabbed a plate, and moved on to bowls of rolls, oranges, and apples followed by slices of apple pie.

"Here we eat more in a single day than in a week at home," said Ben, whose mouth watered. "In the German Army, there was never enough food for us to do what was expected of us. Cold made it worse."

Having never eaten meatloaf, they wondered what they were eating that was so delicious.

After supper, the lights were turned off at 2200 hours except for searchlights, which cast intermittent glows through the barracks windows. For the first time since leaving Weiss, Karl slept soundly. At 0600, the siren wailed, followed by instructions over a loudspeaker for all new prisoners to report to the mess hall. Darkness exacerbated the cold. They sprinted to the mess hall and wove through the long rows of tables with attached benches.

"Attention!" snapped a guard with closely cropped hair, a square chin, and dull eyes. Private Lowe had served in Italy with his twin brother, who was killed by Germans. His hatred for Germans lay just beneath the surface. His widowed mother was the only family he had left, and he was sent home to finish his tour of duty at Camp Grant, an assignment he hated.

"Private Lowe here, I'm in charge of job assignments, classes, and activities. We have dentists, doctors, libraries, educational facilities, and courses you can sign up for, including English lessons. Movies are shown three nights a week in English. Stationery is available so you can write home. In the office, you will find stocked shelves with toiletries and other amenities. You'll be paid eighty cents a day for work. If you want to spend your money, we have a canteen that sells candy, soft drinks, local produce, cigarettes, toiletries, and beer. Any questions, see me." He waited for the German translator to finish. "Form a line, breakfast is ready." Abruptly, he left by the side door.

Standing in the doorway to the kitchen, Stan Johnson, the cook, considered the new arrivals. Smoking a cigarette, he let his thoughts marinate. Stan had served as a cook in World War I and had been honorably discharged. He came home, married, and started a family just before the Depression of 1929 and worked three jobs to support them. Everything about Stan was big: his hands, his feet, and his laugh. His stained white apron covered his wide girth, and a sparse layer of gray hair covered his large head. His blue eyes took in everything around him and instinctively, he knew trouble before it began. War had taught him this. In anticipation of prisoners of war being shipped to the United States,

Stan received a notice that camps were being built to house them and cooks were needed. He lived three miles from Camp Grant and had been there since it opened in 1942. Under Stan's watchful eye, POWs assisted with all kitchen duties. Working for Stan was popular with the prisoners; he was tough but fair, and usually had a beer available for them at the end of the day.

Stan meandered back into the kitchen, where four burners were lit to simmer stews in large pots. He moved toward a chopping block, picked up his favorite knife—which he occasionally used to emphasize a point—and began to chop onions and carrots. The enormous kitchen had three refrigerators and two sinks so big that toddlers could bathe in them. Hanging pots covered an entire wall. In the Army, all the food was boiled in pots until the tops rattled. Stan changed that practice when he arrived at Camp Gran. He roasted meat, baked potatoes, simmered vegetables, and made fresh rolls.

Curious to see what his new helper looked like, Stan walked out to the mess hall. Karl, Ben, and Eric were among the last POWs still there.

"Anyone cook's helper?"

Eric raised his hand.

"Good," said Stan. "Come into the kitchen."

"Come with me," Eric whispered.

Stan said, "I thought there was only one cook's helper in this bunch." Turning to Eric, he said, "So, you can't cook?"

"Well…"

"It's okay. I'll show you. You look like a fast learner. Our boys are fighting the war, so our manpower is way down. We need you. Some prisoners are bused to work in factories and farms. Last winter, some plowed snow. What are you two assigned to?"

"Getting a garden bed ready for planting," Karl said.

"Give it another six to eight weeks to thaw," said Stan. "We can use a garden."

Stan handed Eric a clean apron. "Well, if you'll excuse us, Eric and I have to get lunch ready for four hundred men."

Eric raised his eyebrows. "How many?"

"You heard me. Don't worry, we have help and are quite organized."

Seeing Karl leave the mess hall, Scarface pushed through the crowd and, scowling, raised his bandaged finger at Karl.

Karl looped his thumb into his trouser pocket; his stomach churned. Returning to the barracks, he tossed his jacket, pulled off his shoes, stretched out on his bunk, and sank his head into a soft pillow. His clothes were American, the food he ate was American, and the language was English, but his heart and mind were German.

He turned on his side. *How much food did they eat today? Was the winter bad? Did they have enough fuel? How was Hans? Had soldiers stopped by? Are they still waiting for me to come back after four months?*

Karl and Ben joined the lunch line. Eric placed bowls of stew on the shelf in rapid succession without spilling a drop. When he saw his friends, he grinned.

"Nice job—"

Karl was interrupted by a voice yelling in German.

Scarface yelled, "Hey traitor! Still kissing the Americans' esels?" POWs seated at his table laughed.

Slamming his tray on the table, Karl yelled, "It's none of your damn business!"

Two guards moved in and stood between the tables. "Enough!" shouted one.

Karl clenched his jaw. Finishing their food, Karl broke the silence and spoke. "Ben, let's write home."

"I don't know where my mutter and schwester are."

"Use your home address."

"It was Hamburg."

"Heavily bombed, wasn't it?"

Ben nodded.

They walked into the office. Private Lowe looked up from his magazine, annoyed by the intrusion.

"What now?"

"We'd like some paper to write home."

"Over there, second shelf."

The shelf was empty.

"Guess you'll have to wait until tomorrow."

"Beg your pardon, Private, the inventory supply of paper is full," said Ben.

"Then go find some, smartass."

Karl followed Ben into the stockroom where shelves were packed with supplies and retrieved the writing paper. That evening, Karl sat in his bunk and wrote:

1944 March

Dear family,

I need to practice writing in English. Hans, translate for Mutter and Papa.

I was picked up by the British and they put me on a ship to America with other Germans. I am in a camp in Chicago, but it is good, and we are fed well and have a good place to sleep. I miss the German dark bread. And miss all of you. Ben Schmid was captured and is here with me. We are good for each other. It was colder here last winter than in Germany. I am fine and hope you are too.

Your loving son,

Karl

Karl went to the office, handed his letter to Private Lowe, and said, "I would like this mailed."

"My brother was eighteen when your people killed him, and I have to mail your stinking letter." Private Lowe pulled a book of matches from the pocket of his shirt. He tapped a pack of cigarettes, pulled one out, lit it, and blew smoke in Karl's face.

"What about my letter?"

"Leave it," Lowe said, pointing to a pile on top of his desk.

"I'm sorry about your brother."

Private Lowe crushed his cigarette in the ashtray. "Where were you when they caught you?"

"Italy. I was helping an American get back to his unit."

"You helped an American?"

"Yes. He was wounded."

"Get out of here."

Private Lowe held all Germans responsible for his brother's death, the only one he had. It was easier than thinking about how much he missed him.

In war, there is enough blame to go around: blame for the Allies who dropped bombs on German cities, killing civilians, and blame for Germans who occupied countries and arrested any who spoke against them. It wasn't the German people who killed Corporal Lowe's brother. It was aggression, power, and loathing for an enemy.

The next day, Karl started his classes. He signed up for English, math, and American history. The teacher was a man who taught at a local high school, whose grandparents were German. He had a rudimentary understanding of the German language. Sitting in the front of class, Karl was captivated by all he was learning. This was not lost on Mr. Thurber, who considered Karl a fine student. It was March 10, 1944—Karl's eighteenth birthday.

On Tuesdays, Karl, Ben, and Eric enjoyed watching movies like *Arsenic and Old Lace* and *Meet Me in St. Louis*. They could hear each other's breath in the packed theater. It was a welcome escape as to why they were at Camp Grant.

Karl and Ben sat on the edge of their bunks, waiting for Eric. Lights-out was in fifteen minutes.

"He's late," said Karl.

"I guess cooking for four hundred people takes time."

Eric arrived, panting. "The Nazi supporters were yelling at the guards, calling them fakes. They refused to clear their plates, and Stan says they refused to stand when the American flag was raised or lowered. We watched from the kitchen. I'm scared."

Eric slumped down on his bunk and wiped his brow. "What if they found out my father was a Nazi supporter? What if they expect me to agree with them? Who knows what might happen if I say no? What if Stan finds out? Maybe he wouldn't want me working for him. Maybe no one would want me working for them."

"There are rules here. Scarface isn't in charge, and you're not like them. And you're not your father," said Karl.

"I'm lonely. I never thought I would be, but I am. For what, I don't know. Maybe for what I never had. My father thought Hitler was the greatest, and my mother disagreed. They fought all the time. I can't go back, there's no one there." He turned to Karl and continued. "You're the only friend I have."

Karl placed his hand on Eric's arm.

"Hold on," said Ben. "I'm your friend, too."

The sirens blasted. They slipped under the covers and night encased them with its dark velvet robe.

After breakfast the following morning, Karl and Ben reported to Private Lowe for instructions. "We are assigned to prepare a bed for the spring," Karl said.

"And what?"

"Where is it?" Karl's courage was reemerging.

"Outside the camp, in back. Anything else?"

"Yes. Do we need permission to go outside the camp?"

"You already have it! A guard is assigned to keep an eye on you. Don't do anything stupid." Private Lowe stood and loomed over Karl, who stared back.

"And the tools?"

"In the shed!"

Karl and Ben departed, walking around the rear of the camp through a gate. There was a sizable patch of hard ground covered in three-feet-tall rocky weeds. A guard leaned against a tree, his rifle across his arms. He wore a patch over his right eye, earning him a nickname, Patch.

"They want us to make a bed from this?" said Ben.

"We'll do it. We'll get help."

Karl and Ben pulled the broken shed door from its hinges. Shafts of light streamed through jagged-edged gaps in the wall, casting light on cobwebs. Shovels and three pitchforks stood like sentries. The sweet musty odor of last summer's straw filled the air. In the corner stood a rusted cultivator.

"Look, a cultivator!"

"What's that for?"

"It's for turning over the soil."

Ben rolled his eyes. "Looks like a piece of junk."

"My father had one of these. I know how to use it."

"You do?" Ben brushed away cobwebs.

"Yes."

"Well, I guess we know where to come when the ground is ready."

Chapter Eighteen

It was early morning, and the full light of day had yet to appear. Eric woke, climbed down from his bunk, dressed, and stood in the doorway. Haunted by his father's Nazi support, his mother's opposition, their heated arguments, the slammed doors, and thrown dishes that he saw growing up, he stepped outside wondering if he would ever find peace.

Stan sat on the steps of the mess hall taking deep drags of his cigarette, flicking the ashes with his finger, his eyes fixed on Barracks Ten. Jeeps and trucks rumbled around, and the night shift kept an eye out for any suspicious movement. One of them spotted Eric.

"Freeze!"

Faltering, Eric raised his hands.

Stan yelled, "It's okay! He's my cook."

"I don't give a shit who he is." Waving his rifle, the guard commanded, "Get over there. Wait for formation. Move."

Eric stood at attention until the siren blew.

Karl woke with a jolt to the sound of the siren. He pulled on his trousers, grabbed his shirt, and threaded an arm through a sleeve. Ben rolled over; his arm hung down from the top bunk.

"What time is it?"

"0600."

A low moan emanated from Ben's mouth. "Them and their damn sirens."

"Without them, we would sleep until noon. C'mon, let's go." They took a position next to Eric.

The drill sergeant eyed the group. "Attention. Twenty sit-ups. Twenty jumping jacks. You're getting fed better than us, you mangy crew." When the exercises were completed, he yelled, "Cooks, fall out, double time to the mess hall. The rest of you stay for roll call."

Eric responded to the order and sprinted to the mess hall. Stan greeted him and said, "Best you stay inside until the sirens blow. You want fresh air, open a window, but don't stick your head out, it might get blown off. Time to start breakfast. Pancakes, sausages, and cereal. The guards get angry when they smell sausage. They know it's not for them."

"Why is that?" asked Eric.

"Geneva Conventions demand that we treat prisoners well. Well-fed, well-housed, and well-treated."

"Do the guards resent us for this?"

"Some do. Some were unqualified to serve, and they're mad that they were sent here instead of going overseas. Some guards live at home where rationing is in effect, and here you get to eat well."

Karl stood at attention, waiting for the drill sergeant to finish roll call, chafing under the drill sergeant's stare. The strands of barbed wire and pacing sentinels were reminders he was not free.

Karl remembered his father bent over the garden, handling vegetables like a priceless commodity. Putting his anger resolutely aside, Karl determined that he would plant a garden his father would be proud of.

With roll call completed, the sergeant declared, "Dismissed!"

Karl and Ben climbed the steps to the mess hall, where the aromas of coffee and sausage filled the air.

They approached the breakfast line, where Eric was dishing out pancakes.

"Made them myself," he said.

Karl and Ben headed for a table to join other prisoners, who grudgingly and without greeting shifted to make room. Fritz Weber, who was a few bunks down from Karl in Barracks Ten, sat across from him. Weber had been captured in Tunisia when he was sixteen. He was polite, addressed the guards as "Sir," and did his job cleaning tables in the mess hall and washing floors. Scarface frowned on Fritz's passivity.

Fritz pushed away his tray and unfolded a thin sheet of wrinkled paper that smelled of home.

"This got through. It's dated January 1944. It took two months to get here. It's from my mother. She writes of starvation, no meat, little bread, and no fuel, but they're alive." Tears blocked his vision. He folded his letter and held it in his hands before placing it in his shirt pocket marked POW.

Karl wiped his chin and set his fork down. "They'll be okay. German people are strong. Write back to them. They must be worried about you."

"Ja, I will do," sniffed Fritz.

The rest of the prisoners ate in silence.

After lunch, Fritz Weber entered the mess hall carrying a mop and bucket. Scarface put his dishes in the container, turned, shoved Fritz, and kicked the bucket, sending water over the floor. Fritz reached for the bucket. Scarface stuck his leg out, and Fritz tumbled. Scarface booted him in the ribs. Two guards apprehended him and another helped Fritz stand. On his way out, Karl heard the commotion and ran to help the guard with the howling Fritz.

"Big baby," Scarface yelled over his shoulder as the guards dragged him out.

Fritz was taken away and Karl joined the others in the yard.

"What happened?" asked Ben.

"Scarface pushed and kicked Fritz. I think he broke his arm."

"Poor kid."

Two days later, Fritz returned with a cast on his right arm and a sling for support. Entering the mess hall, Fritz waved to Karl and joined him for lunch.

"You were pretty brave putting up with that guy. You're a better man than he is."

"I'll avoid him at all costs."

"I had a run in with him. We avoid each other, and I still stay clear of him."

Karl had been alerted to Scarface's attitudes and comments and wondered if they would escalate.

"I better get to Corporal Chase's office, he's expecting me at one o'clock to do filing," said Ben.

Ben worked in the office where Corporal Chase taught him how to file and keep track of camp supplies. He rearranged the file system for better access and developed an inventory to avoid running out.

Impressed, Corporal Chase said, "You saved us time and prevented errors. Where did you learn this?"

"I always liked to keep things organized. Helped Mutti with paperwork after my father left. She sold a few apples and potatoes for income, and I kept track of things for her."

"What did your father do?"

"Papa was a schoolteacher. School was regimented by the Nazis who wanted teachers to prepare us how to be soldiers. Papa refused and taught academics. There were many like him. One day he went to school and never came back. Every day we waited for him. One day they came and took me and left Mutti and my schwester alone."

"Your father was a brave man."

Ben blinked back tears, held his chin high, and continued filing.

Corporal Chase combed through orders.

Chapter Nineteen

After seeing *Going My Way* at the Bijou, Harry and Abby made their way home through the March wind. During the war, Harry developed an aching need to survive the horrors of war and make it home to Abby and Uncle. John's moods concerned Harry and he wondered what else his friend saw or did.

"What ever happened to Emma? She and John seemed to hit it off."

"When I ask him anything, he tells me to mind my own business. He goes to work, comes home, grabs something to eat, and goes to his room," Abby said.

"That last time at Duffy's he made a quick exit, but she slipped him a napkin. I bet her number was on it," said Harry.

"You saw that?"

"I did."

"We'll see what happens. When he was in the hospital, I heard John say the name Karl when he was having nightmares. He said he wants wanted to find him. We need to find out about that. Maybe you could get around to it."

"I don't want to set him off."

"At least try."

"Too much delving into his business. Wait and see. Let's ask him if he wants to go to Duffy's," suggested Harry.

Entering the house, Abby continued. "Then there's Lily. Can't you find out about her?"

"Let it be. Get dressed, I'll get John."

"I am dressed, silly," said Abby, sliding into her boots.

Harry took the stairs two at a time, knocked on John's door, and let himself in.

"We're going to Duffy's. Come with us. Maybe Emma will be there." Harry saw a brightening in John's dark eyes. "Get dressed. We'll wait downstairs."

John lifted himself to a sitting position, stood, opened the drawer to his nightstand, uncapped the bottle, and swallowed a pill.

"It's a beautiful night and officially spring—a new beginning," said Abby as she linked arms with Harry. "Don't you think so, John?"

Shoulders hunched, hands deep in his pockets, he said, "Yeah."

Seated at the bar with her friends, Emma pulled her sweater around her shoulders and glanced toward the door. She slid off the barstool and walked toward John. "Good to see you. How are you doing?"

John searched for words which didn't come.

"Hi, Emma. Nice to see you," said Abby. "Care to join us?"

Emma hesitated long enough to give John the courage to speak. "How about a walk instead?" he said.

"A walk?"

"Yeah, a walk in the spring air."

"Sounds nice, I'll tell my friends."

"I guess we'll just wait and see," said Abby.

Harry grinned.

It was Emma's last year of nursing school. She sat at the nurses' station reading her patient's chart.

Emma caught Dr. Joe Pierce's eye a month ago when he saw her walking in the corridor at Carney Hospital and liked what he saw. His next assignment was on the unit where Emma worked.

Dr. Joe was medium height with a strong build, wavy brown hair, well-liked by the staff, and handsome. He fixed his gaze on Emma; she looked at him and couldn't turn away.

"Hi, I'm Joe Pierce. I've seen you around, thought I'd introduce myself."

Dumbfounded, she closed the patient's chart and said, "Emma."

"Emma. Would you like to meet me after we get off duty for coffee?"

"Of course! I mean ... okay."

"Meet me in front of the hospital at seven. If that's okay?"

"It's fine, just fine."

Emma let out the breath she was holding.

In the weeks that followed, they spent all their free time together and were inseparable. Joe would call for her at the nurses' home. They took the local bus downtown for hamburgers and coffee or a movie. When Emma's roommate was absent, they made love so passionately it took their breath away, not knowing where each other left off.

"You're all I think about," Joe told her. "Let's elope."

Emma wanted to finish nursing school first.

Everything around Emma glowed brighter because of Joe Pierce, and she felt like nothing in her life could go wrong if she had Joe. But Joe's father was heavily invested in his only son, including his wish that he would procure a residency in general surgery at a prestigious hospital. It was a future that did not include Emma, the daughter of a recluse. Joe left for home to be with his family at Christmas, promising to call when he returned. He never returned, never called. Emma didn't think she could love like that again. She nursed her broken heart until the hurt left. Meeting John Conway kindled a spark in her that she thought was dead.

Clearing glasses from the bar, Duffy listened as Emma said goodbye to her friends and watched her leave with John. Duffy liked seeing young people get together.

John placed his hand on Emma's back and followed her outside. "I am still waiting for you to call," she said.

"I was going to, but I started a new job, and it's kept me busy."

"Well, that's a good excuse. Let's cut through the park. What's your new job?"

"Meriwether's—an accounting firm. Got the job thanks to Harry. Doing bookkeeping and stuff."

"Do you like it?"

"I guess so."

"John."

"What?"

"Are you all right?"

"Why wouldn't I be?" he asked, pushing dirt around with the tip of his shoe.

"Just asking."

"Are you still at the hospital?"

"No. I work at the VA clinic. We take care of the men coming home from the war who are physically and mentally wounded. It's the least I can do for what they did for us. My friends and I go to Duffy's after work on Fridays. Kind of a get-together after a long week."

"The only friend I have is Harry."

"Sometimes one is all you need."

John stopped walking and turned to face Emma. He lifted her chin, bent down, and kissed her. His cheeks burned and a surge of warmth ran through him. He kept his face close to hers and touched her soft cheek. She stood still, her head tilted, and her lips parted. He kissed her again, this time longer. He held her close, whispering "Emma" and tightening his arms around her.

"John, it's okay."

He released her and bent over. Placing her hand on his back, she said, "John, you're holding back. Whatever is bothering you, you can tell me."

"I can't. I just can't."

"I have big shoulders."

"I need to figure it out myself."

"How?"

"By finding the people I hurt."

"Like Karl?"

John's lips parted.

"I heard you mumble his name when you were in the hospital. A lot."

"Thanks for the walk. I need to go."

"Hurt that you feel and actions that you regret are hard to let go. I know."

"How?"

"I was hurt by someone I loved."

"How could anyone hurt you?"

"It happens, John. A man I loved left to go home for a visit with his family, who lived in another state. I never heard from him again. Much later, I learned he went to a prestigious hospital for a residency program, where his father was on the board of directors."

"Must've been hard."

"A broken heart takes time to mend, but it does—when another person helps with the healing."

"I'm not ready." He started to walk away.

"John," she called. He turned to face her. "When you are, I'll be here."

Chapter Twenty

Prisoners lined up in front of the barracks and performed calisthenics to the barking command of the drill sergeant, their breath visible in the frigid air.

The sergeant unfolded his arms and shouted, "Dismissed!"

Ben bent over and said, "That guy is going to kill us."

Karl stretched his arms over his head. Walking to the mess hall, Karl said, "Considering what we looked like a couple of months ago, we're in better shape."

"Eating three meals a day helps."

Ben hustled up the steps to the mess hall, put his foot down on the floor that had been recently waxed, and fell backward. Karl heard the crack as Ben's head hit the floor Ben's head hit the floor. Everyone nearby was silent. Ben was sprawled on the floor, lips parted, eyes closed, motionless. Karl knelt beside him, feeling a surge of disbelief. "Ben, wake up, wake up!" Karl's eyes scanned the room. "Someone get a doctor, hurry!"

A medic appeared and shouted, "Move back, everyone!" He leaned over, lifted Ben's eyelid with his thumb, and yelled, "Get a stretcher!"

"Is he going to be all right? Tell me!" Karl pleaded.

"Stand back, everyone!"

An ambulance arrived. Ben was placed into the back and it roared off, sirens blasting. Karl was rooted in place with fear. He wandered back to the barracks, placed his hand on Ben's bunk, and closed his eyes. Karl felt his papa's strong arm circle his shoulder. He reached up, but there was nothing there. His breathing slowed. Ben was his link to his family and his best friend.

Prisoners filled the barracks with chatter, which annoyed Karl. The room was in fast forward. For the next few days, he slept little, ate little, and said little, and he was oblivious to Eric, who followed him everywhere, trying to break through the fog that distorted Karl's thoughts.

In the evening, Eric sat on the edge of Karl's bunk. "Say something, Karl."

"Nothing to say."

"You have to eat."

"What makes you think I'm not?"

"I see your tray. Ben will get better. You'll see."

"It's been three days and no word. He could be dead."

"Stop thinking like that. I'm going to bed. See you at breakfast."

The following morning, oatmeal simmered in a large pot, sausages sizzled on pans, dozens of eggs were cracked and stirred. Platters of donuts were at the end of the counter next to an urn of coffee and glasses of orange juice. Prisoners lined up with their trays.

Dishing out the oatmeal, one of them asked Eric, "Any word about your buddy?"

In a voice edged with tension, he said, "How am I supposed to know? Keep moving."

After breakfast, Stan removed his apron and said to Eric, "Start the cleanup, I'll be right back."

Miffed, Eric started washing the pots. Moments later, he felt a tap on his shoulder.

He turned, a pot scrubber in one hand and a pot in the other, and said, "Corporal Chase!" Stan stood behind him. Eric's brow knitted. "What…?"

"I can't find Karl, but I have some good news about Ben. He's going to be okay. A couple of stitches in his head, and he has a concussion, but after a week's rest, he should be fine. Pass it along to Karl. I have to leave camp for a while."

Eric pumped Corporal Chase's hand. "Thank you." He turned toward Stan, who tilted his head toward the door. Eric sprinted to the classroom building and peered through a glass into a classroom looking for Karl. An older man holding a briefcase approached Eric. "Can I help you?"

"I'm looking for Karl Baum."

"He didn't show up for my history class this morning. Bright kid. Is he all right?"

Eric frowned. "Yeah, I'm sure he is." Instinct told him otherwise.

Karl walked around the buildings under the watchful eyes of the guards in the watch tower. He detested being a prisoner, the injustice of his capture, and Scarface's bullying tactics. A fire rose within him. He needed to talk to someone. He'd find Eric. His pace quickened—but first, he needed to use the latrine.

Entering the latrine, Karl saw Scarface standing at the urinal, zipping up his trousers. Without turning his head, Scarface blurted out, "Better teach your buddy how to walk."

Karl lunged at Scarface, arm-wrestled him to the ground, and battered his head against the floor.

Scarface reached up and squeezed Karl's throat.

Walking in the yard, Eric heard loud voices coming from the latrine. Standing in the doorway, he saw Scarface squeezing Karl's throat.

"Guard! Guard!" he yelled.

Eric seized Scarface's wrist, loosening his grip on Karl's neck, and pushed him off Karl, who gagged and rolled over. Scarface stood, his face crimson, his chest heaving. He wiped blood away from his mouth with the back of his hand. Karl staggered to his feet.

Two guards entered with rifles drawn. "Halt!"

Scarface swung at Karl's cheek and knocked him off his feet.

A guard slammed the butt of his rifle against Scarface's shoulder. The other guard stood, rifle shouldered, snug against his cheek, and commanded, "Outside! Now!"

Karl and Scarface stumbled and were taken away at gunpoint. Eric ran to the mess hall where Stan was stacking canned goods.

Gasping, Eric blurted out, "Stan, there was a fight. Karl and Scarface. They almost killed each other. They were taken away at gunpoint. What'll happen? What should we do?"

"Nothing," Stan said, holding three cans in his hand. "Karl will return. Scarface and his like will get transferred to another camp." Placing the cans on the shelves, he continued. "The government found a camp where they could keep Nazi supporters in one place. More supervision, more guards, and tighter controls. The government doesn't want any problems."

"Scarface has taunted Karl since the beginning," said Eric. "Surely they won't send Karl away."

"No. You gotta understand. Scarface is loyal to Hitler. Karl didn't serve, and Scarface resents it. Scarface isn't there to fight for his country, and he notices a lot of you working, obeying the rules. He sees this as disloyalty to Hitler and Germany. Weber was attacked because his English is good, he was friendly with the guards, and he did everything he was told. A nice kid—but not according to Scarface."

"Poor Weber."

"Camp officials don't want problems. All hardcore Nazis are being transported to a camp in Alva, Oklahoma."

"How do you know?"

"Word gets around." Stan wiped his hands on a towel. "In 1939, the Nazis invaded Poland, and by 1941 they had invaded and conquered eleven countries. Eleven! Hitler felt invincible and didn't believe there would be a successful invasion of Europe by the Allies. Then the Americans got into the war. Scarface hated that."

"I remember when the Americans joined the war and hoped it would come to an end. I was glad it was the British and not the Soviets who captured me."

"There's no glory looking at a man with his guts hanging out, and where he's from don't matter. I know. My service in World War I taught me that," said Stan. "War is bad all around."

Eric sat and held his head in his hands. "There's no one back home for me."

Curious, Stan said, "Want to tell me about it?"

"Papa thought Hitler was the answer to Germany's problems—no work, no money, and little food. My mutti disagreed, and all the time they fought, until one day Papa left and I never saw him again."

Stan pulled over a chair and sat next to him. "Your father wasn't a bad man. He just held on to his beliefs."

"But he left me. I needed him," said Eric, his voice breaking.

"I imagine that must've felt pretty damn awful."

Eric blinked, remembering the feeling and searched for the words to describe it. There were none. "Yes, it did. My mother had a boyfriend. They escaped to Switzerland. Said I couldn't come because it was too dangerous for me." Eric let out a snicker. "I was sixteen, and the war was raging in Europe. That's why I'm not going back. Bad memories and I need a new life."

Stan rubbed his chin and said, "Finish your coffee. Karl will be back. I have time off this weekend. Come have dinner with me and meet my family. Corporal Chase will okay it."

Humbled, Eric replied, "I couldn't—"

"Sure you can. Try some home-cooked American food."

"Thanks, Stan."

It was dark when Karl got back to Barracks Ten. He stumbled to his bunk. He needed something cold to calm the fire in his cheek.

Rising from his bunk, Eric said, "Are you okay?" Karl waved a hand. "Corporal Chase told me Ben is okay. He got a concussion, but he will be back in a week."

"Ben is okay?"

"Yes. Get some rest. See you in the morning."

Karl rolled over but couldn't sleep. His thoughts kept him awake until dawn, when he finally dozed off.

The next morning, he woke with pains running through his cheekbone. Thoughts of ice filled his mind. The barracks was empty. He had missed roll call. The drill sergeant was quick to find him.

"Baum. Get out here."

Karl rolled out of his bunk and rose, meeting the drill sergeant's eyes. "Outside, Baum. Push-ups and jumping jacks."

Hatless and without a jacket, Karl completed the calisthenics. The drill sergeant watched with narrowed eyes. "Dismissed."

Karl treaded back into Barracks Ten. Sitting on the edge of his bunk, he dropped his head into his hands. Were there more hurdles waiting?

He slipped on his jacket, pulled a cap over his head, and walked to the mess hall.

Stan called to him. "Nazi sympathizers are gone. The truck pulled out first thing this morning. Here, I brought you a present." Stan handed Karl ice wrapped in a towel.

A thin smile of gratitude appeared on Karl's face—the smile of one who had escaped an enemy.

Chapter Twenty-One

John sat on the edge of his bed, rubbing his temples; even the simplest tasks depleted his energy. He swallowed two pills, which pulled him to sleep.

A ray of sunshine woke him. With a moan, he turned, taking the blankets with him. His throat was dry and his head hurt. The noise coming from downstairs was unbearable and the smell of coffee triggered nausea. His mind filled with thoughts of Karl, and he was overcome with a deep sense of remorse. He stumbled to the bathroom and turned on the tub faucet, dreading the day ahead.

He stood outside the office and placed his hand on the doorknob but hesitated to turn it. Alex appeared beside him.

"Morning John, having second thoughts? Come on, we'll face the music together. I'll get us coffee," said Alex.

Taking a seat at his desk, John poured over the figures on the pages and saw double numbers. Alex set coffee and donuts on his desk. John shoved aside his paperwork and squirmed in his seat. Staring into space, office noise competed with Alex's voice, making it impossible for John to concentrate.

"Let's go have our coffee and donuts. Sugar and caffeine always work."

"Thanks, Alex. But I've got to figure things out."

"Okay, I'm around."

John got through the day, carefully placing numbers where they belonged. He looked at the clock on the wall. His appointment with Dr. Burns was at five o'clock. He picked up his work and gave it to Alex.

"Can you check my figures? I'm leaving for the day."

"Sure thing," said Alex.

John rushed out.

John tapped his fingers on the arm of the chair, waiting for Dr. Burns. *He has to give me one more refill and then I'll be fine. Just one more.* The door opened.

"Hi, John. How are you."

"I need a refill on my pills."

"What's going on?"

"Just give me a refill."

Dr. Burns sat next to John and said, "Tell me what's wrong. I've known you all your life, and I can see you are having a bad time—"

"I'm jittery and I need to relax."

"I can't give you another refill. Too much chance of addiction. I can refer you to—"

John shot back, "I don't need a referral. I need a refill, just one more."

"Getting addicted can ruin your life. I know your family. You matter to them."

"I'm a burden to them, and I have no life."

"You would be more of a burden to them with an addiction. Coming home from a war is difficult. Talk to them."

"Forget it. Just forget it!" John bolted from the office.

Dr. Burns dialed the Conway's number. John's father answered. "Henry, Doc Burns. John just left after I refused to give him a refill on those pills. He could become addicted, and when I suggested he go to the clinic, he stormed out."

"What can I do to help him?"

"He has to want the help. All you can do is just be there and try to get him to go to the clinic. If I can be of any help, let me know, Henry."

Henry hung up the phone and rubbed his sore chest. *I failed him. I should have been more understanding.*

"Henry," Louise called from the kitchen. "Who called?"

"Doc Burns. He thinks John has a problem with drugs. He refused to give him a refill and he took off. He said just be there and call him if we need anything." Heaving himself from the chair, he said, "I'm tired, Louise."

Louise held the arm of the only man she had ever loved and kissed him. "Why don't you lie down for a bit." She watched him climb the stairs and whispered, "God help us."

John arrived home, skipped supper, and went to his room. He tossed from side to side, threw the bedcovers off, and stared out the window until dawn. He dressed, drank two cups of coffee, and left the house before anyone was up. He couldn't face them.

During the night, a dusting of snow had covered the ground. An April drizzle had left pools on the sidewalk. John boarded the bus and got off at Duffy's. It was early. He pushed open the door, rubbed his hands together, and slid onto a bar stool.

"Hey, John. Just in time. Made a fresh pot of coffee."

"Yeah. How about that? Just a beer."

"Kinda early." Leaning in toward John, Duffy added, "Look, guys come home from the war, they drink too much to escape their problems. The booze wears off—but the problems never do."

"I don't have problems."

"I see you in here with your sister and her boyfriend. You got nice people. You wear the weight of the world on your shoulders. I seen it."

"Where's my beer?"

A glass of beer appeared in front of John. He took a long swallow, leaving a white line on his upper lip.

"Saw you leave last night with Emma." Placing his elbow on the counter, Duffy continued. "She's a looker—and nice, really nice. I bet you could talk to her. She'd listen."

John gave Duffy a cold stare.

Duffy straightened. "Let me make you a hamburger. Be right back." He disappeared into the kitchen.

John drained his glass and left. He crossed the street and headed for the office. A large man wearing an overcoat and a scarf that concealed half his face emerged from the shadows and kept in step behind John. He caught up with him and brushed his shoulder.

"Sorry."

Annoyed, John blurted out, "Watch where you're going." The man touched the sleeve of John's jacket. "Get away from me," John said, yanking his sleeve away.

"Name's Jesse." He reached out his hand. John ignored the gesture. "Maybe this will help." He thrust a small container into John's hand. "There's more where that came from. I'll be in touch."

In an instant, the man was gone. John looked at the pills. They were a different color from the ones Dr. Burns prescribed. He put the container in his trouser pocket.

John entered the office, avoided eye contact, made his way to his desk, and sank into a chair. He opened the loose-leaf binder and skimmed the rows of client names and daily transactions, none of which made sense to him. He was unable to make an entry as three pages slipped from his grasp and fluttered to the floor.

"Everything all right, John?" asked Alex, seated next to him.

"Of course, why do you ask?" said John stooping to pick up the papers.

At the end of the day, John placed the completed invoices into the ledger. He rechecked his work three times before closing the binder. He trudged home and entered the kitchen.

"Where's Dad?"

Louise wiped invisible crumbs off the table. "Upstairs. He's not feeling well."

John eyed his mother. "What's wrong?"

"Says his stomach is off." She opened the refrigerator door and stared at the contents.

"Can I bring him something?"

"I'll make him some chicken soup."

John grabbed a beer from the refrigerator and made a ham and cheese sandwich.

"Are you sure he's okay?"

"Yes, don't worry."

"Good night, Mom."

Louise looked at her son. "Are you all right? You'd tell me if you weren't, wouldn't you?"

"I'm fine. I'm okay. Just a little edgy with the new job and everything."

"What's everything?"

"It's okay, Mom. Don't worry."

John entered his bedroom and closed the door. He took two of the pills from the bottle, swallowed them, lay down, pulled the covers over his head, and waited to sleep.

He was running for a bus that was pulling away from the stop. He was at work. Karl stood at his desk, tearing up John's work into small pieces. A door slammed.

He woke, staggered to the window, and pulled the curtain aside. No one was there.

In the morning John rose, his brain moving slower than normal. Fighting nausea, he rolled out of bed, got dressed, and went downstairs.

"Where's Dad?"

"Resting."

"Still? I'll go check on him."

"Let him rest. I'll check on him later."

"Did he have your soup?"

"Yes, he did."

John put on his jacket. "I'm late for work. Call if you need me."

Later that day, Henry came downstairs, his face ashen. "Call an ambulance, Louise. I've got terrible chest pain."

Shaken, Louise dialed the number and called Abby at the library. "This is Abby Conway's mother. Please ask Abby to go to the hospital. Her father is ill, and the ambulance is on its way." Louise grabbed her coat and placed a blanket around her husband's shoulders.

John entered the office, the secretary glanced at the clock. He flinched under her cold gaze before sitting at his desk, trying to look confident.

"Morning, John. Thought you might like some coffee," said Mr. Meriwether.

"Thanks."

"How are things going? Need any help?"

"No sir, everything's good."

"Glad to hear it."

Mr. Meriwether watched John eying the mound of paper in front of him.

Alex leaned over toward John. "It will be easier to separate the credits and the charges."

"Yeah, thanks."

"Anything I can help with let me know."

Observing this encounter, Mr. Meriwether returned to his office.

It was five o'clock. John leaned back in his chair. With his work completed, he put on his jacket and left. A light rain was falling. There was a chill in the air, and John turned up the collar of his jacket. Preoccupation with his thoughts replaced reality until a voice said, "Hi, John."

John recognized it—the man who called himself Jesse.

"You again? What do you want?" asked John.

"Just seein' if you need anything."

Two boys tossing a football in the street ran after the ball that landed near Jesse's feet.

"Get out of here," Jesse yelled as he kicked the ball. John turned to walk away. "We need to talk. I have something you need."

"I don't need anything from you."

"Okay. I'll be around when your pills run out."

Once home, John grabbed the pill bottle, went to the bathroom, and flushed the remaining pills down the toilet.

"Mom? Abby?" There were peeled potatoes on the counter, a cup of coffee and a folded newspaper on the table. Louise's apron was draped over the sink. An uneasiness crept over him.

The front door opened. Abby held Louise's arm. Both were sobbing. John shouted, "Where's Dad?"

Abby lifted her tear-stained face. "He's dead, John. He's dead."

"No." John recoiled. "It can't be." He covered his mouth with his hand and choked back tears. "What happened? Why didn't you call me?"

"He had a heart attack," said Abby. "We were too afraid to leave him. And I didn't want to leave Mom to find a phone. We sat outside the room while they worked on him. It seemed to take forever, yet it happened so quickly. There was nothing they could do."

Seated at the table, Abby and Louise continued sobbing. John circled the kitchen. His eyes burned, and the ache in his chest was relentless.

Abby wiped her eyes. "Harry," she said. "Harry should know."

"I'll call him," said John.

"No, I'll do it." Abby left to make the call. When she returned, she blew her nose and said, "He'll be right over."

There was much to do: funeral arrangements, the eulogy, the church service, notifying family and friends, and lunch after the service.

"Father Ryan will do the funeral," said Louise, twisting a wet handkerchief between her fingers. "And Forbes will do the funeral arrangements."

"I'll call Father Ryan," said John.

"And the eulogy?" asked Louise.

"I'll do it," said Abby.

John said, "I'll call Forbes."

Harry came through the door. "Harry, it's awful. We can't believe it," Abby said. He held her close and reached out for Louise and John.

Over the next two days, the family grappled with their loss, making arrangements for Henry's farewell. The church service was well attended, the singing uplifting, and Abby gave the eulogy, struggling with words when she mentioned her love for her father and his love for their family.

The family gathered at the cemetery and said their final goodbye. Back at the house, neighbors bustled about, arranging trays of sandwiches, cookies, and brownies. The smell of freshly brewed coffee filled the air. They ate and talked in whispered conversations. The fragrance of flowers was beginning to overtake the crowded room. John wove through the crowd to get outside for a breath of fresh air. Unable to fully comprehend his loss, he remained numb.

I should have checked on him before I left for work. I should have been grateful instead of hanging around the house, drinking beer, and taking pills while he worked every day.

He crept upstairs to his parents' bedroom, hoping no one would notice. He picked up his parents' wedding picture from the nightstand. They smiled back at him.

"The pills are gone, Dad. I have a job. I will make you proud of me. You'll see," he said aloud.

He placed the picture back and joined the well-wishers.

"John, talk to people and thank them for coming. See if Mom needs anything. We all miss Dad, but we have to think of Mom," said Abby.

John watched people nibble on bite-sized sandwiches. Stifling an urge to tell everyone to get out, he was brightened at the sight of Mr. Meriwether, who stood in the living room, removing his hat. "Mr. Meriwether, thanks for coming."

"John, so sorry about your father," he said, extending his hand.

John grasped it and blinked to avoid the tears that threatened to spill over.

"It was very sudden. That's what's hard."

"Yes, no time to prepare. Take the time off that you need."

"Thanks."

The front door opened, and Emma entered the room. She took off her hat, ran a hand through her hair, and saw John talking to an older man. Over Mr. Meriwether's shoulder, John saw Emma and walked toward her, extending his arms. They embraced.

Letting go, John said, "I want you to meet someone."

He turned to face Mr. Meriwether, who had moved closer. "This is Emma. This is Mr. Meriwether, my boss."

John took Emma's coat.

"Pleased to meet you. You're a friend of John's?" asked Mr. Meriwether.

"Yes, I was his nurse at the hospital."

Clearly impressed, Mr. Meriwether said, "John's a lucky man."

As the crowd dwindled, plates were cleared, food was put away, and the last of the mourners bid farewell to the family, who were left with sorrow and emptiness. John walked outside with Emma.

"It's so bad losing him. I blame myself that maybe I caused it. You know, heart attack, stress—"

"Don't blame yourself. You're a good son." Emma kissed him. "Call me if you need me."

After a sleepless weekend, John bathed, fumbled for his clothes, and barely made it to work. He sat at his desk, overwhelmed by paperwork, and moved piles from one stack to the other. The names on the accounts were blurred. He was unable to enter invoices.

The secretary walked over to John's desk.

"Sorry about your father, John. Why don't you take the afternoon off? I'm sure Mr. Meriwether won't mind."

John rose and left. Hatless, he started for home.

"Dad," he cried aloud. "I'm so sorry. I should have been more attentive to you. It was my fault."

He failed to notice Jesse. "Left work early? Too bad. You may lose your job."

John recognized the voice. "Leave me alone!" he shouted and started to run, but stumbled. An arm kept him from falling.

Jesse said, "You need something to relax. I've got just the thing." He flaunted a pill bottle in front of John. "Two-week supply is four bucks."

John grabbed him by the collar. "You lousy son of a bitch." John released him and swung, hitting the man's jaw. "If you come near me again, I'll kill you."

Jesse scrambled to his feet and warned, "See what happens when you don't get your pills," and left in the direction from where he came.

John leaned over, threw up, wiped his mouth, and walked into the street. Brakes screeched.

"Watch it, buddy! I almost ran you over."

John weaved in the traffic. A car drove around him, the driver blasted the horn.

"Are you crazy? Tryin' to get yourself killed?"

Reaching the opposite side, John stepped on the curb and saw the bus coming. He got on, sitting in a seat close to the driver.

"You okay?" asked the driver.

"Yeah."

"Where're you headed?"

"Market Street."

"It's the third stop."

John counted the stops.

"This is where you get off."

John grabbed the edge of the seat, stood, and staggered to the door.

"Watch your step," said the driver.

Rain splashed around him and soaked his black hair. From the sidewalk, John saw the number on Emma's apartment, first floor. He broke out in a run. Visions drifted before him; voices echoed. Banging on the front door, his last thread of hope started to unravel.

"Emma, Emma," he cried.

Next door, hearing the racket, Addie Sloan, Emma's wiry bird-beaked neighbor, placed her cup on the saucer and adjusted her shawl. Leaning on her cane, she made her way to the window. She pulled the curtain aside and saw a man peering in her neighbor's window, twisting the doorknob. She went to the kitchen, picked up the phone, and dialed the police station.

With the authority of age, she said, "This is Sergeant Sloan's mother. You tell him to come here right away. There's a man trying to break into that nice nurse's apartment."

Sergeant Sloan arrived in the police car and saw John sitting on the front step. He marched toward him.

"Get up! Let's see your ID."

John stood and fumbled with his wallet. He found his military ID card and handed it to the sergeant.

Softened, Sergeant Sloan said, "What are you doing here? You're soaked."

"Looking for Emma."

Emma stepped off the bus and, seeing the police car, ran toward home.

Frightened, she asked, "John, are you all right?" She turned to the police officer. "What's going on?"

"I got a call that he was trying to break in."

"He's my friend. It's okay. Help me get him into the house."

"I can manage." John stepped inside and fell into the nearest chair.

"If there's anything you need, Miss, just call. If you have a piece of paper and pen, I'll write down my number for you."

"Thank you."

Chapter Twenty-Two

John rubbed his arms, looked at Emma through watery eyes and said, "I'm sorry to have barged in on you. I should leave." Attempting to stand, his legs buckled and he fell back into the chair. He crossed and uncrossed his legs and mumbled, "It's the pills."

"I know," Emma said. She placed a glass of water on the table and turned on the lamp. She suggested he take his jacket off and handed him a towel to dry his soaked hair. He stared into the distance.

"You needn't ignore me. You're the one who showed up at my doorstep."

He turned toward her and in a low voice said, "I never should have come."

Emma saw his slumped shoulders and tired face and sensed he was struggling, but it was not the time for sympathy. "Make up your mind."

John stared blankly.

"Well?" she said.

"I should go."

"Where?"

"Who cares?"

Emma lifted her chin. "I do."

His eyes met hers. He removed his jacket and towel dried his hair.

"Want something to eat?"

"Yeah."

She placed a platter of ham and sliced white bread on the kitchen table, along with a jar of dill pickles.

"It's hard coming home," John whispered. "Everything is the same, but I'm not. I'm disconnected. I don't fit in. Harry and I never discussed what went on over there. He has Abby, a job, a life. I have nightmares." He rose and walked into the kitchen, leaned forward on the table, and pushed the platter away. "I am a worthless piece of garbage. Save your energy for someone who's worth it."

"You show up at my doorstep unannounced, barely able to stand, but I refuse to help a self-centered, self-pitying man. You need to learn acceptance for who you are, learn how to endure, and move on." Emma folded her arms. "Now what'll it be, soldier? Accept my help, or—there's the door."

He eyed her, his choices were clear. If anyone could help him, it was Emma. His aggression faded, and in a low voice, he said, "What do I have to do?"

"First, you need to eat. Second, you need to talk to me about what is eating you. It can be a word, a sentence, or a thought. A little at a time. You ought to understand why you became addicted and why you have so much anger."

"The war was bad enough—but there were other things."

"What other things?"

"You'll probably hate me if I tell you."

"You can't keep the past locked inside. You have got to let it out. And no, I won't hate you."

John picked up two slices of bread and piled ham in between as his thoughts raced, filled with inescapable images: Running from the Germans in Salerno with Beau. The dreaded feeling of death closing in. All those bodies sprawled over the roads and fields. So many soldiers too young to die. And Karl Baum, who saved his life.

I betrayed him. And Lily...

He pushed the chair back and stood. "It's too much, I don't know where to start."

"Okay, finish eating. The rain stopped. Let's take a walk."

Outside, the air was damp but smelled fresh. John straightened his drooping shoulders.

"The pills kept the nightmares away, but they're back. How long will it take for the pills to completely wear off?" The doubt in his voice was only partially disguised.

"Depends on the drug. Food will help and taking walks."

"Sounds easy. Think I can do it?"

Emma put her hand on John's shoulder. "Yes. It won't be easy but trust me. I'll do whatever I can for you."

Returning from the walk, Emma placed their dishes in the sink and, keeping her back toward John, said, "You'll need some clothes, shaving stuff, toothbrush, and we'll have to do some food shopping." She ran water over the dishes.

"When do we do this?" he said.

"Probably tomorrow."

"I'm tired, Emma."

She turned around but didn't move. "Yes, you must be. So am I."

They stared at each other.

John reached behind her, turned off the faucet, and stood close to her, inhaling her scent. She placed her hand on his chest and stopped him.

"I'll get you some blankets. You can take the couch."

"Good night, John," and she entered the bedroom.

It was dark when Emma heard the crash. She pulled the chain on the lamp and noted the time—two o'clock. She put on her robe, opened the bedroom door, and saw John throwing the quilt and pillows around the room "Get away! Leave me alone!" he shouted. He licked his dry lips. The expression on his face was bleak.

Emma stood in front of him and said in a clear voice, "Stop! John, it's me, Emma."

Drenched with sweat, John covered his mouth and gagged.

Emma grabbed his arm and pulled him to the bathroom. She stepped outside, closed the door, and leaned against it. Hearing the toilet flush, she opened the door a crack. John was rolled up into a ball on the floor.

She bent down and shook his shoulder. "John, are you all right?"

He pushed himself up with both hands and stared at her. "Where am I?"

"You're in my apartment, on the bathroom floor."

"How did I get here?"

"You barged in on me, remember?"

"Oh yeah." He rose unsteadily.

Emma handed him a wet facecloth. "Here, wipe your face."

He followed her into the living room, and they sat on the couch.

"What happened to the lamp?"

"You knocked it over."

"I think I should go."

"It's the middle of the night. No buses are running. Wait until the sun comes up. I'll make scrambled eggs."

He grew silent beside her. Barely acknowledging her presence, John whispered, "Karl and his family saved my life."

Emma waited longer, but none came. John's head fell back against the back of the couch and he slept.

Emma knew Dr. Burns from the clinic and dialed his number. It was five in the morning, but she knew he was a close friend of the Conways and wouldn't mind. After four rings, he answered.

"Dr. Burns, this is Emma from the clinic." She explained what was happening.

"You've taken on a great deal of responsibility, Emma," cautioned Dr. Burns. "But I'm sure you already know that. Your work at the clinic should help. I warn you, if he wants to leave, don't get between him and the door. Just let him go. I gave him the minimum dose to control his leg pain. I suspect he may have found another source when I refused to renew his prescription. There are pill pushers everywhere. I don't know how they get drugs, but they do. John's hiding something he can't face. Must be the war. God only knows what he saw over there. I'll drop by if you wish."

"Not just yet. There is one thing. Can you call John's family and tell them where he is? They must be worried. Ask them to call John's boss. And please explain to Anne that I will need some time off. You can tell her what is going on."

"She'll understand. We're all part of the effort to help these guys. I'll stop by the Conways' before office hours. Be careful."

"Thank you."

Emma went to her bedroom, lay down, and stared at the ceiling until dawn. Had she risked her own safety? What if he leaves in the middle of the night? What if...

She sat upright. She had promised to do whatever she could. I'll bring him to the clinic first thing in the morning. And yet, he's already been off the pills for a day or so. She got up, dressed, and walked into the living room where John was awake and glancing around the room.

"Good morning," she said.

He rose to full height and stretched his arms. "Good morning. I should go."

"I don't think you're ready to go. Especially after last night."

He frowned. "Last night?"

"Yes. Remember, the lamp?"

"It's the pills, isn't it?"

"Yes. Your system is learning to get by without them. We agreed it would be difficult, but together we can get you clean." Emma swallowed hard. "If you leave, you cannot come back."

He seemed about to speak but chose not to.

John watched Emma turn on the burner under the coffee pot, take a carton of eggs from the refrigerator, and beat four of them. She put bread in the toaster and slid the handle down. It was as if he was seeing her for the first time. The knots inside him started to loosen.

"You can set the table. The dishes are up there," she said, pointing to a cupboard. She placed eggs and buttered toast on a plate and poured coffee. John cleaned his plate and helped himself to more coffee.

"Sorry about the lamp."

"It was an accident." She reached for a piece of toast and he covered her hand with his.

She withdrew. "John," she said softly. "Not yet."

"When?"

"When you are clean. Are you up for shopping?"

He looked at the clothes he was wearing. "I guess I should be."

Three hours later they returned, carrying bags of groceries and replenishments for John. For supper, Emma cooked chicken, potatoes, and string beans. John had two helpings.

They ate in silence. John cleared the dishes and saw his reflection in the window. His hair was greasy and he had a three-day growth of whiskers. Dropping the dishes in the sink, he entered the bathroom. Emma heard water running in the tub. An hour later, John emerged clean shaven, his shampooed hair neatly combed.

Emma looked up from her book.

"How do I look?"

"Well. I, I…" Her eyes met his. He reached out his hand and helped her stand. The book slid to the floor.

"Emma," John whispered. He bent down and kissed her. She kissed him back.

Abruptly, she stopped and stood back. "John, no. Not yet. You have work to do, and I'm going to see that you get off the pills completely. This will get in the way."

"But—"

"Let's wait, please."

"Then what? Are you going to hang around until I'm clean?"

"Yes, I'll be here. Your appetite is back. That's always a good sign. Tonight, I'll take the couch. You can sleep in the bedroom. That way, I'll hear you if you decide to walk around in the middle of the night."

"Tomorrow will be my third day off the pills."

"I better be sure to have enough food," Emma said.

The next day, John complained of not being able to breathe and wanted to see a doctor. Emma told him to take deep breaths.

Over the next week, Emma encouraged John to read. "It might help you focus," she said. "There are books, and I have back issues of Look and The Saturday Evening Post."

John browsed the Post and read a few articles. His eyes were brighter and the tremors ceased, but his thoughts fluttered like trapped birds. One morning, he sat on the edge of the bed and rubbed his thighs. The thoughts of Beau saddened him, thoughts of Karl filled him with guilt, and would Lily forgive his bad behavior?

He witnessed things in the war that he wanted to forget but couldn't. Suppressing his thoughts was no longer an option. He stood up, pulled on his trousers, and opened the bedroom door. *I must tell her.*

Emma turned toward him, smiled, and said, "Good morning."

How he draped his jacket over a chair, how he cut his food, how he crossed his legs when he finished eating, and how he looked at her when he thought she wasn't looking—had taken on an intimacy for Emma.

"Yeah, I guess it's good." Rubbing the back of his neck, he said, "I ... that is ... mind if I sit?"

"Of course not."

Balling his fist, he said, "What's for breakfast?"

"How about pancakes with sliced orange?"

"Sounds good."

Emma flipped pancakes and set a platter on the table along with sliced oranges.

"It looks good."

"Set the table. Syrup is in the refrigerator. *Lassie Come Home* is playing. Are you up for it?"

"Yes."

John thought he should tell her over breakfast, but the suggestion afforded him temporary relief. He would hold his story for now.

The theater was three blocks away. They wound their way into the dark theater and fumbled around for seats.

"Lassie found her way home, John."

"Quite a dog."

On the way back to the apartment, they stopped at White Tower for hamburgers.

"Would you call this our first real date?" asked John.

Emma smiled, "Yes, I would."

Two days later, as the setting sun disappeared behind a building across the street, John rearranged books and peered out the window. Pulling the curtains aside, he asked, "I think I'm done with this. Look." He raised his hands in front of him. "No more shakes. And I'm sleeping fine."

Emma put her book down and said, "The worst is over, but you will need more help."

"What kind of help?" he asked, narrowing his eyes.

"Therapy."

"You mean sitting around in a circle telling everyone I was a jerk and now I'm fine?"

"Just wait and see."

John shot her a suspicious look.

When supper was over, John said gruffly, "I'll do the dishes. Supper was good."

"Let's take a walk later," Emma suggested.

John cleared the table, washed the dishes, and listened to the radio.

Without warning, he said, "Emma, I'm going home."

She whirled around. "What? What did you say?"

"I need to sort things out."

"Before you go—if that's what you really want—tell me more about Karl, who saved your life."

John closed his eyes, time slowed.

"Did you hear what I said?"

"I can't talk about it because people will see me for who I really am."

"You have to trust someone some time."

Chapter Twenty-Three

Outside, rain began to fall, dampening John's mood. Emma pulled a chain on the floor lamp; light flooded the room. She considered coaxing him to talk and decided against it. It was his story to tell. The stillness was broken by John's voice.

"In June 1942, I graduated from high school just in time for the draft. I fit the bill. Nineteen, single, and physically fit. Look at me now after serving, skin and bones and totally messed up."

"The war changed people," said Emma.

"It was a terrifying ordeal to step out of the confines of my life. My brother enlisted in the Navy in 1941 and never returned. Fear became a shadow in my life." Leaning in toward Emma he said, "You gotta understand that."

Emma maintained her gaze on John. Familiar with the tales of war, she hoped this would aid in his recovery.

Rubbing his hands on his thighs, he continued. "Most of the guys I was with didn't make it. The few kept getting fewer. We were taught to act, not think."

"They made great sacrifices," Emma said.

Retelling how he'd witnessed Beau's death enabled John to reveal the trauma which accompanied this shocking event.

"I held him in my arms wishing I could breathe life into him. It was the least I could do." Tears welled in his eyes. John felt detached from the world, as if he were watching life and not living in it.

"I am so sorry. How terrible for you to lose a friend like that..."

"I took a lot of pills to forget, but I have to live with it."

"Beau was your friend, and he died a hero."

"What does that make me?"

"Some heroes live. Some heroes die."

"I lay there, waiting to die. I thought I should shoot myself, but I couldn't do it."

John stood, paced, and in a loud voice said, "I heard voices. Germans. I thought they were going to shoot me. I raised myself to a sitting position against a tree, but I was too weak to pick up the rifle to defend myself. They spoke English. It was Karl and his father. They lifted me up and brought me to their house. They saved my life."

Emma's eyebrows lifted in surprise. Her heartbeat quickened. "I heard you speak Karl's name in the hospital. Is he the one?"

"Yes."

Emma shifted her position. "And he was German."

"Yes. His family cleaned my wound, fed me, gave me clean clothes and a warm bed."

"They sound like good people, but when you called out his name, you seemed frightened. Did something happen to Karl?"

Breathing became difficult; John was unable to continue. His choices haunted him. Would Emma understand his panic for abandoning Karl, or would she see him as selfish? He stared at Emma with brooding eyes.

A sudden chill enveloped Emma. She wrapped a shawl around her shoulders and said, "There's more, isn't there?"

"Yes, but I cannot go on. Good night, Emma."

Chapter Twenty-Four

S tan had the day off and Eric was in charge of breakfast and lunch. Karl offered his assistance, and along with the other kitchen staff they fed the POWs. When the cleanup was complete, Eric folded the towels, removed his apron, and said, "Stan's invited me to his house for supper."

"What?"

"You heard me." Eric ran a hand through his blond hair. Karl chuckled. "What? You think it's funny?"

"No, it's just that..."

"Yeah, I'm a prisoner."

Karl leaned against the sink. "Have you accepted?"

"I have. It's tonight. So, you are in charge here."

"Me!"

"We made soup, and sandwiches are in the refrigerator. You can handle it. There's plenty of help," Eric said as he tossed his apron to Karl and cleared out.

Eric took a shower and changed into clean clothes, but the initials POW on his shirt pocket were a reminder of what he was.

Stan arrived at the gate, cut the motor to his Chevrolet, and stepped out. Eric fidgeted with the buttons on his jacket. "This is a mistake, Stan. I don't think I—"

"Nonsense! Joan and the kids are looking forward to meeting you."

"Does your family ... that is, do they—"

"They know you are German and a prisoner of war. They know you work for me, you learned to cook, and you get along with the rest of the crew. They're excited about meeting you. They're just regular kids. My wife is very interested in talking to you about your family and your experience at the camp."

"But my English…"

"Your English is better than you think. Relax and be yourself."

Wounded by his parents' rejection, Eric was left with a fragile sense of self-worth. It fueled his apprehension about meeting Stan's family.

"Tell me about your family," asked Eric.

"Joan and I have two boys and two girls."

Eric bit his lip.

Stan pulled up in front of the house with a white fence around the yard. The porch light was lit. "This is it."

It was freezing, but Eric felt sweat trickle down his neck.

The front door opened, and Stan's oldest daughter, eighteen-year-old Martha, greeted them and kissed her father's cheek.

"Hello, sweetheart. This is Eric Hoffman. Eric, this is Martha," said Stan.

"Hi," she said.

Eric shifted his stance. "Hi," he replied.

She wore a long-sleeved green sweater with a collar and a knee-length plaid skirt. A barrette held back her long auburn hair, which she parted on the right.

"Let me take your things," said Stan.

There were unfamiliar sounds and smells, but the house felt warm and comfortable. Eric cast an eye over the parlor. Family pictures hung on wallpapered walls, a multi-colored afghan was draped over the back of a brown sofa, and a textured rug partially covered the wooden floor.

Stan called to his wife, "Joan, come meet our guest."

Wiping her hands on an apron, Joan said, "Welcome. You must be Eric."

"Yes, ma'am."

"We're delighted to have you. Have a seat. Supper is just about ready."

Martha introduced Eric to her eight-year-old sister, Sara, and her brothers, Tim, thirteen, and Jeff, fifteen.

"Are you a real prisoner?" asked Sara.

Mortified, Martha started to say something, but Stan shook his head.

"Yes, I am," said Eric. "At least for now."

"Did you fight in the war?" asked Tim.

"Of course he did. Why do think he's a prisoner?" said Jeff.

Eric gazed at Martha, whose radiant smile attracted him. Their eyes met and his smile widened. Noticing, Stan suggested they take their seats at the table. Martha sat across from Eric.

The family bowed their heads. Eric wasn't sure why until Joan said something about thanks. Eric forced a smile and muttered thanks. Bowls of mashed potatoes, carrots, string beans, and a platter of chicken were passed around. Eric watched the others to avoid a mishap.

"Is your family still in Germany?" asked Joan.

Eric wiped his mouth and hesitated.

Joan chewed her food, waiting for an answer.

"Well," Eric began. "My father was a Nazi sympathizer. My mother was not. This caused friction between them, and I was caught in the middle."

"That must have been hard for you," said Joan.

"Are they still in Germany?" asked Martha.

"Not anymore. My father left to join the Army, and my mother moved to Switzerland, and I was not invited."

Martha stared at Eric, then looked away. Sadness prevented her from speaking.

"I'm sorry for you. War makes people do strange things. Then what did you do?" asked Joan.

"I joined the Army. They would have drafted me anyway."

"How did you end up here?"

"I was captured by the British in Italy and shipped over here."

"How did you get captured?" asked Jeff.

"It was nighttime. Four of us were in an abandoned house looking for food when we heard the command to drop our weapons..." Eric trailed off, remembering.

"Then what?" asked Tim.

"Were you scared?" asked Sara.

"I think that's enough war talk," said Stan. "Eric is a good cook."

"When Dad cooks for us, you might think he's serving the neighborhood," said Tim.

"Yes, and he gets mad if we don't clean our plates," said Sara.

Stan took the teasing well.

The conversation was lost on Eric, whose eyes had captured Martha's. Stan noticed her reddened cheeks, and the look on Eric's face had a familiarity to it.

"I think I better get Eric back to camp."

"He hasn't had apple pie yet," said Joan.

"Oh yes, apple pie."

"See those books on the coffee table, Eric?" asked Sara.

Eric looked over Sara's shoulder into the living room. "Yes."

"Those are Martha's. She's the reader. Mom says if she had enough money she would build a library just for Martha."

Jeff went to help his mother with the pie. Tim and Sara cleared the table.

"I'm sorry to hear about your family. Do you wonder what happened to them?"

"I used to, and it was hard at first but not anymore. My plan is to stay here after the war is over," said Eric.

"Maybe you can come again to supper," said Martha.

Beaming, he said, "I'd like to." And added, "very much."

They walked into the next room. Stan kept a watchful eye on them but remained at the table, waiting for pie.

Martha handed Eric *Life* and *Time*. "These are good magazines, and I think you'll enjoy reading them. I'll ask Daddy to bring them to you when we're done with them."

The pie was ready. Eric had two slices.

"I better get you back to camp," said Stan.

"Would it be okay if I wrote to you?" Eric asked Martha.

"I'd like that. You can give the letters to Daddy."

Stan dropped his coat and retrieved it as the family came into the living room to say goodbye.

During the drive back to camp, Stan was quiet. Eric chatted about supper, Stan's family, and Martha. Back at camp, Eric thanked Stan for the invitation and stepped out of the car. Stan drove away wondering what just happened.

Eric burst into Barracks Ten. "Karl, I'm in love."

"With who?"

"Stan's beautiful daughter."

"That was fast."

"We're going to write."

"And this is okay with Stan?" asked Karl.

Eric shrugged.

Chapter Twenty-Five

The ground underneath Karl's boots crunched as he plodded his way to the mess hall. He paused, thinking he heard his name being called. Looking around, he saw Ben waving and rushed through the crowd toward him.

"Ben!" he yelled. Ben was a little thinner but otherwise unchanged. Karl ran and grabbed Ben around the waist, raising him off his feet.

"Finally, you're back." Karl released him. "Let me look at you." A jubilant smile crossed Ben's face.

"How was it? Are you okay? That was quite a fall you took. How was the hospital?"

"It was a bare-bones place. The food was lousy, but the doctors were pretty good, and the American nurses are the best—and they're gorgeous. I still get headaches, but they told me they would go away eventually."

"This calls for a celebration."

"Like what, some good German beer?"

"Maybe. Eric can't wait to see you. We'll go to the mess hall. He's preparing supper."

Karl felt the sleeve of Ben's jacket. "That's a flimsy jacket they sent you home with."

Karl removed his jacket. "Here, wear mine until we get you something."

"But—"

"Just put it on. I've got a warm shirt," said Karl as he helped Ben thread his arm through the sleeve. "They say the war is going bad for Germany."

Ben buttoned the jacket. "My mother and my sister—"

"I know. My family, too. I try not to think about it, but sometimes you just can't help it. There is nothing we can do. Let's go see Stan and Eric. By the way, Eric went to Stan's house for supper and met his family."

"He did! How was it?"

"He'll tell you. Especially about Stan's beautiful daughter."

Once inside the mess hall, the comforting aromatic smells of fresh-baked rolls and beef stew stirred their appetites.

Eric, feeding a long line of hungry prisoners, was paying little attention to anything other than piling food on plates. His concentration was interrupted by a shout. "Hey, Eric, look who's here!"

Eric looked up to see Ben. "Hi buddy, I'm back, and I'm hungry enough to eat your cooking."

"Ben! You're okay?"

"I am."

"Good. Glad you're back. Tonight is beef stew, one of your favorites." Eric narrowed his gaze. "Karl told you about what's going on with the war?"

Ben wrapped his arms around his chest. "Yeah."

"Hard to imagine what our people are going through. Stan says when the war ends, we will be sent home. When it does, you and Karl can be on the first ship out of here. You have families waiting for you. Stan's off today, it's his wife's birthday. He left a surprise for us."

"Mutter's birthday is next week," said Ben.

Brushing off the sentiment, Eric replied, "Come to the kitchen after supper."

Later, after most of the prisoners went back to the barracks, Karl and Ben entered the kitchen to see Eric's surprise. A dozen bottles of Schlitz were on the counter.

"It's an American lager—and close to a German beer," said Eric. "Let's sample one."

Eric flipped off the caps and handed a bottle to each of his friends. The first beer went down smoothly. Eric wiped his mouth, hesitated, and said, "He's Jewish."

"Who is?" asked Karl.

"My mother's boyfriend. She knew if they stayed in Germany they would be arrested, and so would I. They went to Switzerland. At least that's where they intended to go. I was not invited. They said it was too dangerous for me to go with them," said Eric.

"How come you're telling us this now?" asked Karl.

"Too embarrassed that she chose him over her own son. Papa left me and then Mutter left, too."

"They had their reasons. We heard rumors about the Jews," said Karl.

"Doesn't matter. I'm not going back. Ever," said Eric.

Ben got up and returned, carrying three more beers. "Let's sit." Ben pulled three chairs to the table.

Eric drained the second bottle. "By the way, I met Stan's daughter, Martha. She's beautiful and we're going to write."

"I heard. How did that happen?" asked Ben.

"Stan invited me for supper with his family."

"He did?"

"Yes, I met his whole family." Eric's eyes drifted around the room.

Karl took a swig of beer and said, "War was all my little brother, Hans, knew. One day, Papa and I had gone into the woods for rabbits and Hans stayed back with Mutti. A Nazi soldier showed up—mean and vicious. He hit Hans and tried to attack Mutti. Hans stabbed him with a kitchen knife and killed him. Brave, but how sad he had to kill someone to protect his mutti. He was only thirteen years old."

"Papa disappeared," Ben began. "One day, he went to school and never came home. Mutti cried for days. He wanted to teach academics, but Hitler demanded they teach how to be physically strong. We never heard from him again. Weeks later, soldiers came by and took me for the Army while my mother and sister watched me go. I hope they are still alive."

Ben's expression turned thoughtful, and he sighed deeply.

Feeling lightheaded, Karl offered a toast. "Prost! To our homeland and our families."

"I'll get the next round," said Karl. He returned with refills, and they took long swigs.

"We're friends, right?" Eric said.

"The best," said Karl, raising his bottle.

Ben started laughing. "Best buddies. How does that sound?"

The spontaneous laughter that followed was interrupted when the door to the mess hall flew open. Laughter was suspended and replaced with puzzled looks.

Corporal Chase stomped in and bellowed, "Get rid of the bottles and get your stupid asses out of here! Now! Return to your barracks, all of you. Now!"

Ben gathered up the bottles and tossed them in the trash. They staggered back to the barracks, fearful of being called to Sergeant Jackson's office in the morning.

No such order came through. Karl attributed it to Corporal Chase's understanding of the POWs' situation.

Chapter Twenty-Six

Karl had grown accustomed to the routine at Camp Grant and the company of his two friends. An announcement over the mess hall speaker interrupted their supper.

"Attention!" Sergeant Jackson's voice was loud and clear.

Karl leaned over to Ben. "What now?"

Chewing his food, Ben shrugged his shoulders.

"A major snowstorm is being forecast for March. Up to two feet. The town is asking for men to help with snow removal in farms, cities, and surrounding areas. The list is posted. Prisoners from other camps have been recruited." Jackson's voice hardened. "There will be no barbed wire, no guards, no restriction of movement, and no roll call. I remind you that you are prisoners of the United States and any attempt at escape will be treated with harsh punishment. The van arrives at ten o'clock. Winter clothes will be provided. Take your gear—you may be gone for a while. You will be courteous, respectful, and do your jobs properly, and remember your status. Dismissed."

Ben poked Karl. "Bet that means you. You don't have a job here at camp."

Karl sprinted across the room and scanned the list: Karl Baum—SPRING HILL FARM.

He rushed back to his seat. "Ben, I've been assigned to a farm. I don't want to go. Suppose they hate Germans?"

"They asked for help."

"But I just got here. I'm used to it, and I've got you and Eric."

"You have a chance to see how American farms are run. Think of it that way."

"Suppose I can't do what they want?"

"You can shovel snow, can't you?"

151

"But this storm is big."

"After what you've been through getting here, you can handle this. Other Germans will be there."

"I guess there's no getting out of it."

"Afraid not. You can tell me all about it when you come back."

Karl drank the last bit of coffee and wiped his mouth as he brooded over this new direction in his life. Leaving the mess hall, dread spread over him like a tidal wave.

In the morning, Karl stirred, and with half-opened eyes he climbed from his bunk and looked out of the window. Dawn had pushed darkness away. He watched as snow fell soundlessly, leaving a thick layer of white on rooftops.

Feeling a surge of love and longing for his family, he hoped they would not lose faith for his return. With a wistful smile he remembered them.

"Ben, wake up. Here it comes."

Grumbling, Ben dressed and followed Karl outside to formation. At breakfast, Ben said, "How long do you think you'll be there?"

Karl looked away and pushed his plate to one side. "They didn't say. I've just gotten used to the routine here. I know what to expect, what the rules are—and then they put my name on that list."

"What's the worst thing that can happen to you?"

Through pursed lips, Karl said, "That I won't come back."

Ben dropped his fork and ran his hand over his mouth. "Don't think that way. You'll be back. All your information is here. They keep track of us. Remember all the forms?" There was a pause. "Look, you're only there to help with snow plowing. After that you'll be back."

"But I don't have a choice, do I?"

"Afraid not. So, let's go back to the barracks. You need to pack."

Karl filled his duffel bag, put on the parka he was given, and pulled on his boots.

Ben embraced Karl, who said, "As the Americans say, see ya."

Ben grinned.

Karl stepped outside and boarded the van that was not much warmer than the outside temperature. For the first time, he would be outside

Camp Grant, mingling with Americans. How would he be received? Karl was the only POW from Camp Grant assigned to Spring Hill Farm.

An hour later, the driver's voice cut through the silence. "Spring Hill Farm coming up."

"Spring" was the only part of the sign that was visible. The driver made a sharp turn into the driveway and skidded to a stop in front of a large two-story house with lights on in every window. Wide front steps led to a wraparound porch. Drifts of snow huddled against the railing.

Consulting a clipboard, the driver yelled over his shoulder, "Karl Baum, this is where you get off."

Gathering his gear, Karl walked off the van and paused. White smoke puffed its way out of the farmhouse chimney. Wind blew wet flakes across his face.

The front door opened. A stream of light crossed the snow-covered foot path that had been tramped down by boot imprints. A tall man with thick dark hair wearing a sweatshirt and dungarees stared out at Karl.

"Come in, come in, you must be Karl Baum. I'm Joe Perkins, manager of the farm. Been waiting for you," he said, thrusting out a hand.

Speechless, Karl shook the hand offered. He stepped inside the large foyer and removed his cap, leaving a puddle from his wet boots on the frayed carpet.

Joe noticed and laughed. "It's only water, it'll dry."

A short, dark-skinned woman entered the foyer.

"This is Juanita. She and her husband, Diego, run the house. Juanita, this is Karl Baum, one of our new workers."

"Hola."

Fascinated by Juanita's dark skin, dark hair, and dark eyes, Karl stared. In a brisk manner, she took Karl's things and glowered at the initials on his shirt.

"Don't worry about that. There are others from different camps wearing the same shirt. You're the last German to arrive. Just in time. We need help with this storm and are glad you are here. Just obey the rules. I know you were warned about escaping. I don't think you would get very far in this weather. We offer all the comforts of home. There's coffee and sandwiches in the kitchen. Let's join the others."

According to the clock on the wall, it was eleven. Karl considered this and wondered what he would do after lunch. He followed Joe around like a stray cat. Floors creaked under their footsteps. Faced with the daunting task of living and working with Americans, Karl entered the parlor. A massive brick fireplace with a roaring fire radiated warmth. On one wall, a bookcase was neatly stocked with paperbacks and family pictures. Men sat in overstuffed chairs and on sofas, making conversation. Plates, matching cups and saucers, and stemmed glassware dominated shelves in a mahogany China cabinet.

Joe asked for attention. "This is Karl Baum, just arrived from Camp Grant."

Some cast furtive glances at Karl, others smiled and waved. Karl wanted to run, but where would he go? Any attempt at escape will be treated with harsh punishment.

Joe leaned toward Karl. "You'll be getting Mexican food at supper. Juanita's an excellent cook."

"Juanita is Mexican?" Karl asked.

"Yes, but a full-fledged American citizen. So is her husband, Diego. Their three kids were born here."

"I've never met a Mexican before."

"They are like family to us."

A dark-skinned man approached them. "Welcome, I am Diego. We were waiting for you to come." Diego's smile showed white teeth below a thick black mustache. "The storm, she is going to be big."

Karl took an instant liking to Diego and thrust out his hand. Diego shook it vigorously.

"Diego assists me with chores," Joe said. "I'll have you shoveling when the snow stops, which is likely to happen tomorrow. After that, we'll see what else you can help us with."

The dining room table was set with utensils and napkins. On the sideboard were sandwiches, pastries, cookies, apple cider, and hot coffee. Karl stood behind a short man, who turned and said, "You won't want to go back to camp after eating Juanita's food and working for Joe. Name's Lukas. Got captured in North Africa."

"Karl. Are you from a camp?"

"Yes. Camp Echo, twenty miles south. Been here three days. Came last fall to help with harvesting and am back for snow shoveling. There are ten of us Germans here. What part of Germany are you from?"

"Weiss, southwest." Karl took two sandwiches and moved to the cookies.

"Worry about your family?"

"All the time."

"Me too. I'm from Frankfurt. When the war is over, I'll go back. When I was captured, I was starving, thought I was going to die. Look at me now." Lukas patted his gut.

"Your English is good."

"I learned it in school in Germany, and being here you speak it every day. After a while it gets easy." Lukas poured a glass of apple cider.

"They don't mind us being here?"

"Some do, but they know they need help. The Americans are over there fighting and bombing our cities, and we're helping Americans over here. Strange, isn't it?" Lukas pointed to two chairs. Once seated, he continued. "Last fall a couple of us went to work in a cannery. Tomatoes were rotting. They had no one to can them. It was scary being around the Americans, but once word got around that we were good workers, it was fine. Big food shortages here, no workers to plant and pick, so the Americans appreciate what we are doing. And now with the storm—I'm back to help again."

"Hey, Karl. I see ya got some food. Good. Juanita keeps the kitchen well stocked. You can come in here anytime to grab a bite. Just put your dishes in the sink and put your stuff away. Otherwise, Juanita gets cross, and we don't want that," Joe said.

Karl lowered his shoulders, and a hint of a smile crossed his face.

Once the crowd was seated, Joe stood and said, "Listen up! Our last recruit arrived today, Karl Baum."

Lukas poked him and whispered, "Raise your hand."

Karl did as he was told and noticed the Germans sat together, as did the Americans.

"I've set up teams to work together. First thing tomorrow morning, even if it's still snowing, we need to get to the barn to feed the animals.

You will be expected to work together regardless of your situation. We have a job to do."

A man from the back of the room shouted out, "I'll do whatever it takes, but I ain't workin' with no krauts."

Karl closed his fist.

Joe pointed at the man and said, "If you fail to do as you are told, Tony, you will answer to me." Men adjusted their positions.

Tony lingered before continuing to speak. "Just give me an American to work with, and there'll be no trouble. That's all I'm asking."

Joe continued with the instructions. "We need access to the barns first to feed the cows, and then access to the roads. I will be here at seven tomorrow morning. Diego will start removing snow from around the houses. Once done, the rest of the farm will need to be plowed. We have the manpower—we can do it if we cooperate. Juanita will have sandwiches, donuts, coffee, and cider anytime you need something to eat. See you back here for supper at six."

Karl clutched the edge of his chair. Another adjustment. Another challenge. Another struggle.

"Karl," Joe called out. "Find Diego. He'll show you where you'll sleep."

Karl roamed around looking for Diego and saw a young woman sitting at the kitchen table. She was eating a sandwich with one hand and holding a sleeping baby in her other arm. Strands of blond hair escaped a hair tie and fell around her face.

What is she doing here? Who does she belong to?

She smiled at Karl. "You must be new."

Diego walked in. "Karl, Joe said you were looking for me." Seeing the perplexed look on Karl's face, he said, "Lily, this is Karl, our newest arrival. This is Lily, the owner's wife."

"Nice to meet you."

"Welcome to Spring Hill," she said, turning her attention to her sandwich.

"I'll take you to where you will be sleeping," Diego said.

Karl remained silent and followed Diego outside. They trudged through the storm, staying close to each other. The wind howled.

"Just over there is a two-story building," Diego pointed. "Where you will live. It is warm inside."

Karl pulled his cap low over his head and bent down into the wind. Arriving at the two-story building, Diego pushed the front door open and warm air blew across their faces.

"Feels good, yes? You can leave your boots in the entry. Follow me. Here is living room."

Shades and blue drapes covered the windows. Two bookcases stood like sentries against a wall. A radio sat silent on a table. Chairs and a sofa surrounded an unlit fireplace.

"You can eat in the kitchen for breakfast or lunch, but supper is at the main house. While we plow, Juanita will have stuff for us in the main house, which you can get anytime. I keep food stocked here." Diego flashed his smile and climbed upstairs. Karl followed.

"Here is your bedroom. Three beds and two bureaus. That one is yours," Diego said, pointing to the bed in the middle. "Bureaus are shared."

Off the hall was a bathroom with a sink, toilet, tub, and mirror. "Plenty of hot water. Supper is at six. You can find your way back to the big house, yes?"

"Yes."

"Adios."

Unpacking his duffel bag, Karl heard a toilet flush. He hesitated and stepped outside his room. One of the bedroom doors was ajar.

"Anyone here?" he shouted.

"Yeah, me. Just had a nap." A burly man in his early twenties with a boyish face stood in the doorway of a bedroom down the hall.

"Hey, you must be the new guy. I'm Ray Carson." Ray reached out his calloused hand minus three fingers, shook Karl's, and pointed to the empty places on his hand. "Lost them in North Africa. Germans. No offense. I'm no good for the Army anymore, so they sent me home. Been workin' for Joe for a year. The pay's good, the food's good. You German?"

"Yes."

"Got no cause against you. The Nazis is what did your people in. Now we're workin' together. Didn't catch your name."

"Karl Baum."

"Good German name, I like it. I'll leave you to get unpacked. Later, we'll walk over to the big house for supper."

Karl slid open a bureau drawer and stuffed his clothes into it. He slid his duffel bag under the bed, stood, and inspected his new surroundings. On the bureau was a picture of a woman holding a toddler. The inscription at the bottom read, *An Friedrich von Mutter*. At least one roommate was German.

Sitting on the edge of the bed, thoughts of Germany, the place his soul called home, and his deep ache for his family grabbed his heart. He wondered how he would fit into this place.

There was a rap on the door. "How're you doin'?" asked Ray, stepping into the room. "You look puzzled."

Karl turned his head away from Ray and wiped his eyes. "Tough being away from home. My family needed me." Karl shook his head, cramming his feelings into a deep hole, and in a voice tinged with sadness, said, "I left home to help someone and never got back."

Ray sat on the edge of a bed and said, "Want to tell me about it?"

"Some other time."

"Suit yourself."

"Where are you from?"

"California, a little town called Sausalito. I might go back when the war is over. Roosevelt will win the war and all this mess will be over. Let's go to supper."

Putting on their boots and jackets, Karl asked Ray about the woman he saw earlier.

"Oh yeah, Lily, a fine lady. Keeps to herself and sticks close to Juanita. Not much to do here for her, but Tom, the owner, is crazy about her. A year ago last September, he went to a town just north of here to visit a friend and came back with Lily as his wife. Years ago, Tom had a wife. Died in childbirth, along with the baby. He was a mess for a long time, but Joe, Diego, and Juanita helped him get through it. Don't think Tom's the father of this one, though. Count the months—The baby was born six months after Tom and Lily married. But it don't matter. Lily's got a husband, the baby has a daddy, and Tom has a family. You can't miss Tom. He's six feet, has more hair than me, and always has a smile."

The muscles in Karl's face tightened. *Lily.*

"Tough story. We all got one, but they're fine together."

"What about your story, Ray? Do you have a family?"

"I'm single, twenty-two, and went to college for a year before being drafted. Anything else?"

The subject was dropped like the lowering of a curtain. They crossed the yard to the house, where lights in every window lit up the snow-covered path.

Chapter Twenty-Seven

Wading through knee-deep snow, Karl followed Ray to the farm-house. They stood on the porch and stomped their boots. Karl shrank from the loud voices coming from inside. Ray took a final drag on his cigarette, blew smoke into the air, and flipped the butt into the snow.

He leaned toward Karl and said, "Just be yourself, it always works."

Ray opened the door and shouted hello to the crowd. He tossed his jacket and cap onto a pile of wet clothes. Karl did the same. He saw a few familiar faces from his earlier introduction, but he was tired—tired of adjusting to new people, new places, and new customs. It was work just to breathe.

Lukas approached Karl and asked in German, "Did you get settled?"

"Ja, danke."

"Hard, isn't it?"

Karl lifted his chin. "It's okay."

"I was seventeen when I entered the war a year ago. Barely made it. Dodging bullets, watching guys get blown to bits. And all the time freezing. I went from being a kid to a man overnight—and then I got captured by the Americans."

Karl remembered German people getting arrested for speaking about the war and questioning why. Not used to this frankness, he remained silent.

"How old are you?" asked Lukas.

"Eighteen."

Diego handed them glasses of apple cider. "Welcome."

Sipping the cider, Karl took a tentative look around the room. Joe's face was florid as he listened to a man who said loud and clear, "Maybe you needed to hire krauts 'til our guys came home from the war, but I told you that I work with Americans only." Tony had a muscular body and a deep baritone voice.

Joe raised the palm of his hand. "And I am trying to accommodate you, but we have a job to do, and the Germans are here to help us."

Juanita's voice was heard signaling that supper was ready.

At Karl's elbow, Lukas said, "Don't worry about Tony. He's all talk. You won't be eating bratwurst and German dark bread here. Instead, it's tortillas and tamales."

"What are they?"

"Mexican, and it's the best."

A pile of stuffed tortillas and Mexican cookies covered a long table that was pushed against a wall. Karl filled his plate and joined Lucas.

"Where did you get captured?" asked Lukas.

"Italy." Not wanting to reveal that he hadn't served in the German Army, Karl asked Lukas about his family.

"Two sisters, two brothers—one brother was killed in the war. The other one is still in it, somewhere." Lukas rubbed the back of his neck and said quietly, "My folks don't know where I am. I write letters every week, but I have no idea if they got them."

"Maybe some got through. Sorry about your brother. Must be hard."

"Hard on all of us, but mostly my parents." Lukas motioned for Karl to follow him to a place at the dining room table. "I got captured in Tunisia, North Africa. Where in Italy were you captured?"

"Close to the Swiss border."

"Were you trying to escape?"

With a mouth full of food, Karl shook his head. He gulped down the glass of cider.

Grinning, Lukas said, "I should have warned you. Some Mexican food is spicy hot."

Joe stood and signaled for silence. "Everyone! Welcome! I guess we're all set for snow removal tomorrow. I've posted duties on the counter in the kitchen. It's shaping up as a snowy spring. We have a front loader and tractors with attached blades that we'll use around the barns. You're to dump the snow in the far end of the fields and push it as far back as possible to allow for access. Some will be shoveling around the house.

Again, my thanks to all of you. Enjoy supper. Anyone have any questions, I'll be around."

"Mind if I join you?" Ray asked as he sat down next to Lukas.

"You just did," laughed Lukas.

Karl remembered when his world was destroyed, robbing men of life and women of their hopes. Food and warmth in the room conflicted with his recollection of the ache of hunger and the desperate faces of the displaced. People were interested in his war experience, but his fight was against tyranny. At that moment, his reluctance to share his war status faded and he said, "I didn't fight in the war."

A scowl crowded Lukas's face.

Ray's eyes widened. "What did you say?" he asked.

"I didn't serve in the war. Just wanted to let you know." Karl shifted in his seat.

"How did you get captured?" asked Ray.

Karl paused. Was he ready to share his story?

Ray put down his fork. "Whenever you're ready."

Karl stammered through his story and when finished breathed deeply.

"If the Germans found you, you wouldn't be here to tell the story," said Ray.

"We fixed his leg as best we could, and I took him to the border of Italy to catch up with his unit."

"You walked from Germany to Italy with an American with a wounded leg?" asked Lukas. "And you lived to tell it?"

"So did he, as far as I know."

"Impossible!" said Ray.

"We stayed with a Swiss farmer for one night. He fed us and drove us close to the Italian border. He offered to meet me the following morning and said he would drive me back to his house to rest and then I could go back home."

"And that's why you're here," said Ray. "You missed your ride."

Karl nodded. "I slid down toward him, lifted him up, and heard the click of a rifle. It was a British soldier."

"Mein Gott," said Lukas.

"What happened to the American?" asked Ray.

"I don't know. They called the medics for him and put me on a truck."

Voices in the background dimmed. Karl pushed his plate away.

Ray cleared his throat. "Look kid, you got screwed, but—"

Lukas interrupted. "It's a good thing the British got you and not the Russians."

"Lukas is right," said Ray, grasping Karl's arm. "We need drinks. Diego has Mexican beer." Ray stood and returned with three beers. "I saw what happened over there, and it was hell," said Ray, placing the bottles on the table.

Karl glanced around, wondering if Ray would be silenced, but he kept on. "Hitler was a mean ruler. People from all over paid a price for his madness."

Sipping their beer, they sat in silence, remembering the degradation, deprivation, the dead bodies of war and the helpless feeling that they were powerless.

Joe approached their table. "How's everything?" he asked. "Am I interrupting? You all look serious. Is there something I should know?"

"Not unless you want to hear our war stories," said Ray.

"My cousin served, and I heard his. As they say, war is hell." Joe turned to Karl. "Thanks for helping out."

"You're welcome, sir," said Karl.

"Name's Joe."

Karl thought of all the restrictions in Germany during the war and at camp, and he was beginning to see a way of life he had not experienced.

The next day the snow stopped. Joe was the first one to appear in the yard. It was difficult to distinguish roads from the farmland. When the crew arrived, Joe addressed them.

"Lukas, you can shovel the walk in front of the house, and Tony, the one leading to the barn."

Diego arrived driving a tractor with the snow blade attached. Karl watched Diego climb down.

"Ray, you can start clearing around the small barn at the end of the property and push the snow as far away as possible. Just like last year. Karl, go with him. He can show you how it's done."

Karl squeezed in next to Ray. "We don't have these in Germany. Tractors, yes, but not with snow shovels attached."

"Joe's a good boss. He spells out what he wants and listens. Wait until you see the front loader," said Ray, and with a rumble, he steered the tractor to the small barn at the far end of the property.

By the end of the day, mounds of snow had been pushed back and footpaths leading to the barns and houses had been cleared. Reaching the barn, they climbed off the tractor and entered. The sweet smell of hay mixed with the stench of cow manure greeted them. Karl grinned.

Ray asked, "What's the smile for? It stinks."

"Not to me. I grew up on a farm."

Cows mooed loudly and lifted their heads. Karl patted the side of one of them and said, "Okay, we got what you want." The clatter of grain pouring into the food trough brought louder mooing. Karl thought back to his home in Weiss where his family had given refuge to an old man, a woman, and two small children, one of whom had whimpered the whole time. There were no soothing words that could ease that day's sting.

Later that day, Karl entered the farmhouse looking for food but was startled when he saw Lily chopping cilantro and onions with Juanita. She looked up and said, "You can come in."

Shifting his weight from one foot to another he said, "I don't want to intrude."

"Not at all. I come here often to have coffee and help Juanita chop vegetables. She's trying to teach me how to cook, but I'm afraid I'm a slow learner."

"I'll just get a snack, if you don't mind."

"Have a seat," she said, pointing to a chair. Juanita continued to chop. "Well, I guess just for a few minutes."

"How did the plowing go? Looks like the snow is all cleared away."

"It was fun. Do you know Ray?"

"Of course, we all know Ray."

"He did a great job, and we got the cows fed." "Where are you from?" she asked.

"Weiss, Germany."

"Long way from home."

"Where are you from?" he asked.

"Outside Chicago, not too far from here. I graduated from high school there almost two years ago."

Karl's eyes widened. "I must go find Ray."

"He's probably outside somewhere," said Lily.

Brushing snow off the rail on the front porch, Ray looked up. "You got that perplexed look again. What's on your mind?"

"Nothing."

"You go in the house for five minutes, then come out looking as if you stole something and you say 'nothing.'" Ray shook his head. "Suit yourself. I'm goin' to change my clothes before supper."

It was dark when Karl, following the path he and Ray had shoveled earlier, walked into the barn. He stood against a wall and slid down, landing on a pile of hay. He bent his head slightly. Ray said Tom wasn't the father of Lily's baby. Who was? Lily said she lived outside Chicago and graduated from high school almost two years ago. Remembering John Conway's story of having sex with a girl named Lily, Karl raised his head and stared blankly at the cows. One of them raised her head and mooed.

Two hours later, the barn door slid open. In the dark, a voice called out, "Where the hell are you?"

"Right here. I needed to think."

"You need more than that," said Ray. "You got something on your mind, you better spill it out. No good hanging onto things. What's more, it's freezing in here. Come on, you missed supper. Let's get you some food."

"Ray."

"Yeah."

"I think I may know the father of Lily's baby."

"What the—"

"It may be a coincidence. I don't know. I wouldn't want her or Tom knowing. It's just," Karl stood and faced Ray. "The American soldier I told you who—"

"That bastard?"

"He told me he dated this girl through high school, had sex with her, and then never saw her again."

"What a dog."

"Her name was Lily! Same description as the one living here. And, Ray," Karl's eyebrows knitted. "John was from outside Chicago. So is Lily. And they both graduated from high school around the same time."

"Jeezus! Wait, there's lots of girls named Lily, and Chicago's a big place."

"You said yourself. Tom was not the father."

Ray pointed a finger at Karl. "Stay out of it. I came home from the war totally messed up. Tom rescued me from the hell I was in. Tom and Lily are off limits." Ray spat out the last sentence.

"I'm not going to say anything to anyone." Karl's tone softened. "Just trying to figure things out."

"Who is this guy that betrayed you?"

"His name is John Conway. Because of him, I'm a prisoner of war when I didn't even fight. And he's alive somewhere because of my family." A hot anger flushed Karl's face. "After all we did for him—"

Ray paced about the barn, rubbing his bristled jaw. "What's this got to do with Lily?"

"It has everything to do with her."

"Like what? You're not making sense."

"She may know where John Conway is."

"You're here to shovel snow, not figure out the family. Get it?"

Ray's right. Lily is none of my business.

Chapter Twenty-Eight

The last of winter disappeared and the people of Spring Hill Farm welcomed the new season. Lily and Tom's world revolved around baby Eve, who was now a year old.

Becoming a father had diminished Tom's interest in the farm business.

One afternoon, watching workers paint a building and repair fences, he turned to Joe and said, "Joe, since you are responsible for planting crops and maintaining buildings, why don't you order what you need instead of having me do it?"

This made sense to Joe, and he agreed.

Tom hesitated before he added, "And why don't you keep an eye on the workers? After all, you assign the jobs to them."

Joe thought for a moment.

"Before you answer," Tom continued, "You'll get an increase in pay, of course."

Joe grinned. "Done."

They shook hands.

Tom continued paying the bills and doing payroll, but that was about to change.

Karl stepped out of the farmhouse. The faint sound of chirping birds and the smell of freshly planted spring wheat, oats, and corn brought him back to springtime in Weiss before the war, before the hunger, before the fear. He wondered if his family had eaten that day, and if they were safe. He would write another letter to them tonight—his third this month. Karl wondered if and when he would be sent back to Camp Grant.

One morning, heading to the barn wearing grass-stained trousers and a jersey without POW letters, Karl looked toward the rising sun. Morning dew covered the pasture. The sweet smell transported him back

167

to Weiss when he and Papa gathered mushrooms. The revived memory was as sharp as a photograph.

"Karl, got a minute?" Joe asked.

"Sure."

"I want you to work in the barn with Ray and Lukas. Seems like you all get along. I'm buying half a dozen cows, so there will be plenty of work. I heard you worked on a farm in Germany."

"Yes, my family's, but it's all gone now."

"Sorry to hear that. Tough. You'll get home. When the war is over and our guys come home, there'll be no need to keep you here. In the meantime, you're a big help to us."

"Thanks."

Ray and Lukas joined them.

"Karl's going to work with the two of you in the barn."

Hearing the conversation, Tony yelled out, "Working with the enemy!"

"Tony, enough!" admonished Joe.

Ray responded, "Try it, Tony. You might learn something."

Tony rushed off, but not before raising his middle finger at them. Lukas shook his head. "Let's go to the barn. Ray, show us the routine."

Karl felt most at home in the barn. Under his care, the cows produced more milk. He sidled up to Daisy, one of his favorite cows, rubbing her nose while her tail swished. A loud moo came from Hattie.

"Okay, I'm coming," Karl answered. When calving was imminent, Karl would sleep in the barn to be close to the cow. After months of uncertainty and upheavals, the solitude of the barn and the warmth of the cows suited him. Watching the calf nestling against the cow, Karl felt the need to belong.

Karl was sitting at the dining room table eating scrambled eggs and buttered toast, wondering how Ben and Eric were faring at Camp Grant. He remembered the day they arrived at the camp, terrified of being prisoners of war.

Ray rushed into the dining room. His attempt to modify his excitement failed and he declared, "Big news!"

"What?"

"I went to Sadie's Diner for coffee and a muffin this morning. Sadie left England in 1922 and keeps in touch with people over there, so she is pretty up to date on what is happening in England. People were talking about tons of ships arriving in England. American soldiers all over the ports. Some soldiers practicing climbing rope ladders." Ray stopped, catching his breath. "The British intelligence are up in arms about the solution to a crossword puzzle in a newspaper and have interrogated the guy who writes them. Their concern was code words. Sadie said it's all true." Taking a deep breath, he waited for Karl's reply.

"Code words in a crossword?"

"British intelligence is superior, and this crossword puzzle is an example of leaving nothing to chance, especially with the war going on. It all fits. The increase in troopships, Americans all over the place. Put it all together. Something's up. When I was in and orders came down, you knew things were happening somewhere," said Ray.

"You don't mean..."

"I think something big is happening."

Karl's jaw dropped.

"All German workers are returning to their camps first thing tomorrow. I'm no expert, but between the Brits and our guys—"

"All those lives lost. Who will take over? The Russians?" said Karl.

"Roosevelt and Churchill won't let that happen," said Ray.

"That means we'll all be leaving. What will you do?"

"Everyone will pitch in 'til our guys come home. It's the American way. You better start packing."

Karl went to the barn and stayed there until lunchtime. That afternoon, Joe met with the POWs.

"I've got orders to send you back to your camps tomorrow. I know it's short notice, but I have no information as to why this is happening so fast. The vans will be here at 10 a.m. This is a busy time for us, and you will be missed," he said, his voice breaking. "I do want to thank you for your help over the last years and good luck."

Walking back to their rooms, Karl asked Lukas what he thought. "I've been coming on and off for two years and this is unusual. We left when our job was done and not before."

Packing his duffel bag, Karl thought of his life at the farm over the last few months. He experienced freedom of movement, no sirens, wearing Ray's clothes without markings, and the friendship of Ray, Lukas and Joe.

At supper, Karl asked Lukas if he thought there was something going on.

Lukas put his fork down and said, "We've been used more in the last year than previous. Why? Because there are fewer young men here. They're all over there fighting, and I think Roosevelt and Churchill have had enough with Hitler. The United States is a powerful country with smart men. So yes, there is something going on and my hope is that the war will coming to an end."

Karl stopped eating. Was the war going to end? Would he go home?

"I have to pack. Aufweidersehen. Here's my address in Germany if my house is still there. Hope there is something left of our country," said Lukas.

Karl scribbled his address on a napkin and gave it to Lukas. The two men embraced.

Tom asked Joe to come see him after work.

"Have a seat, Joe."

"What's up?" asked Joe.

"I guess I don't have to tell you how thrilled I am with Lily and Eve."

"I've noticed. I see you walking with her pushing the carriage, smiling, and talking to her. She's a beauty."

"Isn't she? I'm forty-two years old, and I want to focus all my time on them. I need someone I can trust to take over the running of the farm—and I think you can do it."

"Wait, Tom. That's a lot."

"You're doing it all now. I plan on increasing your salary again. As far as payroll and paying bills, I am hiring an accounting agency. You will be responsible for ordering supplies and sending the invoices and time-cards to them. Everything else will be in your hands."

"I don't know what to say, Tom."

"Think about it. When you make your decision, I'll tell Juanita and Diego. If you agree, you can move into our quarters. This may take a while, but that is our plan. Lily's glad to get away from the farm and have a home of our own."

"I don't have to think. Tom. I'll accept your offer, but you'll still own the farm?"

"Of course. I am going to ask my lawyer to draw up a contract for us so we both know where we stand."

"Good idea, Tom. What is the name of the agency you are hiring to do payroll and pay bills?"

"Meriwether's."

"I've heard of them. They have a good reputation in town," Joe said.

Tom sat back in his chair. "Lily wanted to go to college, but her folks couldn't afford it, and then she got pregnant—"

"Tom, I don't think—"

"It's all right, Joe. We assumed everyone could figure it out and we didn't care. Lily wanted the baby, and I wanted Lily. The moment I saw her, I knew. Now that Eve is here, Lily can go to college. I haven't asked her yet if she wants to go, but I can watch Eve."

"I'm happy for you that things have worked out."

"Thanks, Joe. I'll be around. It will take a while for us to move."

After supper, Tom and Lily sat on the porch. Eve was asleep in Tom's arms.

"I talked to Joe today, and he is willing to run things here. So, we can look for a house."

"Tom! Really?"

"Yes, really." Eve stirred.

"A place of our own! And a yard for Eve."

"We do have a yard here." Tom laughed.

"But we share it with cows," Lily said.

"There is one more thing."

"What?"

"I've made good investments and the farm is ours, Lily."

"What are you trying to say?"

"Once we buy a place, how would you like to go to college?"

"Tom! Are you serious?"

"Why not? I have the time and we have the money. You're still young."

Lily jumped out of her chair, kissed Tom, and wrapped her arms around her husband and Eve.

Chapter Twenty-Nine

It was midnight. Emma was curled up on the sofa, her feet tucked underneath the afghan.

"Karl and his family took you to their home and saved your life! They must have known the danger for them."

I hope she understands that I was an American soldier living in a German home. "When Karl and his father found me, I was delirious. They took me home and fixed me up as best as they could. But I knew I had to get out of there as soon as possible. If the Nazis found us, we'd all be shot. But I never thought of the risk his family took. I only thought of myself." Leaning toward Emma, John asked, "Can you understand that?"

"It was a difficult situation for all of you. What happened next?"

John pulled himself up. His shirt hung loose on his lanky frame. He opened a window and inhaled the fresh air. Across the street, a neon sign flashed: FISH & CHIPS.

A puzzled look crossed Emma's face. "So you left?"

"Karl knew the way to Italy. I was desperate. I pointed a rifle at him and forced him to leave with me. I don't know what happened to the family after we left."

"Why at gunpoint? And where did you get a gun?"

"I wanted a quick exit. It was a rifle I stole from the German soldier I killed."

Emma placed a hand on her chest. "They saved your life, but you thought it necessary to use a rifle to get away?"

"I was out of my mind with fear. I didn't care about his family, only about myself."

Emma uncoiled her position and gave John a look that made him straighten. His face burned with shame, his breath was short, and his thoughts jumbled.

Clenching his fist, he began. "When Karl needed me, I panicked—lost my head. And not a day goes by when I don't regret that. But I can't take it back and that still haunts me."

"What do you mean when Karl needed you? For what?" Emma waited in silence for what was coming next.

"We made it to the Swiss border and then to Italy. By that time, I was in pain, could barely walk, but I was determined to get back to my unit. The British picked us up and I denied knowing Karl ... he was German..."

"Didn't you try to tell them that Karl saved your life?"

John dropped his head in his hands; he was unable to say what had to be said.

"Karl and his family saved your life, but you didn't try to save his."

"War made me crazy."

"But not to at least try..." Emma said.

He tried to read her expression. She was looking at him as if for the first time—and it wasn't clear to him whether she liked what she saw.

"You gotta understand."

"All I'm hearing is that you denied knowing Karl, who saved your life. What happened to him?"

"I don't know, I passed out."

Emma threw off the afghan and said, "Not to at least stick up for Karl..."

"You have to understand the agony I've gone through."

"What about Karl? What is he going through? What happened to him? And I suppose his family doesn't know what happened to him."

Their eyes connected, but their voices were silent.

"Does telling the truth make you feel better?" Her words were more formal than usual.

John's heart plummeted. "Yes, it does. It's a relief."

"But I'm not hearing remorse, only excuses."

John's chin dropped. "I'm sorry, sorry about everything, even Lily..."

"Lily?" Listening, Emma folded her arms.

I've got to tell her about Lily. "About Lily..."

Emma listened in silence. Her eyes turned away from John's. "Did you ever apologize to Lily for dumping her off like that?"

"No."

"You need help to understand your decisions and take responsibility for them. Call Dr. Burns and tell him what you told me, and I want you out of here in the morning."

Her words stung.

"But you must understand—"

"I'm going to bed."

Early the next morning, John woke, swung his legs over the side of the sofa, and stood. His despair receded. She loved him once; could she love him again? He was lost in thought when the bedroom door opened and Emma brushed past him.

"I'm going back to work," she said.

John called after her, "You can't just lock me out of your life!"

Facing the front door, Emma said, "I need to think this through."

John hung his head, but he was determined to get her back. He dialed Dr. Burns' number and made an appointment to see him later that day.

John sat in the waiting room, drained of self-worth. *I told Emma, and yet I still feel like a piece of shit.*

The receptionist called his name, and he followed her into the room. Dr. Burns stood and shook John's hand.

"Welcome, John. How are you?" Dr. Burns noticed his washed-out look. "Come, have a seat." John sat but didn't speak. Dr. Burns waited. "What can I do for you?"

John remained silent.

"John?"

"I can't do it. I can't."

"Can't do what, John? Tell me. We can talk about it."

"I can't face people. My mother, Abby, Harry. Work. I can't do it."

"What are you afraid of?"

"The truth."

Dr. Burns knitted his brow. "The truth."

"Yeah, I told Emma the truth and she kicked me out."

"And…"

John repeated his story to Dr. Burns, who listened with a concerned expression.

"Secrets have a way of getting in the way of relationships. Being honest with her took courage on your part. You did the right thing telling her. She may come around. Give her time. It will take work on your part to accept what you did. How did you tell Emma this?"

"I blurted it out."

"No preparation?"

"No. Once I got going, I couldn't stop. I just told her everything. I thought she would understand."

"Betraying a friend, especially one who saved your life, is difficult to understand, and sex is serious to a woman. You demeaned Lily. No woman would understand that. Do you know where Lily is now?"

John shook his head.

"A sincere apology might help—if you could find her. As far as Karl is concerned, do you know what happened to him?"

"That's the hard part. I have no idea. Does telling the truth even matter?" John asked.

"It matters to the person telling it, but not necessarily to the person hearing it."

"I know that now. What should I do?"

"You have to accept what you did was wrong. You can't blame anyone else. I recommend you attend a group."

"A group?" John asked.

"Yes. There are groups for people like you trying to understand what they did and why they did it. You're off the drugs, but you need help to stay off. You'll learn how to deal with your problems if you listen and own up to them. I encourage you to tell them everything, just as you did with Emma and me. Words and the choices we make are powerful. We need to understand the effect they have on others."

"Do I have to?"

"Yes."

"They all have problems."

"So do you, John. I know just the group that will help you. They meet every Thursday at six o'clock at the Congregational Church on Broad

Street. It is made up of people who are struggling, just like you. It will take a while, but I'm sure you will benefit by attending. I've known you all your life. You can do it." Placing his hand on the cradle of the phone, Dr. Burns said, "Well?"

"Okay."

Dr. Burns made the call and gave John the instructions. His first meeting was in two days.

Unlocking the front door, John entered Emma's apartment, closed the door, and leaned against it. I'll cook dinner for her, ask her to forgive me, and tell her what Dr. Burns said, and that I will go to a group. She loves me, I'm sure of it. At least she did. He moved about the room, muttering what a fool he was. He searched the refrigerator for supper for himself and Emma. Two hot dogs and sliced ham were all he found. He'd have to go to the market. Leaving the market carrying two bags of groceries, John's mood lightened at the prospect of getting Emma to understand. A figure emerged from a side street and followed him. John stepped off the curb and accidentally dropped one of his bags. Leaning over, he saw a foot beside the bag.

John looked up, squinting at the person standing over him.

"Hi, John, it's me, Jesse. Remember me? I have a present for you." Jesse dropped a container into the bag John was holding and disappeared. *Jesse, the bastard that sold me drugs. How did he find me?*

Entering the apartment, he tossed the bags on the table, and searching the bags, he found the container. He dropped it on the floor and crushed it with his foot. A powdery residue remained.

He bowed his head and mumbled, "I'm going to kick this, I've got to. I can't lose her." He grabbed the dustpan and broom, swept up the residue, and emptied it into the trash.

Twenty minutes later, tomato sauce, ground meat, and onions were simmering on the stove. The table was set for two with a lit candle in the middle and sliced Italian bread on one side.

Tasting the sauce, John heard the door open. He placed the spoon on the stove and saw Emma. His voice caught in his throat.

"I thought I told you to leave."

"Please, let me explain. I've been such a jerk and messed up my life, but I love you. I spoke to Dr. Burns, and I'm going to the group he suggested. I cooked supper for us. At least let's eat together one last time. I've got spaghetti with meat sauce and fresh Italian bread." He lit the fire under the pot of water, then pulled out a chair at the table for her. "I know I should have acted better to Lily, but I was waiting for my draft notice, and Karl, I was desperate to get back to my unit and—"

"It's all about you, isn't it?"

Emma walked into the kitchen area, saw the pill residue in the trash and shook her head. John stepped next to her. "I can explain. It was Jesse, the guy I bought pills from. He threw them into my bag. I don't know where he came from. I swear it."

Emma eased into a chair. John stirred the sauce and kept a watchful eye on Emma, whose face was unreadable. He served two plates of spaghetti covered with meat sauce, sat down across from her, and watched her twirl the spaghetti around a fork. He passed her the bread, which she refused. He rearranged the spaghetti on his plate, nibbled on a piece of bread, and watched the flame on the candle flicker and burn out. Emma pushed her chair back, her dinner half-eaten. She walked to her bedroom and closed the door. John washed and dried the dishes, put the leftover sauce in the refrigerator, and stood outside Emma's bedroom door. "Goodbye, Emma. I love you."

John stepped off the bus and walked two blocks to the home he had left four weeks earlier. He circled the block, trying to calm his jittery nerves. Stepping onto the porch, he saw a light in the living room. When he walked in, his mother was sipping tea, listening to Fibber McGee and Molly on the radio.

"Hi, Mom."

Louise dropped her teacup, spilling the contents on the carpet. "John, you're home!" She rose from the chair and wrapped her arms around her son. "Welcome home. I've missed you. Are you okay? It's so good to see you. Abby, Abby! John's home!"

Abby flew downstairs and hugged her brother.

Chapter Thirty

Abby held her brother's hand tight, afraid he would disappear again if she let go. The haunted expression he wore before he went to stay with Emma was gone, almost.

"John," Abby began. "Having you home is the best thing we could've hoped for." She turned to her mother. "Right, Mom?"

Louise placed her hand over her heart and said, "Of course. Now, let go of his hand before it falls off."

Abby obliged. "Sit down and tell us how you are. Are you okay? How is Emma? She didn't come with you?"

I want you to leave.

"Maybe John doesn't want to talk about it," Louise said.

John held up a hand. "It's okay, Mom. Yes, I'm fine. No more pills. Emma went back to work. I saw Dr. Burns and he suggested I should go to a support group."

"A group?" asked Louise, her eyes narrowing. Louise had grieved quietly when her eldest son was killed in Pearl Harbor and again when her husband died. Nothing would bring them back, but she held on to their memories and kept her sorrow to herself. Her faith was the rock that she relied on, not sharing her grief with strangers. She linked her arm through John's. "Come, sit in the kitchen. I've got brownies. You used to like them."

"I used to like a lot of things." John cast an eye over the kitchen. "Thanks, Mom, but I'm kind of tired. I'm going to bed. I'll see you in the morning. Goodnight." He climbed the stairs to his bedroom, fell across his bed, and begged God for help.

That night, the phone rang in Harry's apartment. "Hello. Abby." He listened and said, "Great that he's home. How is he? He's had a rough time. I'll come over after work tomorrow. Tell him I said hi."

Driving to the Conway's, Harry thought of the war and its impact on those who served. Was John going to be okay? What was it like for him? War changed men, and coming home to family and friends was no guarantee of lessening the effect. Something triggered his drug use other than his leg, but the wound was a reminder of something.

Arriving at the house, he knocked once and let himself in. "Hello!"

"Harry!" Abby called out. She met him with outstretched arms.

Harry looked over Abby's shoulder at John.

"Hey, old buddy," John grinned.

Harry pumped John's hand. "Good to see you. How are you?"

"Better than I was."

"Is Emma here?"

"No, she's back at work. Want a beer or coffee?"

Harry thought it odd that after all Emma had done, she would not be with him today, but he put that thought away.

"This calls for a night at Duffy's," said Harry.

Louise held up her hand. "I've had enough excitement. You go and enjoy yourselves."

"Maybe I'll stay home with Mom," said John.

"Nonsense, Duffy has been asking about you."

John rubbed a hand across his forehead. *This is the hard part. Facing people. What will they ask? What do I tell them? What do I say? "I've been away." I'm such a fool to think I could do this.*

"John." Abby circled her arm around her brother's waist. "It's a start, and you know everyone there. It'll be fine. You'll see."

Doubt crept in, but John knew he had to start somewhere.

There was a sparse crowd at the pub, but when Duffy saw John, he yelled, "Hey, welcome!"

John shook Duffy's hand and said, "Thanks. It's good to be back."

John followed Abby and Harry to a booth and slid in. A waitress arrived with a platter of fried chicken. John took a piece and bit off a chunk.

Harry spoke. "Your old boss called me last night. He didn't want to pressure you, so he called me. He has a client he wants to assign to you when you are ready to come back."

John swallowed the chicken and wiped his mouth.

Harry said, "Well?"

"I guess so."

"Did you call Emma today?" asked Abby. John remained silent. "She helped you, and it looked like you two were good together."

John cast a furtive glance at Abby and bit off a smaller chunk of chicken. The truth had driven Emma away, and John was reluctant to tell Harry and Abby, fearing the same results. But he remembered the words of Dr. Burns advising him to acknowledge his mistakes, so he lowered his voice and told them about Lily and Karl and his guilt. Harry and Abby sat in silence, their chicken grew cold, and their drinks went untouched.

"You betrayed the guy that saved your life. In the Army we were all brothers. I know this guy was a German, but he saved your life! And he wasn't a soldier!" exclaimed Harry.

Abby remained quiet. Her brother slipped from the pedestal she had him on.

Harry continued. "So, you had sex with Lily and didn't think a thing of it. Never called her to see how she was?"

"No."

Harry wiped his mouth with a napkin. "What a crazy mess."

"Harry…"

"Well, it is."

John eyed Abby, who was staring at him.

"I can't believe what you just told us. It's … bizarre," said Abby.

"It's all true, and I have to live with it."

"And you have no idea what happened to Karl?"

"No, and that's the worst part, but at least I can call Lily and apologize."

Abby paled. *He doesn't know.*

"Abby, what it is?" asked John.

"John, Lily's married."

"What? That's impossible." John glanced at Harry, then back to his sister.

"There was a rumor about town. She married a friend of her father's."

"An old man! Why would she do that? What happened?"

Abby shrugged. "That's the rumor."

"That's impossible!"

Harry looked John in the eye and said, "You've got a heap of stuff to deal with. No wonder you took pills."

"Harry, you're my best friend. In fact, my only friend. Please don't hate me."

"I don't hate you. I'm trying to understand. Just give me time." Harry glanced at his watch. "Let's go. I have to work tomorrow."

Walking outside, John said, "Go on ahead. I need to take a walk." He walked ahead, leaving Abby and Harry behind.

Abby stopped and turned to Harry. "The rumor was she got married."

Startled, Harry said, "You don't think—?"

John didn't hear Abby gasp.

It was late when John arrived home. He dragged himself upstairs and waited for sleep.

April turned to May and John had been attending the group every week. People opened up about their personal lives; some solved their problems; some clung to them like lifeboats. Unable to unlock the door to his secrets, John remained silent.

One evening, a woman seated near John asked him if he had a match. He did not. She paused, fingering her cigarette, and said, "I guess you don't smoke."

"No, I don't."

"What else don't you do?"

Someone handed her a match. She lit up, inhaled, and blew smoke through her nose.

"I don't do drugs," John said.

"Why are you here?" asked the woman.

After a brief stillness, John told his story. The group grew quiet and listened.

The woman was the first to speak. "I remember having sex for the first time. Afterward, the guy ignored me at school like I had some disease or something. What a creep."

The group facilitator, Bobby, asked if anyone else had anything to say.

"Yeah," said a guy named Kenny. "You told the Brits you didn't know the kid who saved your life. Why did you do that? You could've saved him. That's betrayal. Do you ever wonder what happened to him?"

"All the time."

"And he saved you."

John shifted in his seat. "My only hope is that he made it back to Germany."

"Suppose he didn't?"

John bent his head forward.

"A big step in healing is acknowledging what we did," said Bobby. "And you just did."

"It doesn't feel any better."

"My dad was in the service. His Army buddies were like brothers. He kicked me out for using and told me not to come back until I was clean. I don't know what he would've done if I did that. There were five of us, and he didn't tolerate us messing up," said Leo.

"All I could think of was myself. I witnessed my buddy getting his head blown off and that image haunts me. I wanted to die, too. But I survived and when I felt threatened by being with a German, I panicked."

"Do you know where they sent him?" asked Leo.

John shook his head.

"Many here have obstacles that made them make bad choices and caused harm to others, but we need to forgive ourselves and accept who we are. Healing and acceptance take time and work," said Bobby.

The group nodded in assent.

John turned to Leo. "You're clean now?"

"Yes—because of my dad. Once I stopped using, he came with me to the group. Have a year of college under my belt."

"I told my girlfriend, my sister, and her boyfriend. They weren't happy about it. So, I have a few things to figure out. My dad is dead. My mom doesn't know anything, and it's going to stay that way," said John.

"They'll come around," said Bobby, looking at the clock. "Time's up. See you all next week. John, how about joining me for coffee?"

John considered the offer and agreed.

Chapter Thirty-One

Tom Brewster straightened his tie and kissed Lily and Eve. "I won't be gone long."

Lily watched Tom back out of the driveway and waved to him. Her first sexual contact was with John Conway on the lawn overlooking the lake. Her world unraveled when what she thought was love was only fun for John. Her second was with Tom, whose passion had died with his late wife. Tom was kind and generous, and Lily had grown to love him. Their passion for each other intensified after the birth of Eve.

Hearing Eve call out, "Mama," Lily picked her up and murmured soft sounds into her ear. She searched Eve's face, looking for a resemblance to John, but there was none—at least, not yet.

Tom sat in Mr. Meriwether's office, scanning the room. The tapping of a typewriter and the ringing of phones competed with his thoughts. The loss of his wife and child twenty years ago had plunged him into an abyss but marrying Lily and the Eve's birth had brought him a renewed zest for life.

"Mr. Meriwether will see you now, sir."

"Welcome, Tom. Have a seat. We're delighted to have you as a client and hope we live up to your expectations."

"I'm sure you will."

"I have drawn up a contract which states what services you would require. Our fees are on the last page. Why don't you have a look at it while I get us coffee."

Tom turned the pages of the contract, read the contents, and satisfied, placed it on the desk. Mr. Meriwether arrived with the coffee.

"It looks fine," Tom said. "I have a young wife and child. Semi-retirement will allow me more time with them, and I don't want to miss anything."

An unexpected twinge of envy toward Tom presented itself to Mr. Meriwether.

"I lost my first wife in childbirth," Tom continued.

"I'm sorry to hear that. It must have been difficult."

"Yes, it was. But that's all behind me now."

"Yes, very well. Do you have German POWs working at your farm?"

"Yes, but they've all left," Tom replied. "Quickly, I might add. I was given short notice."

"The reason I ask is because we will not include them in our payroll. You pay the government for their work, and the prisoners are paid in scrip, which must be forwarded to the camp for their use. I've heard that some farmers pay their POWs in cash, which is allowed."

"I paid mine in cash. The list of my employees includes the POWs. I'll have Joe do an update and go over it with the new accountant."

"He has been out but will be back next week. I put him in charge of your account. I think you will be pleased with him. He's a bright young man. Top student in math in high school."

"What's his name?"

"John Conway." Mr. Meriwether stapled papers together. "I'll have my secretary call you to set up a date to meet him. He was wounded in the war but has recuperated and is doing fine."

Tom stood and extended his hand. As Mr. Meriwether grasped it, he said, "Good. I guess our business is finished here."

"Thank you, Tom. It's been a pleasure."

Tom left the office, his spirits lifted by a bright sunny day.

Chapter Thirty-Two

"There's a diner two blocks from here. We can get coffee and maybe a bite to eat," said Bobby.

"Good idea."

A waitress with red hair piled on top of her head walked over to the booth and placed menus on the table. "Evening. Anything to drink?"

"Two coffees," said Bobby.

"Cream and sugar?" she asked.

"Yes."

She waved to a customer leaving the diner and stopped at the next booth to collect their bill.

"How do you like the people in the group?" asked Bobby.

"They seem okay. What I said didn't surprise them."

"They've seen, heard, and experienced a great deal of stuff. If you choose, you can turn your life around."

John thought for a moment. "Turning my life around is a big order. Seems like when I share the truth about what I did, I get the cold shoulder."

"That's okay. It's what recovery is all about. You need to prove to yourself that you are worth it. You've done some bad things, but you gotta accept what you did and look at what you have. It's easier when you're clean. You can think better."

The waitress arrived with their coffee. "Have you decided?" she asked.

"I'll have a cheeseburger."

"French fries with that?" she asked, pen poised over a pad.

"Yeah."

"Same for me," said Bobby. He sipped his coffee and continued. "You've got Emma. You've got a family. You dumped stuff on them. Of course they're upset, but they'll come around. Give it time. What about your job?"

"I go back on Monday and already I'm nervous. What if I fail?" said John.

"A little advice for your first day back at work. Get a good night's rest. In the morning, shower, eat breakfast, arrive on time, and be yourself. You also might want to tell your boss you hope to do a good job. Saying it out loud will help you believe it. Trust me, I remember."

The following week John asked Leo if he served in the war.

"No. I was drunk as a skunk when I went to sign up. They told me to get lost. So I did, with more booze. My dad dragged me to AA and forced me to sit there and listen. I've been sober two years, got a good job, a wife, and a baby. My dad lives with us. My wife likes it. Says having him with us keeps me in line."

"You're lucky. I do see things more clearly now, but it's still hard to face," said John.

"Sure, the fog of drugs kept you from thinking about it. Same thing with booze. Bring your sister and her boyfriend to the next meeting. They know you're coming, right?"

"Yes, but I have to talk to them first."

"Start with your sister."

John thought of his days in the hospital when Abby sat by his bed, encouraging him to get better. Growing up, she was always following him and Robert around. *Robert and our dad are dead, and now she's left with a brother who's an addict.* The incessant ache in his throat reminded him that he might never know what happened to Karl.

"I got a few things to work out before I ask her to come."

John was never far away from his past. It snatched his energy. It stole his sleep. It stoked his fears.

Chapter Thirty-Three

The alarm buzzed. John reached out, fumbled, and turned it off. Then he remembered; it was his first day back to work and Bobby's advice rang in his ear. Shower, dress, eat breakfast, arrive on time, and be yourself.

The first part was easy; it was the last part that John struggled with. Who was he? Was he the same person who had left his job six to eight weeks ago, or was he a new version of that person? What was on his coworkers' minds? And the gatekeeper—how would she react to him? He left the house and walked to work rather than taking the bus.

The morning sun warmed his face and helped calm his apprehension. Determined to do well, he squared his shoulders and opened the door.

Miss Nelson, the secretary, looked up from her desk. John smiled and said, "Good morning."

"Good morning," she said. "Welcome back." John thought he saw a faint sparkle in her eyes. In fact, it was unmistakable. John sat at his old desk. A new ledger awaited him. Unsure of what to do, he pulled out a chair, sat, and opened the ledger.

Alex, his coworker, stopped by. "Welcome back. I thought you would like some of our awful office coffee to start your day. If you forgot anything I taught you, just let me know."

Grateful for the welcome, John took a sip. "Thanks. It's good to be back."

John saw Mr. Meriwether coming toward him with an outstretched hand. "Good to see you. Come into my office." Mr. Meriwether pointed to a chair. "Have a seat."

John reached up and pulled at his tie.

"First day back to work. How are you?"

"I'm okay, Mr. Meriwether."

Mr. Meriwether raised his hand. "Emma called me while you were out."

John stood. "Maybe I should—"

"Sit down. Let's talk." Mr. Meriwether leaned on his desk. "I applaud your recovery. It must have been difficult for you, but I see a brave young man who has come through the worst of times. Alex says you have a fine mind for details and numbers. I observed the same thing seeing your work. Both of us want you to succeed, and we are here for you. Emma is, too."

John let out the breath he was holding. "Thank you. I hope to do a good job."

"Glad to hear that. I don't doubt it."

"I go to a group every week," John offered.

"I've heard of them. Something new. Does it help?"

"So far."

"Anything I can do, just ask." Mr. Meriwether opened a file. "I have a new client that I would like to assign to you. We, that is you, will be doing the invoices and payroll. He has a farm outside of town and is going into semi-retirement, and he's asked us to take over his account. How does that sound?"

"Is this the only account I'll have?" asked John.

"For now, yes. It's a new account, and for the time being, I want one person to handle it. I'll be here, and so will Alex, in case you need help. Here is a copy of the contract and a description of your duties. Take time to read it over, and maybe after lunch we can discuss it. When you're ready, Miss Nelson will make an appointment for you to meet Joe Perkins. He's the manager of the farm and the one you will be dealing with."

John stood and left Mr. Meriwether's office with the contract containing his new job responsibilities. He read the wording, jotted down questions, and satisfied, contract in hand, went back to see Mr. Meriwether.

"I've read the contract. I have a few questions for Joe Perkins. Do you think it would be okay for me to visit the farm?"

"Good idea. Why didn't I think of that? Give Joe a ring, introduce yourself. I'm sure he'd be glad to show you around."

He read the contract again. The wording was familiar: services, payment due date, payroll. Alex had explained invoices to him, but that was before … everything.

"How does the contract look?" asked Alex.

"It's well spelled out, Alex, but I don't know if I can do this."

"I'll get you through the first phase. Once you get the hang of it, you'll be fine. They must have a template they use for invoices and a list of their customers. A farm probably deals with only one or two suppliers. All you have to do is fill in the blanks. Just be sure the billing is correct. I'll have a look at it if you want."

Relieved, John said, "Thanks." He opened the ledger and ran his hand over the page.

"Payroll is trickier with timecards and hourly rates of pay," Alex said. "But the farm boss has this information already. You'll need a list of the workers and what they do. It's complicated in the beginning, but you can handle it."

On his way home, John passed a newsstand where a man hollered, "Cassino captured! bombed! Getcha' copy right here!"

John gave the man a dime and read the headlines in *The Washington Herald*:

Polish troops finally capture Monte Cassino
Allied Air Power Devastates Cassino
Italy in Record Bombing

The newsman said, "Had enough of this war. Bring our guys home!"

A crowd emerged and didn't disperse until the last copy was purchased. War memories flooded John's mind, but he was spared and had reasons to live: to get Emma back, find Lily, and pray that Karl was still alive. He raced home and rushed in the door, waving the newspaper.

His mother was reading her copy.

"More lives will be lost, but hopefully this will be over soon," she said.

Chapter Thirty-Four

John dialed the number for the farm, but after three rings, he replaced the phone in its cradle. *Maybe I should just wait until Miss Nelson sets up the appointment.* Alone in the office, his chest tightened, and he found it hard to breathe.

He reached into the pocket of his shirt, pulled out a piece of paper, and dialed Bobby's number.

"Where are you?" asked Bobby.

"I'm at work. I'm scared."

"Of what?"

"That I won't be able to do this."

"What makes you think that?"

"Bobby. It's too soon. I need more time."

"You can't put it off."

"I've got a contract with responsibilities. My boss is depending on me. I can't handle this."

"Yes, you can. Does he know why you were out?"

"Yes."

"He must think you can do this. Show him who you are. Go home. Tomorrow is another day. The first steps are hard, but you're ready. You'll see."

John left the office and walked home. He had opened up to Emma, Abby, and Harry, and they weren't happy. John needed relief from responsibility and the pain of his past. He thrust his hands into the pockets of his trousers and walked home.

Abby and Harry were sitting on the front porch when John arrived.

"How was work?" asked Harry.

"I have a contract doing payroll and handling invoices."

"That's great," said Abby.

"Big job," said Harry. "You can do it."

"Thanks, Harry. I appreciate that. You're my best friend. Maybe you could come to a meeting with me."

Harry's eyes narrowed. "A meeting? You mean the group?"

"Yes."

"I won't go that far."

Heat rose in John's face. "It would mean a lot to me."

"Okay. Let me think about it. Would I have to say anything?"

"No."

"Thursdays, six o'clock. The Congregational Church on Broad Street."

The next morning, John contacted Joe and asked if he could come out to meet the workers and see the farm.

"Good idea. You can meet the staff and see how things are done."

"Thanks," said John.

"The farm is about a twenty-minute drive from the office. Cross the bridge downtown. At the third traffic light, take a left on Moonstone Road. The farm is about five miles on the left. You'll see the sign."

John scribbled down the directions.

Having skipped breakfast, John felt an urgent need for food. He noticed a sign across the street from the office that advertised homemade bread, cinnamon rolls, and sandwiches. "ALICE'S" was etched on the window.

On the way out, he said to Miss Nelson, "I'm going to ALICE'S."

"Get a cinnamon bun," she said.

The door to ALICE'S was propped open with a brick. The scents of cinnamon and coffee filled the air. Glass-enclosed cases displayed pastries, breads, and sandwiches. On the wall were pictures of a young family with four children. A picture of a young Mr. Meriwether, a woman, and a young boy hung next to it. Curious, John looked closer. The third picture was Mr. Meriwether with a woman and her four children.

A slender woman with silver-threaded hair that was tied loosely and hung down the nape of her neck came through a doorway, wiping her hands on her apron. She said, "Those are pictures of my family and friends."

"I work for the man in the picture."

"I know." She smiled. "I've seen you coming and going into Meriwether's. Now, what can I get for you?"

"A cinnamon bun and coffee."

"Have a seat."

The woman arrived with a cup of steaming hot coffee and a warm bun. "I'm Alice. Welcome. Mind if I join you?"

It wasn't a question. John rose from his chair.

"Don't get up. How do you like working for Phil?"

"Phil?"

"Meriwether. He's Phil to me, my kids, and my employees."

"It's fine."

"Phil Meriwether used to work at the bank with my husband. Our kids went to school together. My husband died of cancer. I had four children and no way of supporting them."

John put his cup down. "What did you do?"

"Phil got me a business loan. I purchased this building, and there was room on the second floor for an apartment. Every Monday, he would have coffee and a bun here, and on weekends he would bring his family. He opened his own business right across the street. His son was killed in the war, and six months later his wife was hit by a car and killed. He still comes here on Monday mornings. We're best friends, and he's like a father to my kids."

"I had no idea."

"He doesn't talk about it. People do get over tragedy, but it takes time. Sometimes a long time."

Two women walked in. "Morning, Alice," they said.

Alice stood. "Excuse me, John Conway. Come again."

John drained his coffee and crossed the street to the office. Phil is a fine man and only hires fine people.

"Did you meet Alice?" asked Miss Nelson.

John gave her a small grin. "I certainly did."

"How was your cinnamon bun?"

John let out a breath and said, "Delicious."

Passing Mr. Meriwether's office, he said he would be meeting Joe Perkins at one o'clock.

"How was Alice's?"

"How did you know?"

Laughing, Mr. Meriwether said, "Miss Nelson keeps tabs on all of us, including me."

Gathering his papers, John stood and left the office and drove to the farm. Following Joe's directions, John arrived at Spring Hill Farm promptly at one o'clock. He adjusted his tie and stepped out of the car. The farm felt tropical. Greenery exploded in the humidity. Shading his eyes, he saw in the distance crews wearing broad-brimmed hats, picking corn and tomatoes and placing them in crates.

The farmhouse was shaded by large trees; a moving van was parked outside a smaller house. Cows grazed on a hillside, oblivious to their surroundings. Staring at the bucolic setting, a peace settled over John. He felt safe.

From the back of the house, a man approached, removed his hat, wiped his forehead and said, "Can I help you?"

"Nice place."

Diego's eyes shifted over John. "We don't give tours."

"Tours—? Oh, no, no. I'm here to see Joe Perkins."

"He expecting you?"

John detected an accent. "Why else would I be here?"

"Just asking. Wait here."

Diego swept his hat across his leg and placed it on his head.

Inside the house, Diego found Joe. "Some wise guy looking for you. You know about this?"

"Yes, I do."

Diego stomped off, mumbling in Spanish. Joe opened the door and waved John in.

Walking to the field, Joe explained to John how they got help during the war from German POWs. Along the way, he introduced John to workers returning from the field. Hearing the German accents, John's heart beat like a drum.

"Are there Germans here now?" *Karl could be here*, he thought.

"Some are, but not for long. All the farms I know used them to help us out. Just for the summer. The government wants all the POWs back at camps as soon as possible. They may be getting ready to send them back to Germany."

Joe handed John a list of names. Deeming them irrelevant, he had removed the names of the POWs. "The list is updated and complete. I included each worker's hourly wage and how we do payroll," said Joe.

"Are there German names on the list?"

"No, just the Americans."

John's face was blank.

"John?"

"The Germans. Where did they live?"

"In that big house along with the Americans. We have a few of them here, but as I said, they will be leaving when the job is done."

Shoving the papers into his briefcase, John said, "I'll read it over, and if I have any questions, I'll call. Thanks."

"Okay."

Karl, he thought. *Here, on a farm. In a camp. Is it possible?* A surge of hope rose in his throat. He fumbled with the keys, swung the car door open, and fell into the driver's seat. Letting out a sigh, he gripped the steering wheel, preparing to drive off, but a moving van blocked his departure.

"You're in my way," he shouted.

"Sorry, buddy. We're almost finished. This is the last load. Can you wait?"

He tapped his fingers on the wheel and undid his tie to ease the pressure in his chest. He debated whether to go back and ask Joe if Karl Baum had been there. *What if he was? What would I do?* He thought knowing might lessen his guilt, but he knew an apology was the only thing that could really do that. His past was about to confront him, which didn't include John Conway.

John watched a woman wave to the van driver and close the trunk of a car. Looking closer, a sense of foreboding grew. *It can't be.* He got out of the car and was about to speak but changed his mind. They faced each other, wordless.

"Lily, it's good to see you," he mumbled.

"You made it home from the war. I'm glad."

A quiet tension filled the air.

"Thank you." Rubbing the back of his neck, he said, "Lily, I'm sorry—"

Holding up a hand, she said, "It was a long time ago. I'm married now and have a life."

"You're married!"

"Yes. My husband owns the farm, and we are moving away."

The ground shifted beneath John's feet and the air thickened. He stood there, a solitary figure, grappling with the revelation that he was working for Lily's husband.

"Goodbye, John." And she drove off.

Chapter Thirty-Five

Standing at the entrance of Camp Grant stood a grim-faced guard with a rifle slung over his shoulder. He waved the van through. Karl looked out the window. There were no meadows of white flowers waving in the breeze, no thick green grass, just sporadic withered tufts.

The driver pulled the door open, Karl stepped off, and a voice shouted, "Halt! Name?"

"Karl Baum."

The guard scanned his clipboard. "Barrack Ten."

Walking past two guards he overheard their conversation.

"Rumor is the war might be coming to an end."

"Can't come fast enough for me so I can leave this godforsaken place."

"All the krauts that left for work are back."

"Wonder what Roosevelt has in mind for them."

"Send them back to Germany, I guess."

"To what? From what I hear, nothing's left there."

Karl arrived at the mess hall, and he saw Ben on the steps, his connection to home and his best friend.

Waving, he shouted, "Ben, I'm back."

Ben flew down the steps, grinning, and the friends embraced. "Good to see you. About time you got back. You put on a few pounds," said Ben.

"All that good food and beer. How are things here? I heard two guards talking."

"The war is going badly for Germany. The British and Americans are bombing everything. It's in all the papers. The atmosphere here has changed. Guards are jittery. Like we're all going to revolt."

An unquenchable hope replaced a dark cloud that had reached inside Karl. He had stored his past away until enough time elapsed and he could sort it out. The rage he carried for John Conway died. He had no place for it anymore.

"How was the farm?" Ben asked.

"It was a great experience. The Americans are fair and fun to be with. Mexicans did the cooking—their food is delicious. And I had the freedom to come and go around the farm. It felt good. No sirens. My friend Ray, an American, gave me some of his clothes to use. No 'POW' on them. I met a few Germans there."

"Where were they from?"

"One guy I was friendly with was from Frankfurt. He hopes to return when the war is over. He lost one brother already in the war, and another is still fighting somewhere."

"It's bad on all fronts."

"When the war is over and the Americans come home, our usefulness here will be over. Getting us back to Germany will take time."

"We waited this long, we can wait longer," said Ben.

They headed to barrack ten but were interrupted.

"Halt!" A guard with a rifle approached. "What's your name?" he asked Karl.

"Karl Baum."

"I haven't seen you around."

"I was sent to a farm in March, just got back." Karl raised his hands. "I'm unarmed."

The guard pushed him with his rifle. Karl staggered but did not fall.

"What the—" yelled Ben.

"Get out of my sight."

"Look—" Karl took a step in the direction of the guard.

Ben tugged his arm. "Don't. Let it go. Everyone's on edge."

They passed Private Lowe, who said, "Baum, you're back, you have mail. It's in the office."

"Mail!" Karl repeated.

"That's what I said. It's in the office."

Karl made a dash for the office with Ben close behind. On the desk was a worn envelope. The handwriting was unmistakable. It was from home. He kissed the envelope and opened it carefully. It was dated

30 March 1944. He felt comfort reading a letter written in his native language.

"It's from Mutti, Ben. They are okay, but my brother is sickly. They huddle together to keep warm, and they are waiting for me to come home. Papa still traps rabbits and no soldiers come by." Karl cried openly, glad that Ben was the only person present. Ben cried, too, making Karl's sadness bearable. "Ben, they're alive! They're alive!"

Ben read the letter, remembering his visit with the Baums. "Karl, we'll go back together and find our families."

The calendar page turned to June 1, 1944. Karl and Ben woke to the sound of sirens. Karl reached under his pillow to reassure himself that his mutti's letter was real and still there. They dressed, entered the yard to answer roll call, and performed calisthenics. Before their exercises were complete, there was an announcement on the loudspeaker. "Karl Baum, to the office immediately."

Ben glanced over at Karl, who hurried to the office.

Sergeant Jackson had heard rumors of the war going badly for Germany and of a major invasion. The last thing he wanted was a revolt or escapees. Karl entered the office and felt a quiet tension. Standing next to Sergeant Jackson was the guard who had pushed Karl.

"Baum. You're back." There was a menacing tone to his voice. Sergeant Jackson was thinner than Karl remembered, and his expression was tight.

"Yes, sir."

"How was the farm?"

"Fine."

"Got a taste of living like an American?"

"Sort of."

"Why did you tell Baxter here you were unarmed? Did they give you a gun?"

"No, sir. I was just joking."

"Look, you little shit," he said, pointing a finger at Karl. "We're still at war. And you're the enemy. Got it?"

"Yes, sir."

Sergeant Jackson got up and walked around his desk until he was facing Karl. "What did you hear about the war?"

"There were rumors that it was coming to an end."

"Have you told anyone about this?"

"No, sir."

"Not even that insipid Schmid?"

"No, sir."

"Keep your mouth shut. Get out."

Sergeant Jackson signaled to Baxter. Karl followed him out.

That night, Karl listened carefully and heard his mother's voice, low and calm. No words, just sounds, soothing him. If the war was ending, what was left of Germany? The thoughts kept him awake until sunup. He thought of a letter he would write later and wondered what he would say.

Karl's loneliness shook loose as Ben called out from his bunk, "Hey, Karl! Time for formation."

The heat of the day was just beginning as the two friends lined up.

†

In Germany, catastrophic losses had begun to convince many Germans that the war would not be won. The Reich lacked the resources necessary to fight on so many fronts at the same time. The people prayed for rescue and relief.

On June 3, 1944, Allies dropped 8,000 tons of bombs in a raid on German coastal positions around Boulogne, a coastal city in northern France.

On June 4, 1944, the Italian capital of Rome fell to the Allies.

On June 5, 1944, the battle of Anzio ended after 236 days in an Allied victory.

On June 6, 1944, hundreds of thousands of troops, sailors, and airmen awaited General Dwight D. Eisenhower's orders to begin the invasion of Europe.

Eisenhower gave the order and set in motion the largest amphibious invasion in world history: an armada of over 4,000 warships along with 160,000 invasion troops and nearly 10,000 aircraft. Troops waded in waist-high, unforgiving water toward the beaches of Normandy; some shed their blood before stepping onto French soil. Half of northern France was in flames. The beaches devoured men. Allied forces broke out from the Normandy beachhead and began their long heroic struggle to liberate Europe from Nazi tyranny—but not without significant loss of young lives, their bodies left on the beaches for the medics to identify.

Chapter Thirty-Six

Stacks of newspapers were flung out of an open-backed truck by a young boy who shouted out, "Compliments of the company!"

The guard rushed over, tore into the packet, and blinked reading the headlines. He ran through camp and thrust the paper under the Sergeant's nose. "Read it yourself, Sarge. First Rome, now this."

FRANCE INVADED

ALLIED TROOPS LAND IN GREAT STRENGTH ON NORTH COAST; BATTLE FOR BEACHHEADS

EISENHOWER TELLS MEN,

"WE TAKE NOTHING LESS THAN FULL VICTORY"

Sergeant Jackson read the article. "Call everybody to attention," he barked.

Newspapers were strewn over the yard and picked up by POWs and guards.

"What does this mean?" asked Ben.

"The Allies are in France. It's the war, Ben," said Karl.

A sharp voice came over the loudspeaker. "Attention, everybody to the yard, immediately."

The mess hall, cabins, and buildings emptied as POWs and guards filled the yard. At that moment, they were all the same, human beings caught up in a war that had killed fathers, sons, uncles, and brothers on both sides.

Stan undid his apron and called for everyone to go outside. "What's going on?" Eric asked.

"Gotta be the war. Let's go."

Sergeant Jackson stood on a platform and read the headlines. Guards whooped. The prisoners stood silent. What did this mean for them? Back to a broken country? Back to family? Back to nothing?

Sergeant Jackson spoke. "This is only the beginning. Our boys are doing their best to end this war and come home. At Camp Grant, we will keep all of you informed with any information we receive pertaining to the war. President Roosevelt is addressing the nation. Quiet."

A radio was set up near the loudspeaker.

"In this poignant hour, I ask you to join me in a prayer," Roosevelt began. "Almighty God … our sons, pride of our nation, this day have set upon a mighty endeavor … to set free a suffering humanity. Lead them straight and true. Give strength to their arms, stoutness to their hearts, steadfastness to their faith."

When Roosevelt was finished, there was a strained silence. Heads turned slightly. No one moved. Elation that the Allies had landed on the beaches in Normandy was replaced by reality that some soldiers would lose their lives in the water before stepping on land.

The June event hung over Karl's head like smoke in a closed room.

What would happen to Germany? What will they do with us?

Sergeant Jackson removed his glasses, folded the stems, and placed them in his shirt pocket and in a loud voice said, "Dismissed."

Walking back to the barracks, Ben said, "I signed up to fight for my country out of a sense of duty. In the beginning, we had no knowledge of Hitler's horrific plans for our people. My own father was taken away for speaking out." Ben's voice trailed off. "Now, I just want the war to end," he said.

Karl picked up a newspaper from the front step at their barracks and read the headlines.

ALLIES HOLD FRENCH BEACHHEADS
FIRST TROOPS SLASH WAY INLAND

Allies climbed single file up the bluff toward the hillcrest into France. The war continued. The beaches of Normandy were littered with bodies; high tide washed corpses ashore and low tide revealed men trapped under wrecked vessels. The grimmest mission was the location, identification, and burial of American soldiers. The loss was on an unimaginable scale. Saint-Lô had fallen under German control on the night of June 17, 1940. After the Normandy invasion, only Saint-Lô stood between the US Army and Paris. "Take Saint-Lô," General Patton had boasted, "and we will be in Paris in two weeks."

Ubiquitous in Saint-Lô were hedgerows. Americans needed to capture the commanding heights that surrounded the city. The prevailing height was Hill 192, and it was essential that it be taken. Saint-Lô was a hub of a network of seven roads and the high ground to the east commanded the Vire valley, in which tanks could operate. Saint-Lô was an essential objective of the First Army's offensive launched in July 1944. Americans focused on the railroad station and the power plants.

†

The Allies continued to advance, and on August 24, 1944, they entered Paris. Confronting pockets of intense German fighting, they proceeded through the city. Soldiers were greeted by millions of Parisians who welcomed the Allies with cheers, flowers, kisses, and tears of joy. After four years of silence, the bells of Notre Dame peeled out in triumph as the city was liberated from the Nazi occupation. The sounds of the bells echoed across the Seine, reaching the ears of a jubilant crowd. They proclaimed that Paris was once again free. Four years of occupation were over.

> *"Since I was still very young during the war, I can only recall what I was told. The best thing that happened was General Patton and his men liberated Luxembourg and the Grand Duchess was able to return home. I, of course, remember all the chocolate, candy, and toys soldiers gave me when they spotted me."*
>
> — Lilli Baird, Luxembourg,
> wife of the late William Baird,
> Specialist, U.S. Army 249th Engineer Battalion.

Chapter Thirty-Seven

Karl and Ben weeded the garden. Patch stood with both hands in front of him, clutching his rifle, and stood ramrod straight.

"Wonder who will take over Germany?" said Ben.

"Hopefully, the Americans or the British. If it's Russia, we're doomed. They'll be no better than Hitler."

"These are the vegetables Stan started in March. Remember what the plot looked like last winter?" asked Ben.

"Last winter seems far away."

"That's because you were away shoveling snow, taking care of cows and eating Mexican food."

Sergeant Jackson walked into his office, picked up a large manila envelope from his desk, and opened it. He read "Mandatory education for all German POWs." Out loud he said, "What the hell..."

There was to be mandatory education for all German POWs on the US Constitution and other aspects of democracy, along with films and open discussion touting American culture and values.

"A crash course in democracy. What next?"

The last sentence was "We hope to influence the future of Germany." Sergeant Jackson grabbed the papers and headed to the mess hall. Once inside, he roared, "Stan!"

Sitting on the back step, warmed by the sun, Stan snuffed out his cigarette and thought, now what?

Waving the papers, Sergeant Jackson said, "I need teachers who can reeducate prisoners and show them the positive aspects of American life."

"Why?"

"Because we have to. It's all in here." Sergeant Jackson spit out the words.

"What is?"

"Goddammit, Stan. The government figures these men will return to Germany, and as a group they will have a powerful voice in the future of German affairs. We have to get along after the war is over. And the government thinks this will encourage an attitude of respect for American traditions. They call it denazification. You must know some teachers."

"Sarge, there are no Nazis in our camp."

"Doesn't matter. It's mandatory for all POWs. We have 400 men here."

"My wife knows a lot of people in town. The libraries might have movies we could use. I'll see what I can do."

Sergeant Jackson stomped out of the mess hall. Stan called his wife.

Ben ran to the barracks and shouted, "Americans are in France."

Napping POWs woke. Karl looked up from a book he was reading. "Attention, everyone to the yard," a voice shouted. The barracks emptied in minutes.

Sergeant Jackson took over, and in a voice like the rumble of distant artillery said, "Our troops are in France and Italy, but the war is not officially over. For the POWs, you are still prisoners." He paused.

The mood was euphoric, guards were grinning, their arms hung loose at their sides. German faces were downcast, wondering what was left of their country.

Sergeant Jackson continued, "Classes on the American form of government will be starting soon. Time of classes will be posted in the mess hall. All prisoners must attend."

Two days later, two cars drove up to the gate at Camp Grant. Stan's wife, Joan, got out and spoke to the guard. "Sergeant told us you were coming, Miss. His office is the third one on the left." Joan directed the convoy to the office. A dozen men and women got out of the car carrying books, film canisters, and movie projectors. Classes started that day and were held five days a week until all POWs had a basic understanding of how democracy worked.

Leaving class, Ben said, "The Americans don't understand what it's like living under a dictatorship. We had no say, and it's going to be difficult to speak up for change."

"There must be thousands of us here in America, all in good health and ready for change at home. Maybe we can make a difference. I saw how the Nazis treated us back home. It has to change. It will be up to us."

"Changing from a dictatorship to a democracy will be impossible."

"It depends on who takes over after Hitler."

Karl and Ben picked produce and carried it to the mess hall. Stan and Eric boiled pots of ham, cabbage, carrots, and potatoes until the air became salty.

Eric turned to Stan and said, "I'm going to make some good German dark bread to show Americans what real bread tastes like."

Entering Stan's office, Eric rummaged through stacks of shelves containing food and noticed three letters on Stan's desk. They were addressed to Martha. What were they doing here? Stan stood in the doorway.

"Want to tell me about this," Eric said, pointing to the letters.

"I needed to speak to Joan."

"You've had six months. Why didn't you tell me?"

"I invited you to my house, and you took it into your head to write letters to my daughter. I needed to think about it some more."

Eric retrieved the wheat flour from the shelf, entered the kitchen, and was soon lost in a cloud of flour.

He could've told me. He should've told me.

Chapter Thirty-Eight

An urgent request came to Camp Grant for POWs to assist with end-of-summer farm chores.

"It's temporary," Sergeant Jackson told Karl. "Once it's finished, you will return."

Karl lowered his eyes, conflicted by his unwillingness to leave his friends again but aware that the choice was not his.

"Baum, did you hear me?"

Karl lifted his eyes and said, "Yes, sir."

That afternoon, a van pulled up at the front door of Spring Hill Farm. A dozen POWs stepped off. Most had been there the previous winter and through the spring.

With a clipboard in his hand, Joe greeted the men. "Welcome back and thanks for coming. Put your stuff in your old rooms. Get something to eat, and first thing in the morning we'll start picking carrots and peas. There's a ton of it, but it should go smoothly."

Karl asked Joe if Lukas had come back.

"Not this time. They sent a replacement."

Ray came running out of the farmhouse. "Hey, old buddy! Never expected to see you again." He shook Karl's hand.

"I couldn't stay away."

"War's coming to an end," said Ray. "Have you seen the headlines?"

"Yes, the officer in charge of our camp keeps us up to date. There's nothing left of my country. I'm glad it's over. All I want is to return home."

"The government won't keep you here. Once our guys come home, we won't need your help. Tom's moving off the farm with his family.

Some guy from an accounting agency has been hired to do the books, but Joe is in charge here now, and I'm his assistant."

"Good for you! Did they give you a raise?"

"Yep. Ten a week! Don't think it's going to take long to bring in the harvest, but there's plenty of weeding. Heard anything from your family?"

"My mother wrote. The letter took three months to get here."

"So, what's going on?"

"My brother is sick. Things are hard—but my mother says they intend on staying alive until I come home."

"If they made it this far, chances are they will be okay." Ray wrapped an arm around Karl's shoulder. "Let's go into town to see Sadie. You remember Sadie? She's a Brit and has friends over there. Maybe she knows something."

"You're sure it's okay? I mean for me to go?"

"Sure. I'll tell Joe."

Karl opened the door to Ray's truck, climbed in, and held on to the dashboard as the truck roared off the grounds of the farm. Ray pulled into a parking spot and got out of the truck.

"What are you waiting for?"

"I've never done this, Ray."

"Just be yourself."

"Hey, Ray," a voice called out.

"Sonny, good to see ya. How's things?"

"Pretty good. Got back from Italy last fall."

"This is Karl, a German helping out at Spring Hill Farm."

Sonny shook Karl's hand. "Heard about you guys helping us out. My father lives near a POW camp and some Germans built a fence for him. He was much obliged."

Karl swallowed hard and said, "Glad to hear it."

"See you around, Ray."

Ray opened the door to the restaurant and said, "Loosen up, Karl."

Most of the tables were full, but there was a small one available near a window and they seated themselves.

Ray waved Sadie over. "Do you have a minute?"

"Sure."

"This is my German friend, Karl. He's helping at the farm, and I told him about you having relatives and friends in England. What have you heard about the war that we don't already know from the newspapers?"

Sadie looked at Karl and wondered what he had been through. "Your country has been decimated and will need you. I am sure the Americans have a plan for you to return. You must remain hopeful. Now, order your food. Is this your first visit to an American restaurant?"

"Yes."

"This calls for English fish and chips." Sadie headed to the kitchen.

"The truth is hard to take, but you may as well know what is going on over there. If you had stayed, you might have served, and chances are you would be dead," said Ray.

"Papa has a friend in our village who has a radio hidden his basement. They trusted each other. They must have heard stories from London. Papa will be careful." Karl shredded his napkin.

"Here comes our fish and chips."

Sadie was carrying two plates. After eating, there was not a chip left on Karl's plate.

A man at the next table overheard the earlier conversation. He finished his third beer and, with a snarl, pushed his chair back. "The krauts killed our boys, and now we have them sitting in our restaurants."

Sadie's reaction was swift. She stood between the tables and said, "Gordon, this young man—"

Karl stood and said, "The German people have suffered under Hitler. We lost many of our people in a war we didn't want."

A collective unrest rippled through the restaurant, silent but unmistakable. Gordon rose to his full height of six feet and took a step toward Karl, who remained still.

Gordon's wife grabbed his hand and said, "It's not his fault that Timmy was killed."

Gordon shook her hand loose and lunged at Karl, who stepped aside. Gordon fell across the table, scattering dishes everywhere and pushing Ray to the floor.

Karl reached for Ray, who got up and said, "Let's go."

Sadie nodded to them as she and Gordon's wife knelt over the sobbing man.

Shaken, Karl headed to the truck, leaned over, and threw up. His head ached. The sun warmed his shoulders, but he shivered.

"Ray, I have to get home. I have to."

"Yeah, I know. It'll take time, but we'll get you there. Come on, let's go."

Ray pulled up outside the farmhouse. Karl's ashen face had turned back to its natural color. He turned to Ray. "Don't tell Sadie I left her fish and chips in the driveway."

"Your secret is safe with me."

Karl crept upstairs and lay down.

The next morning, Ray rapped on Karl's bedroom door. "Time to go! Peas and carrots need picking."

Karl leaned on his elbow. "I'm coming." He pulled on shorts and a tee shirt Ray had given him and followed Ray to the big house.

"We work until noon or so, then come in to cool off. You can always come in whenever you need to, but if we work fast, we can get this done in maybe three days. Joe, Diego, and the kids are going to pitch in."

After breakfast, the workers headed to the fields. Jugs of water and large-brimmed hats were provided. Crates were strategically placed for the harvest. When the crates were full, workers would place them at the end of the row to be picked up by drivers.

The noon whistle blew. Sweat ran down Karl's face. He stood and arched his back; he had lost count of the number of crates he had filled. He watched the truck pull away and took a long swig of water, handing the jug to Ray when done.

"Need a break?" Ray asked.

"There's not much left in the row. I think I'll finish it."

"Me, too."

Chapter Thirty-Nine

The sun set, casting a long shadow across the farm's fields, when Karl's thoughts became tinged with luck for being alive, and melancholy for leaving Ray. Their days of working together were coming to an end. Ray stood, arching his back. "It's easier to shovel than to pick," he said.

"You're getting soft, Ray."

Ray laughed. As he hoisted his basket to the end of the row, he spotted a man wearing a shirt and tie talking to Joe.

"Hey, Karl. We have a visitor. Must be the new guy taking over the books for the farm."

"Where?"

"He's gone inside. Think I'll go in, clean up, and get a cold beer."

"I've a few more to pick and then I'm done," said Karl. "I'll see you back at the house."

Ray stretched his arms and walked to the house, unaware of who was awaiting him. The door opened, and Joe said, "Ray, come meet our new accountant."

Ray grinned, stuck out his hand, and grasped the accountant's hand. "Pleased to meetcha."

"John Conway."

Attempting to make sense of what he heard, Ray experienced a sudden rush of anxiety. He instinctively pulled his hand from John's grip.

"Are you all right, Ray?" asked Joe.

"Fine, fine." He pivoted and ran out of the house.

"He must have an urgent matter," said Joe. "Let's go to the field where the workers are, and then we can go over the list."

Ray bolted across the driveway and saw Karl walking toward the house.

"Ray, what is it? Now you're the one who looks baffled."

"Let's take a ride."

"A ride? What is the matter with you?"

Taking Karl by the elbow, Ray led him to his truck.

"Ray—"

"I'll explain." He never did.

"Let's get a hamburger at one of those places on Columbia Street. I hear they're pretty good. Joe won't mind. Time off for lunch. My treat. Fifteen cents for a hamburger."

Remembering the last time he went into a restaurant, Karl said, "I don't want to go inside.

"I'll go in, and we can eat in my truck."

Ray's uneaten hamburger sat in his lap. Karl's wrapper was in a wad.

"That was tasty. What's the matter? You're acting strange and you haven't eaten," said Karl.

"Got something eating at my gut and I have to work it out."

"You always told me to get it out when I felt like that."

"Let's go," said Ray. "We have to finish picking. I'll drive around back and park near the field. That way we can go straight to the rows." Ray tossed his hamburger to Karl. "Here, eat mine."

Karl ate it in four bites.

Chapter Forty

R ay and Karl drove back to the farm in silence. Karl wondered what was bothering Ray but decided not to ask.

Diego came running out of the house, yelling and waving a newspaper. "Americans are in Paris. We've won! We've won!"

Karl jumped from the truck and grabbed the paper from Diego.

GERMANS IN PARIS SURRENDER

Ray joined them and clapped Karl on the shoulder. "Better pack up! You'll be going home soon."

"Rationing will be ending. I can order all the food I want," said Diego.

Ray thought of the horror and waste of lives all because of Hitler's aggression. He heard the engine of a car start up and watched John Conway drive out of the yard. Regret for his inaction hung heavily, but maybe there would be another time. Maybe.

"When will they let us go back, Ray?"

"Who knows? Your country has lost everything. They'll need you back there to rebuild, and you're in fine shape. I'm sure Roosevelt wants our guys home and POWs sent home as soon as possible. Let's finish picking and get you back to camp."

At supper, talk was nonstop about the troops in Paris. Everyone was eager for the war to end and things to return to normal.

Ray signaled Joe. "Given the state of things, how about letting Karl go back to Camp Grant? We're almost done picking, and he misses his buddies. And if plans are made for sending them back to Germany, he should be there. What do you say?"

"I'll finish picking," said Karl.

"Tell you what. There are two rows at the back. In the morning, finish picking that and we'll have you out of here by noon tomorrow."

"See what happens when you let me talk?" Ray said to Karl.

"Doesn't always work out that way, Ray. It depends on what you're saying," said Joe.

Ray flashed a smile at his boss.

Grateful for Ray's friendship, Karl said, "Americans make things look easy."

That evening, Ray joined Karl on the front porch.

"I was beginning to think I would never get back home."

"It may be a while yet, they gotta get Hitler first. But you've got a warm bed and plenty of food, so you're better off at camp now. They'll be getting updates on what to do with the bunch of you, and you'll be with your German buddies. When the war ends, they'll be no need to keep you here."

Karl fell silent. He dreamed of hearing those words. "My family. Do you think they know?"

"My guess is yes. French resistance is big, and word does get out. But when Hitler hears this, he might go crazy. One last-ditch effort. Things can't get any worse for Germany, so if your folks can hang in there…"

"I'll write to them. Diego must have notepaper."

"If he doesn't, we'll find some. Let's have a beer. It's a hot night."

Flushed with anticipation, Karl sipped his beer and wrote:

20 August 1944

Dear family,

I am well and doing fine. We know the Americans have marched into Paris and the Germans have surrendered. It's in all the newspapers here. My American friend tells me we will be sent home when the war ends. I worked on an American farm and helped over the winter, shoveling snow and feeding cows—just like at home. I am here now, picking corn and tomatoes. I will have a lot of stories for you when I come home. Stay strong, Hans. I think of you all.

Your loving son and brother,

Karl

Karl tucked the letter into his pants pocket. He would give it to Private Lowe when he got back to camp.

Karl completed his work and prepared to leave. In an hour, the van would arrive to transport him back to Camp Grant. Ray had become a beacon of friendship for Karl that was etched into his memory. It brought a smile to his face but was swiftly erased by a surge of sadness. He and Ray had different paths to follow. He neatly laid the clothes Ray had loaned him on the bed, put on his POW clothes, and stepped outside where Ray awaited him.

"Take care, Buddy," Ray said, his voice crackling. "Hope you make it home soon."

They embraced. Karl swallowed his tears. The van's horn interrupted their farewell.

Karl sat next to a window, and as the farm faded from his view, he felt a rush of gratitude and sorrow mixed with fear and anxiety. Closing his eyes, he prayed for peace.

The weight of the conflict weighed heavily on Ray's mind—the lives lost, the devastation—all because of Hitler's aggression. His gaze shifted to the driveway as the van disappeared. Watching the dust settle, he wondered when aggression by a leader would flare up again, but for now, he would only wonder.

Chapter Forty-One

Emma held John's hand, following him to a path in the woods, her bare feet barely touching the earth. She felt like a feather floating and circling in the air. Sun filtered through trees. Smiling, John squeezed her hand. She lifted her face and brushed her lips across his neck. They came to a clearing. He wrapped his body around hers and lowered her to the ground. There was no part of John that Emma was reluctant to touch.

Emma woke with a persistent gnawing sensation. *I sent him away. Do I love him?* When it was phrased plainly as a question, she knew only one answer and found her heart behaving in a most unexpected way.

She dialed Dr. Burns' number.

"Dr. Burns, I must see John. I didn't want to contact his family. Can you tell me where he is?"

She scribbled down the information. It had been five months since John left. She bathed, dressed, and took the bus to work. Her chest hurt and her head ached.

At seven o'clock that evening she stood outside the Congregational Church, waiting for John to appear in the doorway. The church door opened, and she saw him among the people coming out. She raised her hand and waved.

"John!"

"Emma!" He grinned and rushed down the steps. "You came."

She ran to him with open arms. Embracing, they laughed and cried and laughed and cried some more.

Standing on the steps, the people in the group understood what was happening and smiled. Bobby locked the church door, turned around and, seeing the couple said, "I'll be damned."

Letting go first, John said, "I was so ashamed for what I did. I covered it up with pills and anger. I can't go back, but I accept what I did. The blame is mine."

"It took courage for you to tell me. I know that now."

Tilting his head to the dispersing crowd on the sidewalk, he said, "They were a big help."

"I love you, John Conway. Come home with me."

Opening the door, John's eyes scanned the apartment where, with help from Emma, he fought a drug-induced state for weeks. Taking her hand, he said, "I love you, Emma."

They slept together that night and made love for the first time, neither of them wanting it to end—two halves of love making a whole.

The next morning, John made coffee, whipped up eggs, and slid the knob down in the toaster. Wrapping her robe around herself, Emma opened the door to her bedroom and, seeing John, smiled.

"Morning my lovely woman."

"I'm a mess," she said, patting down her unruly hair.

He took her by the arm and sat her down in front of a glass of orange juice, placing a kiss on top of her head. "Eggs, scrambled, as I recall, toast and hot coffee."

"John Conway, you are a charmer!"

Laughing, he put the food and coffee on the table and joined her. John told her about his job and seeing Lily.

"She forgave you?"

"She said she was glad I made it home from the war. I waited so long to apologize for my behavior, and it was a relief. So at least she knows."

"And you'll be working for her husband?"

"Yes, he owns the farm. But I'll be dealing with Joe Perkins, the manager, because the owner will be semi-retired."

"Think you will get to meet him?"

"I hope not. It would feel awkward. I'd have to go back to the group if I did. I also found out that the farm hired German POWs to help out because of the manpower shortages here. German POWs were sent to camps all over the country, and work wherever they are needed. Did you know that?"

"I may have heard something about it."

"I keep thinking," John hesitated. "Maybe Karl made it to a camp. He could even be here in Chicago."

"Do you know where the camps are?"

"Only the one I visited, and he could be in any one of them. But it would be nice to know if he was…"

"Alive?"

"Yeah. Then there's Beau's family. I want to visit them. I can find them through the Army."

"We'll do it together."

They finished breakfast and headed back to the bedroom.

Chapter Forty-Two

On Sundays, after church, Louise Conway came home and put on her apron in preparation for Sunday dinner. It was either a roast of chicken, beef, pork, or lamb. Abby stood by, waiting for instructions, which boiled down to stir the gravy, get me the sharp knife, not too much butter on the peas. The family was delighted to eat Louise's delicious meals that started promptly at two and lasted well into late afternoon.

One Saturday, John and Emma were sitting on a park bench. Relieved to hear that the Germans had surrendered in Paris, John's mood was thoughtful. He sighed and leaned back on the bench. A mix of emotions swirled within him. He was relieved that the war had ended, but he felt a profound sadness for all the lives lost. Emma was a comforting anchor and he loved her. Sensing his mood, she squeezed his hand and whispered, "The world is healing. Just like you."

"I want Beau's family to know how brave he was. How he saved my life." He eased away the sadness that engulfed him.

"If you're talking a few years, does that mean we'll still be together?"

John caressed Emma's cheek. "Marry me."

"I will."

The next day at Sunday dinner, John and Emma waited until dessert to tell the others, but when the meal was served, Harry made an announcement.

"I'm being transferred to Evanston. My agency has opened a branch there. And—" He turned to Abby.

Unable to contain herself, she burst out, "Harry and I are getting married!"

"So are we!" John blurted.

Louise clapped. It was the best news for the family in a long time. They went to the porch, leaving dishes on the table, and toasted Henry Conway, father and husband, and Robert Conway, son and brother, long gone but always in their hearts.

Louise, Abby, and Emma shopped for dresses, tried on shoes and hats, and bought new underwear—which Louise thought unnecessary. Remembering her wedding with Henry, she blushed.

Six weeks later, Father Ryan performed the dual ceremony in the church where Henry's funeral had been held. The celebration was held at Duffy's, where the jukebox blared out songs: "Don't Fence Me In," "The Trolley Song," and "Swinging on a Star." Father Ryan sang his rendition of "When Irish Eyes are Smiling." Halfway through the song, Mr. Meriwether stepped up and joined him. They were joined by the crowd, who stood and sang with delight, pushing aside the war which had consumed them for almost four years. At the end of the day, the family felt optimistic about the future and grateful for each other.

That night the family said goodbye to Harry and Abby.

"We're not far, Mom." Abby held her mother close. Louise whispered something into Abby's ear that brought a wide smile to Abby's face. "I love you, Mom."

They loaded suitcases in the car and drove away. John and Emma stood next to Louise until they could no longer see the car.

Louise wiped away a tear that crept down her cheek.

Emma and John left with promises to see her in the coming week. Inside the house, there was a stillness that spoke to emptiness. Louise picked up a family picture. Henry was seated next to Louise and standing behind them was Robert, flanked by Abby and John. Grateful for the love she felt for her family and the gift of happiness they gave her, she replaced the picture and sat in her chair until darkness fell.

Chapter Forty-Three

Eric picked at his food while Karl, sitting across from him, cleaned his plate. Seeing his friend's lack of appetite, he asked, "What's the matter? You've barely touched your food."

"He didn't mail the letters," said Eric.

"What letters?" asked Karl.

Exasperated, Eric pushed his plate away. "The ones I wrote to Martha! Remember?"

Karl's thoughts of mail were on his letters to his family and the one he received from them.

"Sorry, I forgot. I just gave Private Lowe a letter to my family, and he was actually pleasant."

"I found my letters to Martha in Stan's office."

"What were you doing there?"

"Looking for wheat flour. What do you think I was doing?"

"Start over," Karl demanded.

Eric blew a faint whistle and repeated what happened.

"Eric, you're a prisoner of war and it's Stan's daughter you're talking about."

"I must be a jerk to think it would be okay," Eric said.

"Wait and see what happens."

Eric continued cooking under Stan's guidance, but their relationship had cooled.

Days were getting shorter, and the air was dry and cold. Karl kept on with classes. His English improved. He read books on American history. Maps of the United States hung in the classrooms, and he read newspaper accounts of the war, waiting patiently for it to end. He had not heard from his family again, which troubled him.

Preparations were underway for Thanksgiving, a week away. Stan assembled his cooks and assigned duties to each one. He asked Eric to stay.

"I need to talk to you."

Eric folded his arms and waited.

"My wife and I had a talk about you and our daughter."

Eric unfolded his arms. "And…"

"She reminded me that her father had no use for me as a husband for her."

"I don't see what that has to do with me."

"It has everything to do with you, smartass. I'm acting like Joan's father did."

He handed Eric a letter. "It's from Martha. I gave her yours."

As Eric slit open the envelope, a bright smile crossed his face.

Dear Eric,

Daddy gave me your letters and apologized for keeping them. I guess he thought I was too young. I am eighteen. I have a job at a real estate agency. I answer the phones and make appointments. When the soldiers come home from the war, they will be buying houses and the GI bill will be giving them mortgages, so the agency needed help. Mama is getting her real estate license. She said to invite you for supper again. I'll check with Daddy to be sure he is okay with it. I kept your letters.

Your friend,

Martha

Eric held the envelope to his mouth and kissed it.

Stan was thinking of Joan and how much he loved her. Eric and Martha deserved the same.

"What did she have to say?"

Eric folded the letter. "She's going to ask you if it's okay if she invites me to supper."

"It's fine with me. Do you still plan on staying here when the war is over?"

"Absolutely!"

"What do you have in mind?"

"I don't know, but I'm sure I can find out."

"First, get your citizenship."

"How do I do that?"

"You have to do the work, but I'll help you."

"Thanks. When do we start?"

"Right now. Here's the number to call. Use the phone in the mess hall."

"What about my English?"

"It's fine."

"And supper…"

"This Sunday. I'll tell Joan and Martha."

Stan left. The weight lifted off his shoulders, he exhaled feeling a flow of gratitude. Eric kissed Martha's letter again.

Chapter Forty-Four

Emma and John took the day off from work and decided to shop for their apartment. In the morning, after kissing and caressing Emma, John bounded out of bed, lifted the window, and inhaled the fresh air. He loved the sound of Emma's voice, but it was how she made him feel that filled him with joy.

They drove to the local store with no particular purchases in mind, but they were sure they would find something to their liking.

"A hand mixer. Do you have one?" asked John.

"No."

John placed it in the cart. "An electric coffeepot, Emma!"

"My percolator will do just fine. We have to decide between needs and wants."

John tried on an apron with ruffled edges. Emma laughed and said he looked charming.

John removed the apron. "I'm many things, but definitely not charming." He put it back.

A set of mixing bowls, Pyrex baking dishes, a roasting pan, measuring cups, dish towels, and bath towels made it into the basket.

"We need more glasses, dishes, and silverware," said John.

"Are you planning a party?" Emma grinned.

"Actually, I was thinking about Thanksgiving."

"Can you cook a turkey?"

"No."

"Can you carve one?"

"No."

"I guess we can learn," Emma said, placing a Fannie Farmer Boston Cooking-School Cookbook in the basket, which was overflowing.

"We don't need that. We'll invite my mom."

John invited his mom, Abby, and Harry, who invited his uncle and Mr. Meriwether, who invited Alice, who invited Felicia, her assistant in many things.

The turkey took up all the space in the oven. John reached over Abby's head to get the plates; Louise opened the oven door and bent over to baste the turkey. She was bumped into by Felicia, who was checking the potatoes boiling on the stove. Mr. Meriwether emptied the pickle jar onto a small plate and squeezed between Abby and Alice to put it on the table. Glad to be on the sidelines, Harry grinned with amusement at the crowd.

"Harry, how come you're not pitching in?" asked John.

"No room. And besides, you folks are doing just fine."

"Excuses, excuses," Abby declared.

The meal was served, and everyone found a seat. They bowed their heads and said a silent prayer. There was much to be thankful for this year. John held Emma's hand until their guests had helped themselves.

†

The Battle of the Bulge took place from December 16, 1944, to January 25, 1945. Weather was a formidable enemy. It was overcast, and most days the temperature didn't go above 20 degrees. Soldiers washed in cold water, wiggled their toes to keep them from freezing, and skidded over flat, frozen ground that was covered with snow. Canteen water froze. K-rations were eaten cold. Soldiers found out what hell really was. But by the end of January 1945, American units had retaken all ground they had lost; the defeat of Germany was only a matter of time.

Chapter Forty-Five

Decorations for the upcoming Christmas holidays had gone up in the camp, but they failed to improve the mood of restless prisoners waiting with apprehension for the war to end. Some refused to do calisthenics and sauntered to the mess hall for breakfast. Some slept through lunch and went to the mess hall, asking for food. The guards responded by yelling and poking them with the tips of their rifles, further aggravating a tense situation. Noticing this, Patch asked to see Sergeant Jackson.

Annoyed by the visit, Sergeant Jackson asked, "What is it?"

"Sir, the Germans are breaking rules, and the guards want to break their heads."

"Why haven't I been informed of this?" He ran out the door and made an announcement. "Everyone in the yard immediately."

"You yellow bellies are housed, fed, and babied while our troops are freezing in Belgium trying to win the war. You will obey the rules as usual, or you will get bread and water for seventy-two hours in isolation. Do I make myself clear?"

There was a low murmur in the crowd.

"As for you guards, if I see any poking with rifles or any aggressive behavior toward prisoners on your part, you will answer to me—and it won't be pretty. Do I make myself clear?"

The guards nodded. Patch stood by, maintaining his composure.

Over breakfast, Ben asked Karl, "What do you think will happen?"

"Ben, it's over. Roosevelt and Churchill will get a deal for Germany."

"A deal for what? Rebuilding a country? I saw what happened over there, and it must have gotten worse. It'll be years."

Karl, his voice filled with determination, said, "I want to find my family first. Ben, it's our duty to help rebuild our country."

Ben hesitated, his cup lifted halfway to his mouth.

"It has to start somewhere, Ben, and it's up to us POWs."

"If all of us think like you, maybe it's possible."

The sting of the wind, the crunch of the snow, and frosty branches gave way to warmer breezes, softer ground, and budding trees, but news that no one could have imagined happened. On April 12, 1945, the headlines read simply,

PRESIDENT ROOSEVELT DEAD

America stood still; the shock was universal.

The news spread through the camp. The president who had guided them through four years of war was gone. A genuine sympathy emanated from the POWs. In consideration for the loss of their president, the prisoners avoided actions which could offend or aggravate their captors. Eighteen days later, on April 30, 1945, Hitler committed suicide.

On May 7, 1945, the war ended in Europe. Euphoria erupted everywhere across the United States. Lights blared in cities. At Camp Grant, lights were left on in every building, sirens ceased, and music was played over the loudspeaker.

Karl had been a POW for a year and five months. *When the war ends, there'll be no need to keep you here.* Time had a way of curbing one's appetite for revenge, and Karl was no exception. John Conway was forgotten; Karl's main focus was returning to Weiss. He had gained twenty pounds, grew two inches, and absorbed a knowledge of American culture that inspired him. He embraced new concepts like democracy and ideas of inclusiveness. His self-confidence had been strengthened.

Karl wanted one last visit to Spring Hill Farm to say goodbye to Ray. He approached Stan to ask his advice.

"Guards are in a good mood right now, but they can't leave until you guys are shipped out. Giving you permission to visit might not go down too well with them. Start with Corporal Chase. The sergeant has a lot on his mind. He's got to figure out closing the camp, shipping you guys out, and letting us go. Chase will know what to do."

Karl visited the corporal and made his case. After thinking it over, Chase said, "I'll okay a visit for one hour. Patch will drive you. Let's make it Thursday, June seventh."

On the first Thursday of each month, Joe would arrive at Meriwether's to discuss farm matters with John. Finishing their meeting, Joe asked John if he would join him for lunch at the farm instead of meeting at the office.

"Has Tom moved away?"

"Yes. He's minding his daughter while Lily finishes her first year of college, and they're taking a trip this summer."

"Nice. Lunch would be fine."

Karl woke early. He was looking forward to seeing Ray—perhaps for the last time. At eleven o'clock, he went to the gate where Patch was waiting and climbed into the vehicle. Patch's rifle loomed between them.

Arriving at Spring Hill Farm, Diego came running out of the house.

"Mr. Karl. Good to see you. Thought you would be sent home by now."

Karl laughed. "Not yet, Diego. This is Patch, a guard from the camp."

Patch sat rigidly behind the wheel of the truck, barely acknowledging Diego.

"I came to see Ray, and I can only stay for an hour."

"Come into the house. Juanita made tortillas. We have a guest coming."

Karl entered the house. The evocative smell of Mexican cooking stirred memories in his mind.

With outstretched hands, Ray welcomed Karl. "Came for a last visit. Good to see you. Have a seat. Too hot for coffee—how about a beer?"

"I'd better not. I'm only on loan for an hour. I wanted to thank you for being my friend—and to invite you to visit me in Germany."

"Might happen. Who knows? You heard anything about going home?"

"No."

"Here's the address to the farm, write to me," Ray said.

"I will."

The door opened. "Hey, Karl. Good to see you," said Joe. Standing next to him was John Conway.

Feeling a surge of anger and disbelief, Karl stared with eyes he was unable to shut.

"Hey, Karl," said Joe. "This is John Conway, who does our books. Karl is one of the German POWs who helped us with chores, and Ray Carson is—"

John staggered. His face resembled rare beef. Joe caught his arm.

"John, are you okay? What is it?"

"It's just..."

Karl was motionless.

Ray looked from one to the other. "Joe, can I see you?" he mumbled.

Yanking Joe's arm, Ray led him to the kitchen. Windows were wide open, but the curtains remained still.

With a cold stare, Karl said to John, "How are you?"

"Fine. How did you get here?"

"It was a long trip."

Pulling at his tie, John said, "How can I make it up to you?"

"Make up for what? That you denied knowing me after my family saved your life?"

The conversation stalled. John was unaware of the passage of time. Was it seconds? Minutes?

He avoided Karl's gaze and in a low voice said, "I can never undo what I did. It was selfish and I'm sorry."

Karl's memory of his capture and living at Camp Grant was in his recent past, and he knew he could separate himself from it and live a free life in the future.

Caught in a web of memories, they hesitated. "My family risked everything to save you."

"I was scared. I didn't know who to trust. Survival was all that mattered."

"Survival? How do you think my family survived after you forced me to leave them?"

"I still carry their kindness to me. I'm sorry. For everything."

"It's behind us, John. We were trying to survive, and we did. The faces of war are the same on either side."

"Tell your family I'll be forever grateful to them. When do you expect to go back to Germany?"

"It will take a while, but at least I know it will happen."

John looked at the man who saved his life. He seemed so ordinary, but John knew how courageous he was.

"Goodbye John."

Tears welled up in John's eyes. They clasped hands, bridging the gap between them.

Walking toward the vehicle, Karl heard Ray's voice. "Karl, how did it go?" asked Ray.

"I'm glad we met. We settled unfinished business, and now we can get on with our lives."

Chapter Forty-Six

The Japanese surrendered on September 2, 1945, and demobilization of US troops and repatriation of POWs finally began in earnest.

By the summer of 1946, one hundred prisoners had been sent back to Germany from Camp Grant. Fritz was among them; Karl and Ben were not. Eric had begun his application for American citizenship.

Every day, newspapers arrived at camp with the grim news of conditions in Germany. Entire cities had been destroyed. Displaced families wandered among the ruins. Germany had been divided provisionally by the United Kingdom, France, the United States, and the Soviet Union.

In December 1946, Ben and Karl went to Sergeant Jackson to ask if they could be sent back to Germany on the same ship.

"You two have asked for more favors than any of the other prisoners," the sergeant said in exasperation. "I just fill out forms, and the men in charge of sending you back arrange everything. Got that?"

Two weeks later, a list of the next departure of prisoners appeared on the mess hall bulletin board. Above the list of names were the instructions: Prepare to leave at 0700 on February 16, 1947. Karl traced his finger down the list. He traced it twice. His name was not there.

Ben peered over Karl's shoulder. He let out a yelp. "I'm getting out of here! I'm going home!"

"Ben, you lucky devil!"

"Where are you?" Ben asked, searching the list.

"On the next list, I hope."

The guards no longer appeared in the watchtowers and calisthenics were no longer required. Prisoners reported for daily roll call. They filled their days reading and writing letters. Some painted, some discussed politics, history, culture, and the latest news of the war among themselves.

Occasionally Patch would join in the conversation. Sergeant Jackson's mood softened gradually, and his intermittent laugh could be heard by his staff.

Karl and Ben woke early on the morning of February 16.

"Remember what I said the day you left my house in Weiss?"

"I do."

"Maybe we'll see each other again," said Karl. "And we did. I'm saying it again now. We'll see each other again, only this time in Germany."

Ben gathered his belongings. "As the Americans say, see you soon."

"So long, mein freund," Karl said.

Ben boarded the van along with other German POWs for the first leg of their trip back to Germany.

Karl sat with Eric and Stan in the mess hall. Eric was studying the questions he would be asked when he took the Oath of Allegiance to the United States of America.

"If I don't get it right, will they send me back to Germany?" he whined.

"Stop worrying. All your papers are in order, and you got recommendations from Sergeant Jackson and me," said Stan.

"What will you do when the camp closes?" asked Karl.

"Joan has been selling real estate—and doing well. Martha's working. I'm going to retire. My house has been neglected. There's a lot to do, and I want to build a porch for Joan. The boys will help me, but their schoolwork comes first. And I'll do the cooking. Joan loves that idea."

Karl looked at Eric. "What about you?"

"I'm scared to leave camp."

"Eric, a friend of mine needs help at his diner, and I told him about you. He's interested. He has a room in the back of the diner that you can rent for the time being. With soldiers coming home, families will be eating out. He plans on expanding. You'll be all right."

"Does he know about me?"

"What is there to know? You're a POW and about to become an American citizen."

"I wish I had your confidence."

"You've learned how to cook. You know how the mess hall is run. It's the same, only on a smaller scale. I'll need help with the work I plan to do on my house. Maybe on your days off you can come around. The pay's good—and Martha will be glad to see you."

"Stan, I can't thank you—"

"Save it. Just do your best."

Eric returned to his studies. Karl continued reading books on American democracy. He concluded that the American form of democracy was workable in Germany, but it would be a long haul at best.

On March 2, 1947, another list was posted. Karl's name was on it. He had been a prisoner of war for more than three years and he was going home to a different country—a country he would have to learn to live in all over again, but where he hoped to make changes. Coping in postwar Germany would be the challenge of his life.

Afterword

U.S. Veterans Friends, a nonprofit organization, was founded on October 5, 1992, on the initiative of Constant Goergen of Luxembourg, with the help of an American friend, Galen Cole. Their main objective was to keep alive the memory of the Americans who had come to liberate them from occupation by the Germans during World War II. They are hosts to visiting Americans. My husband and I were fortunate enough to be their guests for three days in 2014. Constant Goergen was our official host with Nico Schroeder, now deceased, and Daniel Reiland, who guided us through American and German cemeteries; the Siegfried Line; Bastogne, Belgium, site of the Battle of the Bulge, and the memorial to the 249th Combat Engineer Battalion at the Luxembourg-German border where the battalion built a "Bailey" bridge over the Our River allowing Patton's 6th Armored Division to cross over into Germany from Luxembourg and pierce the Siegfried Line. This visit and the next five days spent in Normandy were the inspiration for this novel.

MORE BY JANE MCCARTHY

Other works by Jane F. McCarthy include her first novel, *All the Rest of Her Days*, a poignant and provocative tale that touches our minds as well as our hearts. It is an epic multi-generational saga that confronts its characters with difficult choices. It is available on Amazon.

Jane wrote an essay in *Befriending Death: A Compilation of 100 Essayists on Living and Dying*, edited by Michael Vocino and Alfred Killilea. *The New York Times* listed it in their Book Review section under *Discover New Titles, Great Stories, Unique Perspectives* in 2014.

About the Author

Jane McCarthy is a Registered Nurse with a Bachelor of Science degree in Health Care Administration and is a Certified Infection Control Practitioner. She grew up in Providence, Rhode Island, and attended school there. She is a member of the South County Writing Group and the Association of Rhode Island Authors.

Jane lives in Narragansett, Rhode Island, with her husband, Gerry. Together they have traveled extensively, visiting Europe, Greece, Morocco, and Ecuador. Jane has three daughters, seven grandchildren, and numerous friends who complete her circle.

Jane's web site is: www.janefmccarthy.com

The Faces of War is her second novel.